yeah, he wanted her...

Angel's gaze drifted to the woman sitting next to him, to her mouth, ripe and moist. He wanted so badly to sample those tempting lips, to taste her and find out if she was as delicious as she appeared. He was already anticipating fitting himself against her lushness, and was unable to prevent the tightening of his body in response.

"I know what you're thinking," Sedona said.

Angel arched one eyebrow at her. "Oh, I don't think you do, *mina,* or you'd already be halfway back to the safety of your hotel room."

To his surprise she smiled, a slow sensual curving of her lips. "That's where you're wrong. I might be anxious to get back to my room, but only because I'd be dragging you with me." She turned slightly toward him in her seat. "I want you, Angel Torres. And I know you're hungry—you said so yourself."

Then, stealing the last of his sanity, she leaned over and traced the edge of his ear with her tongue. "So what do you say, Angel?" she whispered. "Shall we skip dinner and go right for dessert?"

Blaze™

Dear Reader,

I'm so excited to share my debut novel with you! This book includes two of my favorite things— a sexy military hero and lots of superhot romance.

My work with the Department of Defense has taken me around the globe. I've worked side by side with members of our armed forces in each of the military services, and they are some of the best, brightest and bravest men and women our country has to offer. So when I decided to write a story about a navy fighter pilot, I knew I had to pair him with a woman who was equally intelligent—and courageous—even if she didn't realize it herself. Thankfully, this supersexy hero is ready for whatever mission she has in store for him.

So climb aboard and soar along with Angel and Sedona for a wild ride I hope you'll enjoy.

Happy reading!

Karen

FLYBOY
Karen Foley

TORONTO • NEW YORK • LONDON
AMSTERDAM • PARIS • SYDNEY • HAMBURG
STOCKHOLM • ATHENS • TOKYO • MILAN • MADRID
PRAGUE • WARSAW • BUDAPEST • AUCKLAND

ISBN-13: 978-0-373-79357-0
ISBN-10:   0-373-79357-X

FLYBOY

ABOUT THE AUTHOR

Karen Foley is a native New Englander who actually looks forward to the long, cold winters. When she's not curled up near a crackling fire writing sizzling romances, she works for the Department of Defense, supporting America's war heroes. Karen lives with her husband and their two beautiful daughters, as well as an overgrown black dog and a Maine coon cat, on the banks of a tidal river in northeastern Massachusetts.

This book is dedicated to my husband, John,
and to our girls, Caitlin and Brenna,
for enduring many weeks of benign neglect
and never once complaining.

Huge thanks also go to Lieutenant Commander
John "Z-Man" Zrembski and Bobby Ascolillo, my
"go-to" guys for all things related to naval flight.
You guys are awesome.

And a special thanks to Brenda Chin,
for believing in this book.

_1_

IF WHAT THEY SAID about reincarnation was true, Sedona Stewart decided she was coming back as a man in her next life.

She snatched her sheet of paper from the copy machine and marched back toward her office, determined to ignore the sounds of merriment coming from the small conference room to her left. Another promotion was being celebrated, the third in as many months, all of them going to her male counterparts.

Despite the fact that she had as much education, experience and time on the payroll as any of them, she had been passed over yet again for the position of senior engineer, and for Bob Lewis of all people. It was like a slap in the face. The guy was a total dork. She'd be damned if she joined them in their good-old-boy ass-slapping and shoulder-punching congratulations.

She threw her paperwork down onto her desk, flung herself into her chair and acknowledged it was time to look for a new job. As an aerospace engineer for the Department of Defense, she'd worked damn hard to earn a promotion. She'd played the game, tried to be one of the boys, in an environment dominated by the opposite sex. She'd taken on additional duties, worked long hours, traveled when nobody else was willing to, sacrificed her personal life for her career, and where had it gotten her? In exactly the same position she'd held for five years now.

She gave a snort of self-disgust. So much for the edicts her father had imposed on her when she was younger. He'd disapproved of any activity, extracurricular or otherwise, that didn't further her chances of being accepted into the best technical college in the country. How many times had he expressed his opinion that women could only expect to get ahead in a man's world by emulating them? A woman who came to work dressed in a manner that distracted men shouldn't be surprised when she bumped her head on a low glass ceiling.

As a teenager, cheerleading hadn't been an option. School dances were prohibited as frivolous and rife with opportunities to go astray. Her father had been unrelenting in his belief that short skirts, makeup and jewelry would only result in an unwanted pregnancy and the end of all her dreams.

His dreams, really.

Her father hadn't had a clue about her dreams. But she hadn't dared oppose him, and in the end, had reluctantly boxed up and gotten rid of her feminine frills and fripperies. She'd even given up her dream of pursuing a career in fine arts, though she hadn't been able to give up her sketchbook. Some people kept a journal, others took photos; Sedona documented life through her drawings and sketches, not that she'd ever share them with anyone. Nope, drawing had become her secret thing, her escape when her overbearing father became too much to handle.

She'd obediently followed his advice and obtained an advanced degree in aerospace engineering. When she'd accepted her current position, the artist in her had secretly thrilled at the beauty and power of the fighter jets the company produced. It seemed impossible for so sleek and elegant a machine to contain so much strength and speed. She'd thrown herself into her job with a determination that surprised even her. It was only now, looking back on those years, that she realized she'd spent so much time trying to be one of the guys, she'd all but forgotten how to be a woman. These days, she didn't even know what it was like to feel feminine.

What would her dad's reaction have been learning that despite all of her hard work and sacrifices, she'd been passed over for promotion yet again? Her shoulders sagged. Her father had been gone now for three years, and while there were times she missed him terribly, she told herself she no longer had to please him. She could do what she wanted without fear of his criticism or censure.

She thought briefly of her two younger sisters, Allison and Ana. Allison was the good girl, who'd opted to stay at home and take care of their mother. She ran a small shop that sold bath and body products, but had never shown any ambition to do more with her life. She was sweet and unassuming, and their father hadn't pushed her to excel. He'd acknowledged the benefits of having one grown child remain at home to help out.

Ana, on the other hand, had violently opposed her father's strict edicts and gone completely in the opposite direction. As an exotic dancer in Las Vegas, she derived great satisfaction in telling Sedona how much money she made doing nothing more than shaking her stuff.

In some ways, Sedona envied Ana. Comfortable in her own skin, Ana had a natural sex appeal that attracted men wherever she went. For as long as Sedona could recall, Ana had been able to charm and manipulate the opposite sex, including their formidable father. He hadn't even argued when, at nineteen, Ana had declared her intent to move to Las Vegas. He'd just hugged her and gruffly said to call him if she needed him. To Sedona's knowledge, she never had.

While Sedona might never possess the kind of allure or kittenish appeal that Ana had, she told herself it didn't matter.

She was an aerospace engineer. She didn't need to exploit her body in order to make a living.

She scrubbed a hand over her eyes. Aerospace engineers were in high demand in private industry. As much as she hated the idea of embarking on a new job search and having to relocate, neither did she want to throw her career away working for an agency that obviously didn't appreciate her talents. Her boss, Joe Clemons, was a good guy and she actually liked working for him. He'd be disappointed if she left, but it didn't seem like a good enough reason to stay.

She wasn't getting any younger, either. She felt about twice her age, which, at twenty-eight, wasn't a good thing. To think, when she'd first taken the position right out of grad school, she'd actually harbored hopes of meeting a guy who would respect her for her intelligence and abilities. Ha. That was such a joke; the guys she worked with were a bunch of uptight misogynists who wouldn't recognize a good woman if they tripped over her. Although, it seemed they had no problem squashing them underfoot as they muscled their way up the career ladder.

She looked around the office where she'd worked for the past five years. Maybe the reason she'd never brought anything personal in, like framed photos or a potted plant, was because on some level she knew she wouldn't be sticking around.

Beside her desk hung a large poster of a jet engine emblazoned with the words, Thrust You Can Trust. The poster had to have been designed by a guy. Only a man would come up with a motto like that. Even the shape of the engine was phallic, right down to the afterburner with its smooth, curved cap. The poster never usually failed to wring a wry smile out of her. Now it just made her grimace.

She wrenched open a side drawer in her desk and bent over

to rummage through the hanging files, looking for a copy of her old résumé. It was way past time to get that baby updated and on the street. Maybe she could teach some engineering courses at one of the local colleges; all those fresh young minds would definitely be an improvement over what she was accustomed to working with.

"Excuse me, Miss Stewart?"

"Yes?" Sedona recognized the voice of the administrative assistant, Linda, but didn't look up.

"Um, there's a gentleman here to see you. An, um, officer gentleman."

Sedona shot upright in her chair so fast she nearly threw her back out. Linda stood in the doorway to Sedona's small office and, despite her round proportions, was completely dwarfed by the man behind her. Linda stared at Sedona in a meaningful way, mouthed the word *wow* and fled, leaving Sedona alone with her visitor.

She gaped at the man standing there. Her gaze slid over him, from his cropped black hair, past the impossibly wide shoulders and slim hips, to the long legs, all encased in a dark-green jumpsuit emblazoned with the American flag on one shoulder and a flight-squadron insignia on the other. For those who thought Antonio Banderas was hot, all Sedona could say was they hadn't seen Lieutenant Angel Torres.

She couldn't find her voice, couldn't think of a single coherent thing to say. There was only one thought that kept buzzing through her head.

He came back.

"You're back," she said, her voice no more than a squeak. Then she wanted to die. Nothing like stating the obvious.

To his credit, he didn't roll his eyes or look at her as if she'd come from another planet. He stepped into her office and extended a hand across her desk. "Yes, ma'am. I wasn't

sure you'd remember me. After all, it's been almost a year
since I left."

Remember him? Was he kidding? A day hadn't gone by
that Sedona hadn't thought of the navy fighter pilot whose
job it was to test-fly the military jets as they rolled off the production line. When he'd been reassigned to an aircraft carrier
in the Persian Gulf ten months earlier, she was certain she'd
seen the last of him.

Rumor had it he'd been grounded after a combat sortie
went bad, but she hoped it wasn't true. She didn't know any
details about the incident except that he'd apparently disobeyed a direct order from a superior officer. Lieutenant
Torres was a Top Gun graduate, and Sedona knew he possessed more than an average intelligence, so she had to
assume he'd had no other choice in disobeying the order. He
didn't strike her as the kind of guy who would throw his
career in the toilet for pride's sake.

Now here he was, standing larger than life in her office.
He looked even better than her memories—and her fantasies—gave him credit for. His Spanish heritage was evident
in the blackness of his hair and eyes, the thrust of chiseled
cheekbones and his proud nose. He also had a set of dimples
you could drive a truck into, although they were barely
evident until he smiled. His skin was darker than she remembered, burned to a coppery hue by the Arabian sun. He
reminded Sedona of a Bedouin sheikh, desert-hot and just as
fierce.

She'd forgotten how seductive his voice was, deep and
warm, with just the barest hint of a Spanish accent. Once,
during a meeting when he'd given an overview of test-flight
parameters, Sedona had sat in the back of the darkened conference room with her eyes closed and let his voice flow over

her like warm, dark chocolate. In more private circumstances, she'd bet he could bring her to orgasm using only his voice.

Blushing at her own wayward thoughts, she pushed herself to her feet and clasped his hand and tried to ignore how large and warm it was.

"Lieutenant Torres." *Please, don't let my voice wobble.* God. She was like a teenager, but there was no denying the effect he had on her. Every cell in her body responded to him on a primal level. She drew in a deep, steadying breath and released his hand. "I'm happy to see you made it back safely."

He smiled at her across the mess that was her desk and Sedona felt her pulse react. "Yes, ma'am. But it's lieutenant commander now."

"Oh. Congratulations." Sedona's eyes flew to the broad thrust of his shoulders, noting the gold oak leaves embroidered there. Whatever transgression he'd committed hadn't prevented the navy from promoting him. So why was he here, and not aboard the USS *Abraham Lincoln,* keeping the bad guys at bay?

"Thanks." He shifted his weight. "Listen, I understand several changes have been incorporated into the Coyote engine design since I left, and I was hoping we could set up a time for you to brief me on what impact they have on flight performance."

Sedona pushed down the disappointment that surged through her. Of course he was here on business. What had she thought? That he had come all the way over to her office just to see her again? Guys like Lieutenant Commander Torres were too busy saving the world to think about plain-Jane engineers like herself.

Forget about coming back as a man in her next life. She was coming back as a gorgeous, long-legged, sultry blonde.

She forced a smile. "Of course. Just let me know what time is convenient, and we can go over the drawings."

"How about first thing in the morning?"

Forget about looking for a new job. It was suddenly the last thing she wanted to do. This time, she didn't have to force a smile. "That sounds great. I'll bring the coffee and dough-nuts."

He grinned then, revealing the deep indents in either lean cheek. "Thanks, but I'm not much for pastries." He laid one hand over his flat stomach, drawing Sedona's gaze irresistibly to his midsection. "The cockpits on those jets are tight enough as it is."

"Um, okay. Just coffee, then." How was it that those two words, *tight* and *cockpits,* were enough to send her imagi-nation nosediving into the gutter?

He smiled again and Sedona felt her own tummy turn over. God, she had missed seeing his face. The agency she worked for, the Defense Procurement Agency, maintained a government office at Aerospace International, one of the top five aircraft manufacturers in the world. Her agency oversaw the production of the military jets and provided final accep-tance on behalf of the customer, in this case, the U.S. Navy. It had been her experience that when the Navy sent test pilots to their facility, they were on temporary assignments that rarely exceeded three years.

For the six months Angel had initially worked on their flight line, she had lived in hopeful anticipation of seeing him or talking to him. Their brief encounters had never been anything but professional, but Sedona had harbored an em-barrassingly intense crush on Angel Torres from the moment she first saw him. His departure for the Persian Gulf had left a huge void in her otherwise unexciting, predictable world. She'd thought she'd never see him again. And now here he was.

"Great," he was saying, "it's a date. I'll see you in the

morning." He turned away, and then paused in the doorway. He angled his head toward her and his dark gaze traveled slowly over her. "It's nice to see you again, Sedona. You look…good."

And then he was gone.

Sedona sat down slowly and drew in a deep breath. She was trembling. But then, Angel Torres had always had that effect on her. In the past, all she'd had to do was see him from a distance and her heart would pound, her knees would literally go weak and she would start to tremble. It was worse than any high-school crush she'd ever had.

He'd called her Sedona. He typically only ever addressed her as "ma'am." He'd called their meeting a date, but that was definitely just an expression.

He'd said she looked good.

Sedona expelled her breath in a whoosh. What did that mean? Good could mean anything. He hadn't said she looked great. Or gorgeous. Just…good.

She glanced down at her khaki slacks and plain white blouse. Nothing overly exciting there. She didn't have a bad shape, but she certainly wasn't under any illusions about her appearance. Her hair was nice, but she usually kept the thick, auburn mass neatly clipped up on the back of her head. She had her mother's green eyes, and while she privately thought they were her best feature, she admittedly did little to enhance them. She was reasonably slender, although her butt was bigger than she would have liked, despite the fact she worked out on a regular basis.

Still, there wasn't anything about her that would make a man like Angel take a second look. He was probably just being nice. All part of the officer-and-a-gentleman protocol.

Sighing, Sedona pushed to her feet. She'd go pull the drawings they would need for their meeting, and reacquaint herself with the details of the engine changes. If she couldn't dazzle Lieutenant Commander Torres with her beauty, at least she could impress him with her brilliance.

The room where they kept the thousands of blueprints and drawings was aptly named the Drawing Room. It comprised row after row of tall cabinets with long, shallow drawers containing specific drawings, cataloged by number. After compiling a list of the ones she would require, Sedona walked amongst the cabinets until she found the corresponding drawer. It was close to the floor, so she pulled up a low, rolling footstool and sat down on it as she leafed through the contents.

"Hey, looks like that trip to San Diego really paid off, huh?"

Startled, Sedona looked up. There was nobody in sight. She recognized that the voice belonged to Mike Sullivan, one of her fellow engineers, and realized he must have entered the Drawing Room after her.

She groaned inwardly, dreading any confrontation with him. He was nicknamed Hound Dog for his daily practice of strolling through the office to check out what the women were wearing. If that wasn't bad enough, it was common knowledge he sent e-mails to his male colleagues entitled, Hound Dog's Pick of the Day, and identified the woman he considered the hottest that day. While Sedona was pretty sure she'd never been one of Hound Dog's top picks, the complaints she'd lodged against the alleged practice went unheeded.

She was about to stand up and reveal herself when a second voice, belonging to the latest promotee, Bob Lewis, chimed in.

"I'm telling you, man, if I'd known how easy it was to get promoted, I'd have been banging chicks left and right a long time ago."

Sedona blinked. *Excuse me?*

"Yeah, it's a pretty great system. Why do you think we volunteer to do so much business travel?" Mike Sullivan chuckled. "Get laid, get promoted. All you have to do is bring back the proof. Speaking of which, those photos were amazing. I mean, I've gotta hand it to you, not just one babe in your bed, but two! I think you actually put the other members to shame."

Sedona's mouth fell open.

"Well," Bob drawled, "it was all in a day's work, so to speak. You can tell the Membership I was happy to oblige."

"You can tell them yourself," Mike replied. "We're going to have a quick meeting at two o'clock today in the East Wing men's room. You know, to officially celebrate your promotion." There was the sound of a high-five hand slap. "Good job, my man."

Sedona listened to their laughter fade as they left the room. She forced herself to remain seated despite the fact that she wanted to leap up, chase after them and confront them. She could scarcely believe what she had heard. She didn't know what was more shocking, the discovery of a secret club that promoted men based on their sexual exploits, or the fact that dorky Bob Lewis had actually gotten it on with two babes.

She didn't consider herself to be a prude, but this was completely off the charts. It was one thing to have an affair. It was another thing altogether to deliberately use sex as a means of career advancement. Worse, Sedona had been part of the team that had traveled to San Diego with Bob, and she hadn't had a clue about his extracurricular activities. She shuddered. Not that she wanted to. But it drove home the fact that she spent way too much time alone.

Her sister, Ana, had inherited the sultry good looks and the feminine wiles. Sedona had inherited the brains. Ana viewed guys in terms of their potential as bed partners. Sedona's only interest in the men she worked with was whether they would help or hinder her job performance, and how much competition they might pose for the next promotion.

She'd learned early on that most of her male colleagues didn't take women seriously. They made insinuating remarks and casual suggestions with impunity, and it still amazed her that the women in question didn't slap the bastards with sexual harassment suits. While she suspected her male co-workers considered her something of a bitch, it didn't bother her. They might actively dislike her, but at least they respected her.

She couldn't envision any man enticing her into having a one-night stand. The very thought of being intimate with a complete stranger made her go cold inside. There were just way too many risks involved to even consider the idea.

She took a deep breath. What to do? Go to Human Resources and report them? She snorted. Yeah, right. Like anybody would believe her. She'd be laughed out of the office. With his lank hair, oily skin, and seventies-something wardrobe, Bob Lewis was hardly the picture of animal magnetism. And since she had just been passed over for promotion—for the third time—her story would no doubt be viewed as the malicious rantings of a disgruntled employee. Never mind that the reason she'd been passed over was apparently because she wasn't getting any on the road.

She pressed her fingers against her eyelids and tried to think rationally about how to handle the situation. The government had a merit promotion system specifically designed to prevent favoritism or unfair advancement practices, but there was no denying they did, in fact, exist. Sedona understood office politics accounted for many of the recent promotions, but she'd have never guessed they might be based on sexual prowess. It was almost too unreal to be believed. More importantly, why would anyone risk their job—their very career—by taking part in such activity? What was the point? It made no sense.

But one thing was certain; there was no way she could continue working for this particular government agency, not after what she'd just heard. She had to find another job, and didn't that just suck? Because Lieutenant Commander Torres had finally returned, and leaving was suddenly the last thing she wanted to do.

Grabbing the drawings she would need for tomorrow's meeting with Angel, she pushed herself to her feet. There was really only one thing to do.

She would find a way to expose the members of the secret club. Once the truth came out, the agency would have to admit they had a real problem and deal with it accordingly. She had no idea how many men were involved, but she was going to put a stop to it.

All she needed was proof.

2

ANGEL GLANCED UP from his paperwork in time to see Sedona Stewart stride out of the Drawing Room and come to a jerky halt in the corridor, as if debating which direction to go. She didn't seem to notice him sitting in the small conference room just across the hallway.

The Drawing Room appeared to be a popular place this morning. He'd gone in and pulled several drawings of the re-designed tail section, and had taken them across the hall to spread them out on the table in the conference room. He'd watched Sedona go in, followed several minutes later by Mike Sullivan and Bob Lewis. The two men had left after a few minutes, but Sedona remained inside. Angel had refocused his attention on the drawings, but to his mild annoyance, found himself waiting for Sedona to reappear.

When she finally did, she was visibly upset. Twin patches of bright color rode high on her cheekbones, and he didn't miss how she fisted her hands at her sides. He was halfway to his feet when she spotted him.

Their eyes locked.

Hers shimmered with anger. They stared at each other for a full minute. Angel knew the instant she became aware of him, as the fury in her eyes clouded and became softer. The color in her cheeks slowly spread, until her entire neck and face were rosy. She blinked, like a child coming awake after a disturbing dream, and for a moment she looked confused, disoriented.

Angel was already pushing his chair back when she made an incoherent sound of distress, accompanied by a vague gesture of dismissal. Before he could stop her, she turned and fled in the direction of the administration offices, head bent and one hand pressed against her temple.

Curious, he stepped out of the conference room and watched as she hurried down the corridor and stopped outside the Human Resources office. She hesitated, and Angel was certain she was going to turn and walk away. But then she squared her shoulders and he knew if he was closer, he would hear her indrawn breath of resolve. As he watched, she pushed the door open, entered, and closed it firmly behind her.

Slowly, Angel turned back to his drawings. Sedona Stewart was considered unflappable. Cool and levelheaded, she approached every issue with a calm, almost Vulcan-like rationality that infuriated her coworkers as much as it amazed them.

So what had caused her uncharacteristic display of emotion? Of course, he reminded himself, she hadn't known he was watching her. Otherwise, he was pretty sure she'd have controlled her expression before she left the Drawing Room.

He lowered himself back into the chair and drummed his fingers on the table, considering. It had to have been some dumb-ass, chauvinistic thing Mike Sullivan had said to her in the few minutes he and Bob Lewis had been in the room with her. Mike had a reputation for being a prick where women were concerned, and Angel could definitely picture the guy saying something completely inappropriate to Sedona, just to see her reaction.

Recalling the distress in her green eyes, the Cuban part of him—that traditional, old-fashioned part that demanded all women be treated with respect—wanted to hunt Mike down and kick his ass. But the military part of him said that would be a poor decision, especially given his own recent misconduct. It would be an excuse for his commanding officer to bust him back down to lieutenant and stick him behind a desk to push paper for the rest of his career.

He took a deep breath and flattened his hands on the surface of the table. He needed to put Sedona out of his thoughts. She was an adult. Whatever shortcomings she might have, he was pretty sure sticking up for herself wasn't one of them. Hadn't he seen her go into the Human Resources office? He smiled wryly. It wasn't Sedona he should be worried about; it was Mike Sullivan.

"WHAT DO YOU MEAN you can't do anything?" Sedona stared at the woman on the other side of the desk. She'd figured Human Resources would be skeptical, but where else could she turn? "I'm telling you, these guys have been getting promoted based on how many *babes* they bang when they go on business travel."

Gladys Drummond smiled, apparently in sympathy, but Sedona could see it didn't reach the older woman's eyes. Sedona wanted to scream with frustration.

"I'm sure what you overheard was nothing more than a joke. A bad joke, in very bad taste, but a joke nonetheless." The director of Human Resources sat back in her chair and considered Sedona. "I understand how you might be feeling put out about Bob Lewis getting this latest promotion, but I can promise you it had nothing to do with his—his male prowess. All promotions have to be approved by the Promotion Selection Board."

Sedona blew out her breath in frustration. "But they seemed so sure of themselves. This—this 'club' must have influence at higher levels. If they say the promotion goes through, then it does."

Gladys tented her fingers together. "Do you know who the other members are?"

"I have no idea."

"Then we're back where we started, Sedona. You can't make these kinds of accusations without substantial evidence."

Sedona leaned forward eagerly. "I can get evidence. The members are supposed to get together this afternoon for a secret meeting. I could…I could sneak into the room and spy on them. Or…I could record what they say! That would be proof, wouldn't it?"

Gladys smiled, a patently false smile. "I believe there are laws against recording people without their knowledge. Even if it's permissible, it's not something I have the authority to approve. In truth, this whole issue is more or less beyond my purview. I'm only the director of Human Resources."

Sedona shook her head in disbelief. "So you're saying there's nothing you can do?" When the other woman didn't answer, Sedona gave a huff of defeat. "I'm sorry to hear that, I really am. I feel as if you're not leaving me any choice but to resign." She shrugged helplessly. "Consider this my two weeks' notice."

The other woman's eyebrows shot up. "Really, Sedona. Don't you think you're overreacting?"

Was she kidding? "No, quite the opposite. How can I even contemplate working for an agency that condones this kind of behavior?"

Whatever Gladys believed, Sedona knew what she'd overheard hadn't been a joke. It had been all too disgustingly real. She watched as Gladys picked up her PDA and consulted it. After a moment, she scribbled a number down on a piece of paper.

"This is the number for the Defense Criminal Investigative Service. They can put you in touch with an agent who might be able to help you." She handed the paper to Sedona. "I'm sure you'll find this whole thing is just a misunderstanding. I hope you'll reconsider leaving."

Sedona took the slip of paper. Fat chance. As expected, Human Resources didn't believe her, and it was unlikely DCIS would, either. Like HR, they'd probably decide she was just trying to get even with her male coworkers. And they'd be right, to a certain degree. Exposing and putting an end to the Membership would be her last effort to level the gender playing field.

"Thanks," she muttered, and pushed the slip into the pocket of her pants.

Leaving the director's office, she determined she *would* contact DCIS. She'd already declared her intent to resign, and she wasn't going to change her mind about it. Therefore, she had nothing to lose. She strode toward her office to make the phone call. As she passed the Drawing Room, her footsteps faltered, recalling that moment when she'd realized Angel had been sitting in the room directly across the hall.

Watching her.

And for just a moment, she'd been so completely flustered, she'd all but abandoned the idea of exposing the Membership. For one brief, crazy instant, the thought of leaving the agency just when Angel had finally returned seemed too high a price to pay.

Now, as she passed the conference room, her gaze was drawn irresistibly toward the chair where he'd been sitting. She shouldn't have been surprised to find it empty, but there was no denying the disappointment that surged through her. In every way that counted, he was so gone from her life.

3

FROM HER HIDING place in the women's bathroom, located directly beside the East Wing men's room, Sedona peeked through a crack in the door and watched no less than eight men slip covertly into the adjoining lavatory. With the entire East Wing closed for renovations, it was the perfect choice for a clandestine meeting. While she wasn't personally acquainted with all the men, she knew who they were. With the exception of Mike Sullivan, she was shocked by who she saw.

There was Tony Webber, whose intensity and single-minded dedication to the job she'd always found a little intimidating. She'd never have guessed his determination to succeed went this far. Then there was Alberto DeMasi, whom she'd always categorized as the warm, grandfatherly type. Apparently, there were no age restrictions on becoming a member, either. She knew he was a widower, but she cringed just thinking about him hitting on some strange woman in order to get promoted. Kevin Donnelly was middle-aged and divorced, and it was common knowledge he was struggling to raise two teenagers. Was his financial situation so tough that he needed to prostitute himself in order to get ahead?

Sedona pushed down the sympathy that threatened to sap her determination. She couldn't allow personal feelings to interfere. But of all the members she saw, none surprised her more than Ken Larson.

In his midthirties, Sedona had first noticed him because of his quirky sense of humor and easy camaraderie with the other engineers. He wasn't good-looking in the traditional sense, but he was friendly and likable, and there had been a time when Sedona had briefly considered dating him. And then Angel had come on board, and suddenly every other man she knew paled in comparison.

Still, she felt a huge sense of betrayal to discover Ken was involved with the Membership. She'd worked with him on several engineering issues and had found him reliable and knowledgeable. He was one of the few guys she actually enjoyed working with. Clearly, she'd given him way more credit than he deserved.

Biting her lip, she stepped back inside the women's bathroom and gently closed the door all the way, careful not to make any noise. She'd made the call to DCIS and had spoken with an Agent Curtis Denton. Despite his gruff voice and clipped manner, he'd taken her allegations seriously. When she had suggested confronting the members while wearing a recording device, he'd approved, with the promise of a full investigation to follow.

She adjusted the small tape player she had tucked into the waistband of her pants, beneath her blouse, to a less conspicuous position. Her finger was on the Record button when the sound of male laughter startled her.

Her fingers slipped on the buttons.

They were starting. Not wanting them to disperse before she had time to confront them, she stepped quickly into the corridor. She paused outside the door to the men's room and drew in a deep, fortifying breath. Then, placing her palm on the door, she gave it a mighty push so that it burst inward, slamming back against the inside wall with a resounding *bam!*

A group of men, including Tony and Kevin, leaped to attention from where they'd been lounging against the sinks. Under any other circumstances, their expressions of dismay and horror might have been amusing. The bathroom, tiled in turquoise-green, was awash with stark, fluorescent light and smelled faintly of disinfectant.

"Hello, gentlemen," Sedona said silkily. "Oh! Am I interrupting something?"

Mike Sullivan stepped forward. "What are you doing in here, Stewart? I mean, come on, this is a men's room!"

Sedona forced herself to smile into his face, despite her pounding heart. "I heard there was a meeting going on to discuss future advancement opportunities, and I didn't want to miss it. Actually, I heard there's a new upward-mobility program that practically guarantees promotions." She ignored his gape-mouthed expression and sidled past him to stop directly in front of Bob Lewis. "It must be one hell of a program. After all," she murmured, tracing a finger down the front of his madly patterned silk tie, "it's worked so well for Bob."

She stared directly into Bob's horrified eyes until a slow flush crept up his neck and suffused his face.

"I—I don't know what you're t-talking about," he stammered, his gaze darting to Mike.

"Oh," Sedona crooned, "I think you do. Or have you already forgotten the two babes you banged in San Diego?"

In the mirror behind Bob, she saw Alberto's appalled expression as realization slowly dawned. She also noticed Ken Larson holding what appeared to be several photographs. He looked even more horrified to see her in the men's room than she had been to see him enter. He was trying to slide the photos covertly into the pocket of his pants, only they were too large, so he oh so casually palmed the pictures and tucked his hands behind his back. Poor Bob looked as if he wanted to die. His gaze swung back to Mike Sullivan with something like desperation.

"I don't know what you've heard," Mike said in a hard voice as he stepped forward, "but I'm going to have to ask you to leave. Now."

Sedona turned away from Bob to stare at Mike. "I'm not going anywhere, Hound Dog, until you tell me everything there is to know about the Membership."

Mike laughed, but it sounded forced. "I have no idea what you're talking about, Stewart."

"Oh, yeah?" Before they could guess her intent, Sedona darted forward and snatched the photos from Ken's hands. Turning her back on the men, she swiftly flipped through the half dozen prints. Oh, God. It was true. There was Bob Lewis, sprawled half-naked in an enormous bed with two California-blond bombshells. Who would have guessed the guy had so much body hair? Ew.

As Mike reached over her shoulder for the photos, Sedona shot him a warning glance and turned away again.

"Oh, this is a good one," she said, holding up a photo of Mike sitting in a hotel-room chair with a scantily clad brunette on his lap. "It certainly doesn't look like your wife."

Mike visibly sagged. "Okay, Stewart, what do you want?"

"What do I want?" She thrust the pictures beneath his nose. "I want this to stop! It's not only illegal, it's immoral. And degrading." She turned to the other men, fixing the chagrined Tony and Alberto with a disapproving frown. "I'm surprised at all of you. I'd expect this kind of juvenile behavior from teenagers, not grown men." She gave Alberto a look that she hoped conveyed her deep disappointment. "And certainly not men with small grandchildren."

"Oh, get real, Stewart." One of the men—she recalled his

name was Brad Something-or-Other—stepped forward, his expression contemptuous. They had once worked together on an engineering investigation, and she hadn't much liked him then. He was a cocky man, with pale blue eyes and skin that bore evidence of what must have been a horrific case of adolescent acne. Now he shrugged. "So what if we like to indulge in a little extramarital activity? What are you going to do about it? Huh?"

"I could care less what you do on your own time," she snapped at him. "But when this kind of activity is not only condoned by management, but encouraged as a means of getting promoted, then I definitely have a problem with it. Big-time."

"You'll never prove it," Brad taunted. "Anyone can tell you our promotions were based purely on performance."

Sedona snorted and held up the photos. "No kidding."

"So what's your big plan?" Brad took another step forward, his smile mocking, and before Sedona could protest, snatched the photos from her fingers. "Going to report us to Human Resources? Tell the director about our evil club?" He laughed. "Go right ahead. I can hardly wait to see what kind of reaction you get."

Inwardly, Sedona rejoiced. This was what she had been hoping for. The photos be damned. If she could get the men to discuss the club openly, it would all be there on her tape recorder.

"Considering your…inclinations," Brad continued smoothly, "this will actually be something to look forward to."

Sedona frowned and noted the expressions on the other men's faces. They ranged from cautious amusement to outright smugness. "What do you mean by that?" she demanded. Inclinations?

"I mean that you're considered to be something of a man-hater, Stewart."

Sedona's mouth fell open, then snapped shut. The anger

and frustration that had been simmering just below the surface finally bubbled over. "Careful," she warned in a falsely sweet tone. "Your insecurities are showing. If I have a limited tolerance for the opposite sex," she continued, turning hard eyes on Ken Larson, "it's no wonder."

She wasn't at all mollified when Ken flushed and turned his gaze downward, clearly embarrassed.

"So tell me, Ken," she asked, "have you been banging babes, too?"

Ken turned a darker shade of red. "No," he mumbled. He raised his gaze to Sedona's and gave her a sheepish grin. "I mean, I haven't been promoted, have I?"

"So why are you doing this?"

Mike Sullivan stepped forward, effectively preventing Ken from answering. "You want to know why, Stewart? I'll tell you why. Because women like you are taking away our job security and our promotional opportunities."

Sedona gave him a bewildered look. "What are you talking about?"

Mike snorted. "It isn't enough to be a good engineer anymore. Hell, being a great engineer isn't even enough. Especially if you have one qualified female thrown into the mix. I'm telling you, it's reverse discrimination at its best. Call this our way of getting what we deserve—in every way that counts."

Sedona stared at him, appalled. "But why degrade yourselves?"

"You call it degrading. We call it proving our worth." Mike's voice was contemptuous. "Do you know how tough the competition is for the higher grades? Being competent and conscientious doesn't cut it anymore. These days, it's about being completely dedicated, about proving you'll do *anything* for the job, no matter what."

"Even if it's something incredibly intimate, or personally

repugnant?" Sedona couldn't believe what she was hearing. They were like a bunch of frat boys.

"Especially if it's intimate or repugnant." Mike gestured to the men around him. "Each of these guys deserves to be promoted. But how to determine which one is the right one for the job?" He leaned forward until his face was inches from Sedona's. "By putting it all on the line, baby. No guts, no glory."

Sedona couldn't keep the sarcasm out of her voice. "I can't recall where in the job description it says 'must get laid.'"

"Hey, don't knock it 'til you try it. In fact," Mike said, smirking, "I think you need to get laid in a big way, Stewart."

There was a snort of muffled laughter, and several of the men had to turn away to hide their amusement. Tony and Alberto looked mortified, but Sedona knew the others were getting a huge kick out of her embarrassment.

"Oh, and I suppose you're just the man for the job, huh?" Sedona injected as much scorn as she could into her voice. "Trust me, I wouldn't sleep with you if you were the last man on Earth."

But far from looking wounded, Mike just laughed. "No kidding. Unless I'm mistaken, you wouldn't sleep with any man. Period."

Sedona realized her hands were clenched into fists at her sides, and she forced herself to relax, though every cell in her body wanted to scream her denial at this jerk. "What, exactly, is that supposed to mean?"

"I know that when you go on business travel, you spend every night hiding in your hotel room." He arched an eyebrow at her, as if challenging her to deny it. "Remember when we were in Saint Louis for two weeks? You wouldn't even join the rest of us for dinner, never mind any late-night entertainment. Hell, your idea of excitement is probably finding a mint on your hotel pillow."

Ouch. That hurt, probably because it was no less than the truth.

"Just because I choose not to have affairs," she said tightly, "does not mean I'm incapable of having them."

Mike's eyebrows flew up and he exchanged a knowing look with the man nearest him. "Oh, really? Well, excuse me if I don't believe you. You've been working here for what— five years? And from what I hear, you haven't even had a date, much less an affair."

"So what are you saying, Mike?" Okay, this was it. If she played this right, she would have all the proof she needed to expose them. "Are you saying if I have an affair the next time I go on business travel, I'll get promoted?"

Mike grinned, clearly enjoying her outrage. He turned to the other men. "What do you think, boys? Should we let Stewart join our elite membership?"

"No way," interjected Bob. "She's just trying to screw us. Figuratively speaking, I mean."

"Supposing I agree," Sedona said, ignoring him, "what's my guarantee? I mean, how can you assure me that the next promotion will be mine?"

"Don't you worry about that," Mike soothed. "We have five members who sit on the Promotion Selection Board. All we have to do is give them a name. You just bring back proof of the affair." He smirked. "If you can."

Sedona drew herself up and raked the group of men with what she hoped was a scathing look. "Despite what you think, I'm just as capable of a little on-the-road romance as the rest of you." She looked at Mike. "So, that's it, then? I just bring back some kind of proof? Like a pair of men's underwear?"

Mike laughed. "Oh, no. It's not that easy. Just ask Bob."

Bob mumbled something under his breath.

"What was that?" Sedona took a step closer. "I didn't quite catch that." *On my tape recorder.*

"I said you need to bring back photos." His tone was almost defiant.

"Photos," Sedona repeated. "Photos of what?"

"Sedona…forget it, okay?" It was Ken Larson, stepping forward. His face was still red with embarrassment, but his eyes met hers squarely. "Don't get mixed up in this. It's— it's not worth it."

"Photos of the significant other," Mike continued, interrupting Ken and impaling the other man with a hard stare. "Preferably in a position that leaves no doubt as to the nature of the relationship."

Seeing Mike's censure, Ken ducked his head and retreated to the far wall. Despite her determination to see this operation through, Sedona nearly ran for the door. She'd never been so completely mortified in her entire life. Drawing in a deep breath, she nodded. "Got it. What else?"

Mike laughed. "Okay, then. The picture has to contain something that will clearly indicate the time and location of the event. Like a newspaper and a room key, prominently displayed. You get the idea."

"Fine. The next time I go on business travel, I'll bring back the proof you need. Okay?" Sedona had no intention of bringing back proof of anything. She already had the proof she needed to put an end to this "club."

Ken looked at the other men, and although some of them looked away or down at their feet, Mike nodded his approval.

"Okay, it's a deal. Oh, and Sedona?"

She looked at him questioningly.

"The picture can't be staged. You can't get your brother,

or your cousin, or your good friend to pose for it, just to fake us out."

"Great. So that's it? Okay, then. I, uh, should probably get back to work," Sedona muttered, suddenly anxious to get out of there. The sordidness of the entire scheme made her feel ill. "I'll let you know when I have what you need."

Without waiting for a reply, she bolted for the door. She walked quickly through the deserted corridors of the East Wing until she reached the main part of the building. Only then did she place her hand over the slight bulge in her waistband, reassuring herself that the small recorder was still there. She had it all on tape.

IN THE PRIVACY of her office, Sedona pulled the tape player from beneath her blouse. She stared in dismay at the small device.

The Record button was off.

Maybe she had inadvertently hit the Power button on her way back to the office. Please, let that be the case. With trembling fingers, she pushed Play. There was nothing but the soft whirring of the tape as it wound from one reel to the next. There was no recorded conversation. There was nothing but silence. She rewound the tape and played it again. Still nothing.

With a groan of self-disgust, she tossed the tape player onto her desk, sank into her chair and buried her face in her hands. She had neglected to hit the Record button. She'd been so busy making sure the tape player was hidden, and then so nervous about confronting the men, that she hadn't even turned the damn thing on.

She had absolutely no proof, not a shred of incriminating evidence against the members. It would be her word against theirs. Worse, she had lowered herself to their level by agreeing to have a sordid affair of her own in order to gain access to their disgusting club. Though she had only been pretending, she felt cheapened and dirty.

She picked up the phone and punched in Agent Denton's number, dreading the inevitable.

"DCIS, Agent Denton."

Reluctantly, Sedona identified herself and let the story tumble out.

"So you see," she concluded, "I have absolutely no evidence. I blew it."

"Not necessarily," Agent Denton replied. "You agreed to join the club, to become a member based on the same conditions imposed upon the others. That's definitely something we can work with."

Sedona floundered in disbelief. "I wasn't serious—I mean, I never…I don't think…"

"Miss Stewart," Denton interrupted. "I'm not suggesting you do anything you're not completely comfortable with. I'm merely saying this could be a way for us to get the evidence we need to really nail these guys."

"Agent Denton," she protested, "I could never do what these guys do. I couldn't live with myself. In fact, I haven't told my supervisor yet, but I submitted my resignation to the Human Resources office earlier today."

There was a brief silence. "I understand. Of course, this doesn't change my intent to conduct a full investigation into your allegations. However, if you should change your mind about assisting us, you have my number."

Sedona replaced the receiver in the cradle, completely drained by the day's events. She scrubbed her hands over her eyes.

She sat there, her mind replaying the scene in the men's bathroom. When somebody knocked on her office door she started guiltily, fearful that someone had discovered her clandestine meeting with the Membership, and was coming to confront her.

The door opened, and she found herself staring at Joe Clemons, the director of Engineering.

Her boss.

Her heart sank as for one instant she envisioned herself being fired before she had the chance to tell her boss she quit. Then her gaze traveled to the man standing just behind Joe.

It was Angel Torres, and from the taut expression on his face and the dangerous glint in his black eyes, she knew the reason for their visit went way beyond the Membership and its dirty little secrets.

She stood up. "Joe, come in. What's going on?"

Joe's face was pinched with concern as he entered her office. He didn't say anything, merely placed a memo on her desk. Sedona couldn't prevent herself from glancing at Angel before she picked it up. He was rigid with suppressed anger. Or frustration. She wasn't sure which, but she could sense the coiled tension in his lean, hard body. He dominated her small office with his presence. He was all dark, simmering power held under tight control.

Sedona shivered.

She forced herself to concentrate on the memo, but it was a moment before the words on the page shifted into focus and became legible. She quickly scanned the page, and her stomach tightened in dread. It was an electronic memo, issued by the Secretary of the Navy, and the words *urgent* and *investigation* leaped off the page at her.

"Oh my God," she breathed.

Three F/A-44 Coyote fighter jets had crashed into the Pacific Ocean in three separate training incidents over a twenty-four-hour period, resulting in pilot ejections. Two additional jets had experienced problems when their throttle-levers had locked up, but the pilots had been able to activate in-flight emergency shutdown procedures and conduct single-engine landings.

The secretary of the navy was demanding an immediate investigation into the crashes, as well as an inspection of all remaining Coyotes. Until the problem was resolved, all jets were grounded.

"What does this mean?" Sedona wasn't sure if she was asking Joe or Angel.

"*¡Maldita!*" growled Angel. "It means we have one hell of a problem on our hands. There's a war going on, and with our fighter jets grounded, we can't provide the air power our troops need to stay alive." He looked at Joe. "I'd like to fly out to Lemoore as soon as I can. Tomorrow, if possible."

Sedona frowned. Lemoore was the location of a naval air station in California. It was just her luck that he had finally come back, and now he was leaving. Again. Her hopes of seeing him during the remaining two weeks of her employment were dashed.

Joe sighed and ran a hand over his face. "I agree. The Aircraft Mishap Board is scrambling to get their folks out to the three crash sites. The other two jets are en route to a hangar at Lemoore for inspection. We'll have a full team ready to head out there first thing tomorrow."

Sedona held her breath, hardly daring to anticipate his next words.

Joe looked at her. "Sedona, I want you to head up a team to inspect the engines. You'll be gone for a couple of weeks, so take the rest of the afternoon to make whatever personal arrangements you need to. The other divisions are putting together their own teams to analyze the power-level control and the hydraulics systems." He glanced over at Angel. "Lieutenant Commander Torres will conduct flight tests of the grounded jets and put together baseline evaluations. You'll be working together pretty closely, so I'll reserve a block of rooms for the teams at the same hotel. That way, you can spend the evenings going over your findings."

Angel turned his gaze on Sedona, and she felt her breath hitch as she stared into the fathomless darkness of his eyes. For an instant, she wondered what it would be like to have that gaze heated with passion. To have it directed toward her.

"I think that's a good suggestion," he said, and his eyes drifted over Sedona's features.

Was it only her imagination, or did they linger for a moment on her mouth? Nervously, she ran the tip of her tongue over her bottom lip.

"I'll be making my own travel arrangements just as soon as I get back to my office," Angel continued, his eyes still on her. "If it's okay with you, ma'am, I'll reserve us seats next to each other on the plane. It's a long flight from Boston, so we might as well use the time to go over the Coyote incident reports."

Sedona stared back at Angel. Sit with him on the plane? A couple of weeks in the same hotel together? Working closely with him, and perhaps getting together in the evenings? Holy Coyote, there really was a God!

She looked swiftly down at the Navy memo and pretended to reread it in order to compose her features and hide the fluttering excitement she was feeling. Excitement she had no right to feel, not in the face of such a blow to the Navy flight program.

When, after a brief moment, she glanced back up at Angel, she prayed her expression didn't reveal her feelings. "That, um, sounds fine." She tried to sound cool, but her voice quavered ever so slightly. She cleared her throat. "Just give me a call to let me know what flight we're on. I'll meet you at the airport."

Angel smiled then, his teeth strong and white in his tanned face. Sedona's heart rate kicked up a notch and her stomach did a slow roll.

"Since it looks like we're going to be partners," he said easily, "I'll do you one better. If you give me your address, I'll pick you up in the morning and give you a lift to the airport."

Sedona knew right then that she had been wrong.

She had thought she could never engage in an affair while on business travel. Up until that moment, she couldn't envision herself having an affair, period. But when Angel Torres looked at her like that, she knew she would gladly toss every one of her old-fashioned ideals and morals out the window for just one night—one amazing, never-to-be-forgotten night—in his arms.

4

TUCKED INTO a window seat of the commercial airliner, Sedona tried not to stare as Angel stowed their carry-on luggage in the overhead compartment. She had never seen him wear anything other than his military flight suit, and the sight of him clad in a black T-shirt and jeans was entirely too appealing. From her vantage point beneath him, it was difficult not to admire the impressive bulge of his biceps as he secured their belongings. Apparently, she wasn't alone in that regard.

A trio of pretty young women sat in the row of seats across from them, and Sedona had heard their collective sigh of longing when Angel made his way down the narrow aisle, ducking his head to avoid contact with the ceiling. His dark good looks, combined with his rugged build, were guaranteed to capture the attention of every female on board. But when he smiled at the three women and inclined his head politely in greeting, Sedona thought they might actually swoon with delight. Even now, she could hear them tittering as they ogled his backside. To his credit, Angel appeared oblivious to the attention he attracted.

Satisfied their gear was safely stowed, he bent down and eased his large frame into the seat next to Sedona. His sheer size dwarfed her. He had managed to secure seats next to the emergency exit, which afforded them a little extra legroom.

Even so, the space barely accommodated his long legs, and his knee brushed against hers in the close confines.

He quirked a rueful grin at her. "Well, this is cozy."

When he looked over at her and flashed those incredible dimples, Sedona's brain just about shut down. She pressed tighter against the window to accommodate his wide shoulders. She hadn't counted on being in such proximity with him and was glad she'd taken extra care that morning with her appearance.

Still, she couldn't help but feel completely self-conscious by his nearness. God, the guy even smelled great. An intoxicating blend of clean cotton, soap and something mildly spicy that might have been aftershave, made her want to inhale deeply. She watched as he buckled the seat belt across his lean hips. He had strong hands, with long, tapered fingers and neat nails. And, thankfully, no rings.

One of the airline attendants, a pretty woman with blond hair and large brown eyes, stopped by their seats. Although she smiled politely at Sedona, her eyes barely left Angel.

"I'm required to tell you that you're sitting in an emergency-exit aisle," she said, dimpling down at him. "Do you have any physical…restrictions that might prevent you from opening the emergency door and assisting other passengers in the event of an emergency?"

Angel looked up at her, and his lips curved in the barest hint of a smile. "Uh, no, I don't believe so."

The woman was practically eating him alive with her eyes.

"Well," she purred, "I didn't think that was the case, but regulations require me to ask. Oh!" She lurched forward into Angel's lap, thrusting her breasts into his face in the process, as a passenger squeezed past her in the aisle.

Angel caught her by the upper arms and steadied her as she braced herself against him with both hands on his broad shoulders. Sedona barely contained her indelicate snort of disgust.

"Oh, my," the attendant said, breathless and laughing. "I am so sorry!"

Yeah, right, Sedona thought. Like that wasn't completely planned.

"No problem," Angel assured the woman, and set her firmly back on her feet.

"Well," she said, practically preening in the aisle, "if there's anything you need, just let me know." She indicated her name tag with one pink-tipped finger. "I'm Taffy."

Sedona turned toward the window, rolling her eyes. Angel murmured something vague in response, and she turned back in time to see the woman waggle her fingers at him before sauntering away.

"That was helpful," she muttered darkly, "considering I'm the one sitting next to the emergency door." She turned to Angel. "So just what is it I'm supposed to do in the event of an actual emergency?"

Angel's black eyes danced with devilish amusement as he looked at her, and a lazy smile creased his features. "The only thing you have to do, *mina*," he drawled, "is get the hell out of my way, and I'll take care of the rest."

Sedona's eyes widened in surprise, and she had a vivid image of him bodily lifting her out of the way before assuming the manly duty of controlling the emergency door. Part of her was taken aback by his sheer cockiness. But another part was secretly thrilled by that same arrogance. He was supremely confident, capable of anything. He made her feel both fragile and safe.

"Hey, Sedona," interrupted a masculine voice. "Looks like we'll be working together."

She dragged her gaze away from Angel and nearly groaned

aloud in disbelief. It was Ken Larson, making his way down the aisle. He paused near their seats and smiled almost shyly at Sedona. She stared back at him in utter horror.

"I'm, uh, really looking forward to it," he continued. Was it just her imagination, or did his eyes sweep over her in a proprietary way? "It'll be, you know, a real team-building experience. Who knows? There might even be a promotion in it for some of us." Noticing Angel for the first time, he extended a hand toward the other man. "Aren't you Lieutenant Torres? Good to see you back, sir. I'm Ken Larson. I'll be part of Sedona's team of engineers." He smiled again at Sedona. "Like I said, I'm really looking forward to working with you again. Maybe this time…" He let his words trail off, then laughed self-consciously and shrugged. "Who knows, right?"

He moved past their seats, but his words echoed in Sedona's head. Her heart sank. Ken Larson believed she was interested in joining the Membership. He'd expect her to take advantage of this opportunity to acquire the proof she'd need to claim the next promotion.

She swore silently.

As soon as they reached the hotel, she'd pull him aside and disclaim any interest in joining their club. What he decided to do was his own business, but no way would she have him believing she would sink to the same level.

"You work with that guy?"

Sedona glanced guiltily at Angel. "Yes," she muttered. "We've worked together on investigations before."

There was a momentary silence.

"Oh, yeah? So…you're just coworkers? Nothing more?"

Sedona stared at him in disbelief. "No! I mean, yes! I mean—" She was spluttering in indignation, acutely aware that Angel watched her with amused interest. "We are definitely just coworkers. God." She recalled Ken's expression as he'd swept his gaze over her, and shuddered in revulsion. "Please tell me you didn't think—"

Angel laughed and held up one hand to forestall her. "I'm sorry, it's just that there seemed to be…something between the two of you. I just thought…"

"Well, you thought wrong."

"Fine."

"Fine." Sedona slid him a last sidelong glance before turning to look out the window. This whole trip was fast becoming a nightmare of huge proportions. It was completely unfair that one of the Membership should be part of her team. She needed to set Ken straight immediately, or they'd have a tough time working together. And the last thing she needed was for Angel to believe they were involved in any way.

She sneaked a look at Angel, and then colored hotly. He was watching her, and the expression in his dark eyes was thoughtful.

ANGEL WATCHED as Sedona wrestled her suitcase, laptop and overnight bag through the doorway of her hotel room and then closed the door firmly behind her. He shook his head slightly in bemusement and turned his attention to his own door, directly next to hers.

The woman was a complete contradiction and damned if he could figure out what was up with her. He'd heard the rumors about her, even down on the flight line. Personally, he wasn't convinced she was some kind of man-hater. She just had a zero-tolerance policy for stupidity. He'd heard she was one of the agency's best engineers. He'd even read a couple of her technical reports and had to agree. Personally, he believed the malicious whispers about her stemmed from the feelings of inadequacy she engendered in her male counterparts.

He'd seen the way she looked at him when she thought he didn't notice. He wasn't conceited, but he recognized female appreciation when he saw it. And Sedona Stewart, despite her acerbic and sometimes mannish manner, had appreciated just about all she could see of him in the scant seconds he had caught her looking.

Normally, that would be all the incentive he'd need to begin a pursuit, but there was something about Sedona that made him hesitate. It had nothing to do with her looks. She was attractive enough, but her cool reserve made him reluctant to explore just how appreciative she might be. He liked his women on the adventurous side, and Sedona didn't strike him as the daring type.

Stepping inside, he closed the door to his room, noting it had a balcony overlooking an interior courtyard where the pool and hot tub were located. He could hear the shouts and cries of several kids as they splashed in the water. Dumping his bags on top of the bed, he opened the sliding-glass doors to let some fresh air into the room, and paused when he noticed movement on the balcony next to his.

He leaned against the doorjamb just inside the room and watched as Sedona moved over to the railing of her balcony. She had shed the navy blazer she'd worn during the flight, and she was barefoot. Her toenails were painted a glossy shade of cherry red.

She stretched her arms up over her head and loosely linked her fingers together. Then she arched her back and bent sideways at the waist, first to one side, then the other. The movement pulled the fabric of her modest, button-down shirt taut across her breasts. Angel's eyebrows went up. Maybe not so mannish, after all.

Stepping carefully back into the room, he quietly pulled the drapes closed, reluctant to disturb her. But even with the curtains drawn, he couldn't get the image of those brightly painted toes out of his head. Not that he had a foot fetish; they just weren't what he'd expect to see on her. They intrigued him. Made him wonder what other feminine attributes she kept hidden from the rest of the world.

They'd agreed to meet downstairs in the lobby for dinner, but that was still several hours away. If he hurried, he could head over to the hotel gym for a quick workout before he had to meet Sedona. He'd make a few phone calls first, to let his commanding officer and the guys at the naval air station know he'd arrived, and to confirm they'd be at the hangar to begin inspecting the grounded jets first thing in the morning.

It felt good to be back in California. He'd been stationed at Lemoore Naval Air Station early on in his career. He'd done his initial flight training there in an F-14 Tomcat. He hadn't thought anything could be more thrilling than flying that fighter jet, until he'd climbed into the cockpit of a Coyote to conduct test flights on behalf of the Navy. Then he'd been deployed aboard the USS *Abraham Lincoln,* an aircraft carrier in the Persian Gulf, and life was just about as perfect as it could get.

During the ten months he'd been aboard the carrier, he'd flown more than sixty sorties from her deck in support of the war against terrorism, and he'd accomplished each one flawlessly. At least, he amended, until that last one. Yep, that one had been the last straw for his commanding officer, who had seen to it Angel was taken out of combat flight.

He tried hard not to be bitter that they'd shipped him to a manufacturing plant on the East Coast to perform test flights. He knew he was lucky they hadn't busted him back down to lieutenant. At least they hadn't completely clipped his wings.

When they'd first assigned him to Aerospace International's facility, nearly eighteen months earlier, it was to be a three-year stint. Angel knew he'd been given the assignment as a sort of reward. Extended shore-based assignments were highly sought after by guys who had spent months at sea. It was an opportunity to attend school, to strengthen family bonds and to recharge.

Angel didn't need any of that.

He'd already graduated from the Navy War College, he had neither wife nor kids, and the only thing that recharged his engines was combat flight. So when he'd been deployed to the Navy carrier after just six months of performing test flights, he'd been thrilled. Not that conducting test flights was a bad gig; there was a certain thrill in taking a jet on its maiden voyage into the skies. He just didn't want to do it for the rest of his career.

But according to his commanding officer, after the stunt he'd pulled during his last sortie, that's just what would happen if he didn't straighten up and fly right—literally. So he'd sucked it up and resigned himself to completing his shore assignment, with the knowledge that it would only be for another eighteen months, and then he'd be back aboard a carrier.

Close to thirty minutes later, he finally pushed open the doors of the gym, and stopped dead in his tracks, riveted. The workout room was empty except for one other person.

Angel's brain almost shut down at the sight.

It was a woman, standing with her back to him. Well…sort of. She was bent over at the waist, legs slightly apart as she gently bounced the palms of her hands against the floor. She wore a pair of tight biking-style shorts, and Angel was transfixed by the sight of her perfect rear, displayed to full advantage by her position. It was lusciously heart-shaped, and he wondered rather dazedly how those cheeks would feel in his hands. She wore some kind of sports bra, and above the waistband of her shorts, her skin was smooth and golden. He couldn't see her face, but through the inverted vee of her splayed thighs, her breasts bounced enticingly with each move she made.

Every cell in his body urged him to walk up behind her, grasp her hips and press himself against the feminine softness she so blatantly presented to him. Stifling a groan, he held his towel low in front of himself and moved swiftly to the opposite side of the room. He couldn't remember the last time he'd had such an instant physical reaction to a woman, but yep, there it was.

He scanned the equipment in the room and settled on the treadmill. It was the only piece of machinery that faced the wall, away from the temptress. He decided a quick five-mile run would take his mind off his libido and allow him to warm up before he tackled the weights. He had just settled into a nice stride when he realized there was a mirror on the wall beside him, providing him an unobstructed view of the woman. She was on the floor now, legs splayed wide as she bent forward, head down, and grasped her toes.

His eyes narrowed.

Her auburn hair was pulled back in a thick, glossy braid. When she straightened, she raised her arms above her head and stretched her spine before bending low over the other extended leg.

Angel very nearly fell off the treadmill. As it was, he lost his smooth stride and had to grasp the handles of the machine and do a quick two-step to regain his balance.

Goddamn. It couldn't be. Could it? But when she raised herself upward again and twisted in his direction, her eyes met his in the mirror. She froze, arms stretched over her head, her supple breasts thrust forward beneath the stretchy material of her top.

It was Sedona Stewart.

If the expression of horror on her face was anything to go by, she was just as shocked to see him. Angel swiftly recovered his composure and even managed to give her a benignly polite smile, as if he hadn't just been thinking about thrusting into her, while cradling her sweetly curved backside in the palms of his hands.

In the mirror, he saw her blush and was momentarily transfixed. The flush of color spread slowly downward, until it seemed her entire body was rosy. She gave him a brief nod and scrambled to her feet.

Angel stared. He couldn't help it. He wasn't an expert where women were concerned, but he prided himself on having a good eye. But holy mother of God, who would have ever guessed that hidden beneath her conservative business attire was a body like that? It was better suited to pole dancing than sitting behind a desk.

As he watched, she snatched up a towel and a bottle of water she'd left on the floor. Damn. She was going to bolt. She hesitated, her hand on the door, before she looked over at him.

"So...I'll see you at seven o'clock?"

His breath was coming a little unevenly. He told himself it was from his exertions on the treadmill. "Yes, but I hope you're not leaving on my account."

She turned even rosier, if that was possible. "No," she said quickly, and Angel knew she was lying. "I'm—I'm done with my workout. I was just cooling down when you came in. So...I guess I'll see you later."

As if unable to help herself, her eyes slid down the length of his body. Angel tightened beneath that swift scrutiny. Her eyes flew back to his, and his gaze was drawn irresistibly to her mouth when she ran her tongue over her lips. And in the brief instant before she turned away, he knew.

She wanted him.

But before he could say anything more to her, she yanked the door open and was gone.

Angel was hardly aware of the treadmill churning beneath him. His body was operating on autopilot, his long strides easily keeping pace with the machine. But his mind was spinning. He still couldn't comprehend that beneath the all-business exterior Sedona presented to the world was a lush, tantalizingly feminine woman.

Christ, hers was the kind of body men fantasized about. He felt a little dazed, not only by her physical attributes, but his own reaction to them. He was still slightly aroused, and that was just from looking at her.

He gave a huff of disbelieving laughter. Had he really thought she held no appeal for him? He recalled the habit she had of moistening her lips with her tongue. He wondered if she was even aware she did it, or that when she did, it drew one's eye to the ripe fullness of her lips. He wondered how they would feel beneath his own.

He was sweating.

Glancing down at the display on the treadmill, he realized he was already halfway through his five miles. He felt as if he hadn't even expended himself. He was vitalized, charged with a new energy. He recognized it as keen anticipation.

It was the same way he felt when he climbed into the cockpit of his fighter jet to complete a combat mission—the hot, pounding adrenaline of excitement, the sheer rush of going into the unknown. It was the thrill of the hunt, of finding his target and nailing it. Of coming in fast and low, dropping his payload and streaking away before the object ever knew what hit them.

It was how he felt now, thinking about Sedona Stewart.

He wanted her.

Angel wondered if two weeks would be enough time to entice the prickly, straitlaced Sedona Stewart into his bed, then decided it had to be.

He'd never failed a mission before, and he wasn't about to start now.

5

SEDONA GLANCED at her watch for what seemed like the hundredth time. It was three minutes past seven and she'd been pacing her hotel room for a quarter of an hour. Should she knock on Angel's door? Wait for him to knock on hers? Stand outside in the corridor and cough discreetly until he heard her?

She wished for the first time in her life that her experience with men went beyond competing with them for promotions. Establishing personal relationships with them had never seemed all that important before.

From the time she'd been a young teenager with an uncanny aptitude for math and sciences, her life had revolved around her education and subsequent career. Even now, she could hear her father's voice. *If you want to succeed in this world, you have to be willing to sacrifice. Your looks may get you the job, but your brains will get you to the top. You have to be tough to make it in a man's world.*

She knew he'd only had her best interests in mind. A successful man, he believed his oldest daughter should demand the same respect—and salary—he had. As a senior vice president of a Fortune 500 company, he'd traveled frequently and worked long hours. When he was home, he ruled with an iron fist, ruthlessly steering his children in the direction he thought they should go.

At fifty-five, he died of a massive heart attack. Her mother had found herself alone, lacking any practical skills beyond child rearing and the ability to plan dinner parties. While there was a sizable life insurance policy, nothing could compensate for the years of loneliness she'd endured.

Sedona was grateful for her career and her ability to support herself, but she had to admit, her ambition to succeed in a man's world had done nothing for her on a personal level. She had few friends, male or female. She'd never had a real boyfriend, at least none to speak of, and never for any length of time. She spent her evenings at home watching reruns of *Sex and the City,* vaguely shocked at the blatant promiscuity and sexual freedom the characters portrayed, and secretly wishing she could be more like them.

She thought about how Angel had looked at her in the fitness room. For just an instant, his expression had been taut and hungry, as if he wanted to eat her alive. A primal awareness had surged through her and a slow, pulsing throb had settled low in her abdomen. It had scared her so much she'd bolted, praying he hadn't seen the naked desire she'd felt for him.

Back in her room, she berated herself for being such a coward. She wanted Angel Torres. She'd fantasized about him more times than she cared to admit. She should have stayed. She should have continued with her stretching exercises; maybe acted coy and asked him to show her how the weight machines worked. She'd been a total wimp, but no more. She was going to change her attitude and go for what she wanted.

As she paced, she caught sight of her reflection in the mirror and stopped to examine herself with a critical eye. Lacking anything overtly feminine in her wardrobe, she had finally settled on a pair of faded jeans topped with a sleeveless blouse in a soft, moss green. She had debated over what to do with her hair, and finally opted to wear it loose around her shoulders, where it gleamed in soft waves of red and gold. She wore no cosmetics, unless a quick slash of tinted, fruity lip balm across her mouth counted.

For her, these concessions were huge, but would they be enough to attract Angel's attention? Hopefully, because if he didn't show at least a tiny bit of interest in her as a woman, she wasn't sure she'd have the courage to go through with her plan.

She was going to sleep with Angel Torres.

Well…she hoped it would be more than just sleeping, actually. A lot more. She remembered again all the hard, lean muscle he possessed, and the ease with which he'd worked the treadmill. Her imagination conjured up sultry images of him directing that strength and stamina into a different kind of workout. The images she carried of him in her mind had even inspired her to fill several pages of her sketchbook.

She'd made up her mind about what to do as she'd fled the fitness room, her heart still beating hard from the jumble of emotions he stirred in her. She was going to have him. It hadn't been as much a conscious decision as a physical imperative.

She'd probably end up getting her soft, stupid heart completely broken, but she was determined to know—just once— what it would be like to be with Angel Torres. To be one with him, connected on a level so intimate her chest constricted thinking about it.

She'd never done anything so reckless in her entire life. She recalled Mike Sullivan's comments about hiding in her hotel room each time she went on business travel. She'd always been so concerned about her reputation that she'd pretty much denied herself any enjoyment. Her father would have said there was a name for women who consorted with their male colleagues after hours. He'd have had no respect for those women, and Sedona reluctantly acknowledged it was one of the reasons she chose to remain alone and aloof.

But her father was gone. There was nobody to criticize her behavior except herself. How much worse would she feel if she let this opportunity slip away? If she was ever going to fulfill her fantasy, now was the perfect time. She was at a point in her life when she had decisions to make, both personally and professionally. Her entire life had been spent setting her own dreams aside in order to please others. Well, now it was time to please herself.

Sedona admitted Angel was out of her league. On a sexometer, he was off the charts. She might be able to keep his interest for the short run, but eventually he'd move on. She was prepared for that. This wasn't about keeping him. It was about taking control of her life and finally doing things to please herself. She had the distinct feeling that having Angel in her bed would please her very much.

But she didn't have much time to accomplish her goal. She had no idea how long the inspection of the grounded jets might take. She'd told her boss she was resigning but hadn't been truthful about why, except that her career wasn't advancing as she'd hoped.

While she had initially given just two weeks' notice, she'd finally agreed to stay with the agency long enough to complete the Coyote inspections, however long that might take. They could be on the West Coast for weeks, or they could get lucky and identify the cause of the mishaps within the first few days. Either way, they couldn't stay at Lemoore Naval Air Station indefinitely, and once they returned to the East Coast, her employment with the agency would be over.

She was never going to be this alone with Angel again. Even if she weren't leaving, he could be recalled to combat duty at any time and she might never see him again. That knowledge added a certain desperation to her feelings; made her bolder and more determined.

A sharp knock on her hotel-room door caused her to jump guiltily. She gave herself one last, appraising look in the mirror, smoothed her blouse down over her hips and opened the door.

Her pulse quickened a beat at the sight of the dark-eyed man who stood waiting for her. Angel wore a white, button-down shirt that emphasized the bronze hue of his skin. His black hair gleamed wetly from a recent shower, and Sedona caught the tangy scent of his soap. He smelled good enough to bite. When he smiled, she wanted to trace the deep indents of his dimples with her fingers, pull his head down and crush her mouth against his.

His eyes swept over her, missing nothing. Sedona was glad she'd decided to leave her hair down when his gaze lingered for a moment on the glossy waves. "Ready to go?"

She ducked her head, half afraid he might see her intent in her eyes, and rummaged through her purse to ensure she had her room key. "I'm ready. What did you have in mind for dinner?"

He shrugged and indicated she should precede him down the hallway toward the elevators. "I usually let the lady choose. What are you in the mood for?"

You.

"I'm not familiar with this area, so I'll let you choose. Although," she added with deliberate nonchalance, "we could always stay in and order room service."

She sensed his sudden attention, but they had reached the bank of elevators where several other hotel guests were already waiting, and he didn't respond to her veiled sugges-tion. Her heart pounded at her own temerity.

His casual remark about letting the lady choose had mildly

annoyed her. How many women had he been with? And how many of them had offered themselves for dessert?

As they stepped into the elevator, Sedona was pressed into the corner by the other occupants. Angel stood beside her, his large frame protecting her from getting squashed by those around them. As Sedona determinedly stared at the illuminated numbers blinking their descent floor by floor, Angel leaned down and spoke quietly into her ear.

"Would you rather we order in?"

A warm wash of heat suffused her neck and crawled upward, and she risked a glance at him. He watched her with a careful intensity that made her breath catch. For a moment she worried about what the others in the elevator might think, but they stared fixedly at the closed doors, and she doubted they could hear Angel above the piped-in music.

"Honestly?" she asked softly. "Yes. But it's only our first night here. There'll be other nights when we can opt to stay in."

There. Let him make what he wanted out of that. The elevator came to a halt and the doors slid smoothly open. Sedona started only slightly when Angel took her elbow and steered her past the small groups of people congregated in the lobby. The heat of his hand on her bare arm caused a shiver to course through her.

"Cold?" he asked. "We can go back upstairs and get you a sweater, if you'd like."

"No, I'm not cold," Sedona murmured. "Just the opposite, in fact. But if you'd like to go back upstairs…" She let the sentence trail off suggestively.

Angel's eyes narrowed and a hint of a dimple appeared in one cheek as he considered her. "I think you enjoy teasing me, *mina*. If I weren't so hungry, I might take you up on it." He laughed as she came to an abrupt halt and stared at him. "Relax. Now I'm the one who's teasing."

He looked away, his eyes scanning the lobby. Sedona scowled at him. Dratted man. It had taken a lot of nerve for her to make that comment, and for one heart-stopping second she had actually believed he was considering her offer. Apparently, he wasn't hungry enough. For her, at least. She was definitely going to have to do something about that.

"We can always grab a bite to eat at the hotel restaurant," Angel commented, interrupting her thoughts. "Looks like a pretty popular place."

Across the lobby a dimly lit restaurant and lounge was segregated by a low wall and a row of potted palm trees. Strains of music drifted toward them, interspersed with noisy laughter and loud conversation. It looked like a sports bar, and Sedona's stomach tightened at the thought of having dinner in that overtly male setting. It was exactly the type of place Mike Sullivan and his cronies liked to frequent; the type of place where single women were easy targets for their lewd attention.

As if on cue, she heard her voice being called. Moaning inwardly, she turned to see none other than Ken Larson and a group of men from the engineering division stroll across the lobby toward them.

"Hey, Sedona," Ken called, a friendly grin splitting his features, "you and the lieutenant care to join us for dinner?"

"No!" she said quickly. Then, sensing Angel's curiosity, she hurried to add, "We were actually just heading out to find someplace a little…quieter." She smiled brightly at Ken and tried to pretend she didn't want to wipe the knowing look from his face. "But you go ahead, enjoy your meal. We'll see you later."

"Okay. But speaking of later," Ken continued blithely, ignoring the warning daggers she was throwing at him, "we'll be in the lounge if you want to join us when you get back." He turned to Angel. "We tend to get a little rowdy when we're on business trips…you know how it goes. But we have a good time. We've been trying to get Sedona here to let loose a little bit and join us, but she's a tough nut to crack. But, hey—" he leaned forward to give Angel's shoulder a friendly slap "—maybe you'll have better luck."

"Maybe she's just particular about the company she keeps," Angel replied, looking pointedly at his shoulder, and then at Ken.

Sedona watched as Ken's eyes narrowed, and his features tightened. He stared at Angel for a full minute before he spoke. "Maybe you're right, Lieutenant," he finally said, his tone cool. "In all the years I've known her, I can't recall a single time she's ever agreed to have dinner with one of the team." He cocked his head slightly as he considered Angel. "So what does that say about you?"

"That I'm one lucky son of a bitch," Angel replied, grinning as he took Sedona by the arm and steered her toward the exit.

"Yeah, well, I hope you remembered to bring your camera, Sedona," Ken called after their retreating backs. "After all, I wouldn't want you to miss any of the *sights.*"

Sedona knew he was referring to the "proof" she had promised to bring back to the Membership. It was obvious Ken didn't expect her to go through with it, and as soon as an opportunity presented itself, she'd let him know he was right. There was no way she wanted anything to do with his nasty little club.

As they pushed through the revolving door and out into the dry, cloudless heat of early evening, Angel glanced down at her. "So what was that all about?"

For one instant, Sedona was tempted to tell him about the Membership and how Ken believed she was going to bring back proof of her own illicit behavior. But she knew he wouldn't believe her. He'd probably think she was completely nuts. Nobody would believe such a club could exist in today's world of political correctness, and especially not in a government office.

Besides, telling him about the club might very well ruin any chance she had of getting him to sleep with her. If she told him about the Membership, he might think she was coming on to him in an effort to further her own career.

They reached their rental car and Angel opened the passenger door for her. Sedona paused, one hand on the door frame, and looked up at him.

"Ken Larson has made it pretty clear that when he's on business travel, he's on the make," she said, trying to convey a sense of what Ken was up to, without mentioning the Membership. "I try not to associate with him unless the reason is business related. Ken's the kind of guy where if you're friendly to him, he thinks you want to have sex with him."

Angel's eyes glittered as he stared down at her, looking intently at her mouth. "Oh, yeah? So if what Larson says is true, and you never go out when you're on business trips, why'd you agree to have dinner with me tonight?" He shrugged. "Maybe I'm cut from the same bolt of cloth as Ken."

"Well," she said archly, her insides churning, "a girl can always hope."

She slid into the car and waited while Angel came around to the driver's side and eased behind the wheel. He started the engine and flipped the air-conditioning on, but made no move to put the car in gear. Sedona held her breath when he turned in his seat to face her. His expression was taut. His entire body seemed coiled with tension.

"Okay, Sedona." His voice was low. "That's about the third time in the last ten minutes you've made a suggestive remark to me." One black eyebrow arched in question. "So tell me now, do you get some kind of cheap thrill from teasing guys? Are you the type who likes to string a guy along with your sultry come-ons, but never comes through with the goods?"

Sedona stared at him in dismay, momentarily at a loss for words. Did he really think that of her? That she was a tease? She felt wild color come into her cheeks as she forced her gaze to deliberately travel over the thrust of broad shoulders, down the arms corded with muscle, to the lean, hard body that dominated the interior of the small car. But when she slowly met his eyes, there was no mistaking the heat she saw there, and it lent her courage to say the things that until now, she'd only ever dreamed about. She drew a deep, unsteady breath.

"I never tease, and I never string guys along." She ran the tip of her tongue nervously across her lips. "And I'm definitely not stringing you along. If you really want *the goods,* then come and get them."

6

ANGEL STARED at her, stunned. This couldn't really be happening. It was like a miracle or something. Here he'd been trying to figure out how he was going to get her into bed, and she'd practically offered herself to him on a plate. If someone had told him yesterday that Sedona Stewart would put the moves on *him,* he'd never have believed it.

Want her? Was she kidding? For just an instant he let his imagination soar with all the possibilities the coming night held. He had an incredibly sharp image of Sedona, less her clothes, straddling his hips.

He'd surprised himself with the intensity of his desire for her. When she'd opened her hotel-room door to greet him, his eyes had immediately been drawn to the rich abundance of glossy hair that framed her face and fell softly around her shoulders. She didn't wear any perfume, yet he'd caught the clean, light scent of something floral. Her shampoo, he'd guessed, and his eyes had lingered on her hair. He'd wondered briefly how it would feel beneath his hands. Silky? Cool?

Her breasts thrust gently against the soft fabric of her blouse and for the first time he'd noticed how green her eyes were. And when she'd preceded him down the corridor toward the elevators, his attention had been fixed on her luscious backside, encased in a pair of jeans that were worn nearly threadbare across her buttocks. She wasn't all that tall, but her long legs and curvy hips lent her an aura of height.

Oh, yeah, he wanted her. But as he stared into her eyes, he also realized she was the kind of woman a guy could get serious about. The kind of woman who probably didn't get involved with someone unless she had long-term plans. She probably fell in love with every guy she slept with. He had to make it clear that he wasn't interested in anything permanent or long lasting.

He'd seen plenty of relationships fall apart under the stress and demands of a military career. Add combat duty and extended overseas deployments, and it was a recipe for marital disaster. Nope, it took a special woman to commit herself to a Navy man. So while he was perfectly willing to engage in a fling, he didn't want Sedona to delude herself into thinking it would be anything more than that. He could be recalled to combat duty at any time, or be reassigned to another squadron, and there was no way he was going to ask a woman to wait for him while he was gone. It wouldn't be fair.

But in the meantime…he was already anticipating fitting himself against her lushness, and was unable to prevent the tightening of his body in response.

"I know what you're thinking," Sedona said.

Angel arched one eyebrow at her, and couldn't quite suppress a smile. "Oh, I don't think you do, *mina,* or you'd already be halfway back to the safety of your hotel room."

To his surprise, she smiled, a slow, sensual curving of her lips. "That's where you're wrong. I might be anxious to get back to my room, but only because I'd be dragging you with me." She turned slightly toward him in her seat. "I want you, Angel Torres. So, what do you say? I know you're hungry. You said so yourself. Shall we forgo dinner and go right for dessert?"

A primal response coursed through Angel, a rush of heat that poured through his veins like liquid fire. But although her words were full of bravado, he could sense her uncertainty. This wasn't something she did frequently, if she'd ever done it all. His gaze drifted to her mouth, ripe and moist. He wanted so badly to sample those tempting lips, to taste her and find out if she was as delicious as she appeared.

He leaned toward her across the center console as his eyes swept her features. Why had he never before noticed how damn pretty she was? Her skin was smooth and golden beneath a dusting of freckles across her nose and brow, and her lips...Jesus, her lips could tempt a saint.

Hardly aware of doing so, he reached out and slid a hand beneath the cool, silken fall of her hair and drew her forward. Her pupils dilated, turning her eyes almost black, before her breath escaped in a soft rush and her lashes drifted down to shield her eyes from him. Her lips parted, and then he was covering them with his own.

Her mouth was incredibly soft and pliant, and she tasted vaguely of something sweet, as if she'd recently sucked on a piece of candy. But if he'd thought he was going to be the one doing the kissing, he'd thought wrong.

She made a soft, needy sound that inflamed his senses, and then she arched against him, tentatively seeking his tongue with her own. When he responded, she met him eagerly. She wound her arms around his neck. She drew him closer, gently thrust her tongue against his and did some exploring of her own until he groaned aloud and angled her head for better access. She clutched at his shoulders, slid her hands along the back of his neck and speared her fingers through his hair.

Her mouth was hot and sweet, and Angel's entire body responded to its pull. His hands moved down her back, over her smooth shoulders and the bumps of her spine, to the bare strip of skin revealed where her shirt gaped away from her waist-band. His fingertips caressed the exposed flesh, learning its texture and warmth.

She gave a soft gasp and wriggled closer, slanting her mouth across his. She caught his tongue and tugged on it, sucked it until Angel's world was reduced to nothing more than the woman in his arms and the feel of her hot, insistent mouth on his. When he ran one hand along her rib cage and captured her breast, she gasped and arched her back. He caressed the soft mound through her blouse, reveling in the weight of it against his palm. When he rubbed his thumb across the peak, her nipple hardened instantly, thrusting against him until he rolled it between his fingers.

He was only dimly aware of working the buttons on her blouse until the fabric fell away and he encountered the silken flesh beneath. He dragged his mouth from hers and used his lips to sear a path along the elegant arch of her neck to her collarbone. She gripped his head, encouraging this new exploration. Her breath was warm and ragged against his cheek, his neck.

Slipping one hand behind her, he bowed her across his arm and tugged her bra downward until her breasts spilled free. They were round and firm, pale and smooth except for the ruddy nipples. He bent his head and sucked one into his mouth, pressing the hard nub against the roof of his mouth while he cupped and kneaded her other breast.

Vaguely, as if from a great distance, he became aware of a car engine roaring into life somewhere close by, accompanied by the sound of voices. Slowly, the realization of what they were doing in the parking lot of the hotel sunk into his lust-sodden brain.

"Jesus." Angel jerked himself away from her.

She lay half collapsed against the seat, her naked breasts

pushed high by the bra that was still bunched beneath them. Her nipples were stiff and rosy and gleamed wetly from where he'd suckled them. Tousled hair fell around her flushed face.

She looked like an erotic fantasy.

Her breathing was as labored as his, but her eyes were still closed, her lips moist and parted as she struggled to draw breath. If Angel didn't know better, he might have thought she was still savoring the taste and feel of him. When she did open her eyes, they were hazy with pleasure. She stared at him with a mixture of wonder and longing, and for the first time in years, Angel felt a frisson of fear.

Almost harshly, he dragged the open edges of her blouse together. "Cover yourself, *mina.*" His voice sounded rough, even to his own ears.

Confusion, then embarrassment, replaced the warmth in her eyes, and she struggled to sit up. She bit her lip and turned slightly away from him as she adjusted her clothing.

Angel blew out his breath in frustration and resisted the urge to drag her back toward him. He flung himself into his seat and scrubbed his hands over his face. What the hell had just happened? He'd come so damn close to losing control. Too close. He'd wanted to haul her across the console, tear her jeans off and take her, right there in the freakin' car in the middle of a goddamn parking lot. He still wanted her. He was aching and uncomfortable with need, and it scared the hell out of him.

Sedona wasn't the first woman to come on to him in such a blatant way. In fact, women had been chasing after him or propositioning him since he was in high school. He was, to a certain extent, used to it. The difference was that he was the one who decided whether or not to let the pursuer catch him. He always retained the upper hand, never let his libido rule his better sense. He never let himself lose control. End of story.

Until now.

It was as if an unseen hand had tilted the world ever so slightly on its axis, causing the very laws of nature to redefine themselves. He recalled again those three little words she'd uttered, and the instantaneous surge of reaction they'd elicited.

I want you.

Christ. He'd responded like a horny teenager. How was it that a woman he'd scarcely noticed until a few short hours ago was now the single, white-hot point of focus in his life? He wanted to consume her, to eat her alive.

He raked a hand over his hair. *Madre de Dios.* For several minutes, he'd completely lost control.

What was worse, though, was how much he'd liked it.

7

"LET'S GO GET that bite to eat."

Angel growled the words as he thrust the car into gear and maneuvered out of the parking lot. He drove faster than he should have, but there was no question he handled the car with smooth efficiency.

Sedona risked a peek at him, more unnerved than she cared to admit by the raw hunger and energy that rolled off him in waves. She ran a shaky hand through her hair, still stunned by what had just happened.

The reality of being kissed by Angel was far different than the fantasies she'd indulged in.

Her trembling fingers absently traced the swollen fullness of her lips as she remembered the fierce intensity of Angel's kiss and the all-consuming passion that had both shocked and delighted her.

Any girlish daydreams she'd harbored about him had been completely and utterly destroyed in the scant moments she'd been gripped in his arms. In her feeble imaginings, she'd envisioned Angel as a tender, considerate lover who would woo her with gentle patience and all the gallant consideration of his rank, anticipating her needs and satisfying them with sweet eagerness. Never had she imagined the incredible strength or heat that had accompanied his embrace, sweeping over her like a firestorm, melting her resistance—if she had any—and incinerating her on the spot.

Her breasts ached where he'd touched them; no, where he'd devoured them. Just the memory of his dark head bent over her, tasting her, caused liquid heat to gather at her core. She thrummed with longing.

Neither of them spoke as Angel negotiated the busy local roads and pulled in to the parking lot of a small pub. He was clearly disturbed by their encounter, but Sedona couldn't tell if he was pissed off, disgusted by her behavior or just plain regretted his response to her.

He turned off the engine, but when it seemed he would get out of the car without saying anything to her, Sedona reached over and touched his arm. He stiffened and slowly turned to face her.

Sedona recoiled at the raw flame she saw in his eyes. He waited, not saying anything, but a muscle worked in his lean jaw.

She wet her lips nervously. "I, um—I'm not sorry about what happened back there. So if you're going to apologize to me for your less-than-gentlemanly behavior, forget it. I don't want to hear it."

He smiled then, a predatory smile that caused Sedona's heart to kick into high gear. "I have no intention of apologizing, *mina*." His eyes raked over her, the intensity of his scrutiny as palpable as if he had touched her. "But before we get completely carried away and do something we both regret, we need to talk."

"Oh." Sedona nibbled her lower lip and stared at him uncertainly. Was she right? *Did* he regret kissing her? If there was even the slightest chance of getting him into her bed, she certainly didn't want to give him any opportunity to talk himself out of it. She could almost hear the arguments he'd present: he had a thing about getting involved with cowork-

ers, or his military career made relationships impossible, or
he had too much integrity to screw around with somebody
while they were on official business.

She watched him as he gave a self-deprecating laugh and
rubbed the back of his neck with one hand. "You blew me
away back there. You know that, don't you?"

"I did?" Sedona couldn't keep the pleased surprise out of
her voice. She'd been operating on pure instinct, responding
to him on a primal level. He'd overwhelmed her senses,
reduced her to a quivering mass of greedy nerve endings that
clamored for more, and he was saying she'd blown *him* away?
Maybe she was better at this sex thing than she realized.

With newfound confidence, she slanted him what she
hoped was a come-hither look from beneath her lashes. "Well,
consider that the appetizer, flyboy. Just wait until I serve up
the entrée."

Angel's surprised laugh gave way to a choking fit as he
stared at her in utter disbelief. "You're not serious?"

"Why not?"

Angel made a noise that was part laugh and part groan.
"It's just that I'm having a little trouble convincing myself
you're for real. One minute, you're this no-nonsense engineer
who's all about getting the job done. The next, you're this
smokin'-hot babe who practically gets me off in the driver's
seat of a car in broad daylight! Pardon me if I'm just a little
confused by it all."

Happiness, pure and dizzying, swept through Sedona.
She'd done it. She'd made him want her, maybe even as much
as she wanted him. All her life, she'd been called the brainy
one, the sensible one. Hearing Angel describe her as hot was
amazing. She knew she had the advantage and there was no
way she was letting it go. She was nothing if not determined.

"Oh, I'm for real," she murmured, and leaned toward him,

not at all deterred when he pulled back, as if afraid she might touch him. "And just so there's no confusion, I'm definitely all about getting the job done."

Angel's eyes drifted to her mouth and lingered there for several long seconds. In the next instant, he seemed to give himself a mental shake. "Oh, no, lady," he growled softly, "we're not doing a repeat performance in this parking lot. We're going to go inside and have something to eat. Then, after we've cooled down, maybe we can talk about this rationally without jumping on each another."

Sedona smiled. She did want to jump him. "Okay," she conceded, "but can't we do fast food or, even better, takeout?"

He chuckled warmly and squeezed her fingers. "We'll save that for another night."

Clearly, there would be no more exchange of delicious intimacies until he'd had his chance to talk. But at least he'd said there would be another night. All was not lost.

She gave him a quick smile. "All right. Something tells me we're going to need sustenance, so let's go eat."

She didn't wait for him, but opened the car door and climbed out, taking a quick opportunity to comb her fingers through her hair and smooth her clothing. The sun was just beginning to sink over the horizon, streaking the skies with brilliant pinks and yellows. Even now, Sedona could feel the heat of the day beginning to subside, with the promise of a cooler night in store.

Inside the pub, Angel steered her past the lounge area, with its noisy crowd of young people, to a booth in a quiet corner. Sedona was scarcely aware of ordering her meal. She was completely focused on the man who sat on the other side of the table.

He perused the menu and after the waitress had taken his order, sat back and surveyed their surroundings as he absently drummed his long fingers against the table. They might have been complete strangers for all the notice he took of her. Sedona sipped her drink and played with the stir stick as she watched him from beneath her lashes. Finally, unable to stand his inattention any longer, she cleared her throat.

"So…you wanted to talk?"

Almost reluctantly, he turned to look at her. He held her gaze for several long moments in which Sedona was unable to discern his thoughts, before turning his attention to the beer he cradled in his palms.

"You must know I find you attractive," he said at last. When he glanced up at her, his eyes were banked with heat. "I guess I've made that pretty obvious."

Sedona swallowed. Why was this beginning to sound like a gentle brush-off? "I'm sorry. I know I came on pretty strong—"

"Let me finish," he admonished, taking the sting out of his words by slanting her a quick grin. "I had absolutely no problem with the way you came on to me. But I think it's only fair to let you know I'm not in the market for a serious relationship."

Sedona almost sagged with relief. "That's great. Neither am I."

He gave her a look that clearly said he didn't believe her.

"Really, I'm not," she insisted. "It's just that—well, it's just that I've had this thing for you for so long now. And here we are, together for a couple of weeks… I just thought…"

"You just thought you could indulge in a little sexfest with the itinerant military guy, and nobody would ever know, is that it?"

"What? No! My God, I can't believe you'd even think that!" Sedona stared at him in horror, despite the fact that was exactly what she'd thought. "I've never done anything like this before in my life."

Angel sighed and pinched the bridge of his nose between his fingers. "Okay, forget I said that. You're right, I don't really believe it, anyway." He leaned back in the booth and considered her. "I must be insane to even question your motives. I mean, what do I care what they are? You've made it clear you're interested in me. You're attractive and single, so why shouldn't I take you up on your offer?"

Sedona gave him a wary smile. "Right."

"So long as we both go into this with our eyes open, with the understanding that it will only last for as long as we're out here, right?"

"Right." Sedona moistened her lips, hope flaring inside her. "I mean, it would be too uncomfortable if we continued to see each other when we got back to the office." She didn't see any reason to tell him that for her, there would be no going back to the office.

"Right."

"So…we're on?"

Angel laughed. "We're on. Jesus, this is just too weird."

Sedona tilted her head to one side. "I don't know, I'd think it's what every guy fantasizes about. I mean, think about it."

"Oh, I have," he said, and let his gaze travel deliberately over her.

Sedona blushed. She could scarcely believe she was really going to do this. She hadn't had a relationship of any kind since she'd been in college, and even that had been more physical than emotional. She'd briefly dated a guy in one of her thermodynamics classes, and while the sex had been good, it hadn't been great. Too many times, Sedona had been left unsatisfied, wanting more. Pragmatic to the core, she'd become pretty adept at satisfying herself. After that, having a guy in her life had seemed, well, superfluous.

As a whole, she found men to be self-absorbed, needy

creatures. Thanks, but no thanks. After she graduated and took the government engineering job, she hadn't met anyone who interested her on any level.

But with Angel... Suddenly she couldn't wait to find out what it would be like to have him in her life, even on a temporary basis. He didn't strike her as being egocentric. And she was quite certain that his lovemaking would never leave her frustrated or wanting.

Their food arrived, saving Sedona from having to respond to Angel's words, but as she looked down at her plate, she realized she wasn't the least bit hungry. Her stomach was knotted with nervous anticipation.

"So," she blurted as Angel took a healthy bite of his burger, "I notice you keep calling me *mina*. What does it mean?" She laughed and held up her hand. "I only want to know if it's complimentary. I mean, if it's something like man-hating she-bitch, please don't tell me."

Angel smiled, clearly amused. "No, it doesn't mean that, although I'm not so sure you'll like the true translation." He folded his napkin before he arched her a look that was half-challenging, half-defensive. "In Cuba, it means mine. Or my little one."

Sedona nearly choked on the iced tea she was sipping. *Mine? As in...his?* She coughed until her eyes watered and Angel half rose to his feet. She held up a hand to forestall him.

"No," she finally gasped. "I'm okay." She took another, careful sip of her drink and wiped the moisture from her eyes. "It just surprised me, that's all."

"I know, it sounds a little territorial and corny, but it's actually a common form of address amongst Cubans." He shrugged, and Sedona could have sworn that was embarrassment coloring his neck and jaw. "More like a casual endearment."

"Mmm. It's fine." She nodded, as if contemplating his words; as if she was accustomed to having men call her *little one* every day. But she couldn't bring herself to meet his eyes for fear he'd see her pleasure. Instead, she snatched her napkin up, held it over her mouth and pretended to cough a little more. Anything to hide the silly grin that threatened to spill free.

Mine. His.

The words were more than just music to her ears. They were like a full violin concerto.

"Well," she said, when she could finally speak, "I think it's very…sweet." She gave him a bright smile. "I didn't realize you were Cuban."

He shrugged again. "My parents fled Cuba in the sixties, after the revolution. I was raised in San Diego."

Sedona tilted her head as she considered him. "Not Miami? Don't they have a huge Cuban population there?"

He smiled. "Actually, I was born there. But my father wanted his kids to be raised in a community that was fully American. He said too many Cubans refuse to assimilate, believing they'll eventually return to Cuba. So we moved to San Diego and…assimilated."

"Your mom didn't mind?"

Angel laughed, but Sedona thought it had a slightly bitter edge to it. "My mother still dreams of returning to Cuba. She let my dad move us to San Diego, but refused to speak anything but Spanish in our home." He chuckled wryly. "She'd like nothing better than for me to marry a nice Cuban-American girl and settle down."

"Oh." Sedona looked at her hands. Her pale, WASP hands. "Is that what you want?"

There was silence and after a moment, Sedona looked up to see Angel smiling at her. "Is this a fishing expedition?"

Sedona flushed. "Of course not. I was just making conversation." She knew her voice sounded defensive, but couldn't help it. Yes, dammit, it was a fishing expedition. Just because he didn't have a ring on his finger didn't mean he wasn't committed to somebody.

"Then the answer is no," he said smoothly. "I have no desire to marry."

"Not ever?"

He shrugged. "Not anytime soon. My job isn't exactly conducive to settling down."

Angel's dark eyes locked with hers, and for a brief instant, Sedona thought she saw something in their depths; regret. Then it was gone, carefully shuttered behind his roguish grin and nonchalant shrug. "Maybe someday, when the war is over, or when my flying days are done. Who knows?"

Sedona tried to imagine what it would be like to be married to a guy like Angel. To send him off, not knowing if he'd come home or not, enduring long months without him. It would take a special woman to share his life on those terms, but Sedona was willing to bet she could do it. The guy was incredible, not just amazingly good-looking, but intelligent and funny, too. Not to mention that he kissed like a dream. It'd be hard to go six months without him, but she could do it in a heartbeat. The rewards would be well worth the wait.

Angel took a swallow of beer. "I came close, once, but it didn't work out." He shrugged. "I guess we just weren't meant for each other."

You were meant for me.

For a moment, Sedona thought she might have uttered the words aloud. She glanced at Angel, but he continued to eat his meal with unrestrained gusto.

"C'mon," he urged her. "Eat your salad. The sooner we finish up, the sooner we can get out of here."

She glanced from her spinach salad to the robust burger he'd ordered for himself. She didn't know how he could have an appetite.

"Aren't you nervous?" she finally asked.

He washed down his mouthful of burger with a healthy swig of beer before he spoke. "About us? Hell, yeah, but in a good way. It's when you're not nervous that you need to be worried. You don't want to be too cocksure, because that's when you make mistakes. Crash and burn, baby."

Sedona pushed her salad around with her fork, unable to suppress a smile. "Are we talking about sex, or flying?"

He wiped his mouth and grinned unabashedly. "Is there a difference?"

Sedona raised her eyebrows. "If you're so cautious, then why were you sent back to us? You still had another six months aboard the USS *Abraham Lincoln,* right?"

For the space of a single heartbeat, he looked completely taken aback. Then he shrugged and looked down at his plate and the moment was gone, but not before Sedona saw the quick flash of pain in his eyes. "I took some risks considered unacceptable to the senior brass."

"Oh. That's not how I heard it."

Angel gave her a tolerant smile and pushed his plate slightly away. "And just how did you hear it?"

Sedona flushed, but pressed on. She *did* want to know. "I heard you disobeyed a direct order from a superior officer."

Angel's smile grew wider. Sedona tried not to stare at his dimples, or the perfection of his white teeth. "That's not exactly how it went down," he said, amusement evident in his voice. "Do you want to know what happened?"

"Okay." Her heartbeat picked up a notch. He was actually willing to share his story with her. Was that significant?

Angel sighed. "It was a couple of months ago. I was lead

jet in a five-jet formation to fly deep into Iraq and drop several bunker busters on an area where senior members of al-Qaeda were believed to be hiding out." He picked up a saltshaker and turned it over thoughtfully in his hands. "We'd already nailed our target and were returning to the carrier when we were informed that a second sortie had been deployed to take out another target pretty damn close to where we were."

He glanced up at Sedona. "Intelligence sources on the ground said the target was on the move and would be past the point of engagement in about eight minutes. The second sortie was still fifteen minutes out, and it was unlikely they'd arrive in time."

Sedona stared at him, mesmerized. "What did you do?"

And so he told her that with his remaining ordnance and scarcely enough fuel to make it back to the carrier, he had blown off his wingman and separated from formation, and gone in, low and fast. He'd dropped below the hard deck of ten thousand feet, putting himself into range of enemy surface-to-air missiles. He'd located the target and succeeded in destroying them just seconds before they might have reached a safe zone.

"I made a snap decision that put my wingman in danger when he chose to follow me. In the opinion of my commanding officer," he said ruefully, "that was bad enough, but when I finally reached the USS *Abraham Lincoln,* I did a four-point victory roll across the bow of the carrier." He shrugged. "They saw it as an act of glory-seeking theatrics and shipped me back to the East Coast to cool my heels and contemplate what it means to be a team player."

"Sort of like a military version of a time-out."

Angel gave her a half smile. "Sort of. My commanding officer said he doesn't need any heroes in his jets. He wants team players who put their own safety and the safety of their wingmen first, not hotshot mavericks out to impress the top brass."

Sedona frowned. "But surely he understood the position you were in? Didn't it matter that you'd taken out the target and probably saved countless lives in the process?"

Angel set the saltshaker down with a small thump. "Independent thinking isn't always encouraged in the military. I did what I thought was right, what I was trained to do."

"What you love to do," Sedona finished softly.

"Yes. Exactly." Smiling ruefully, he shrugged. "I have no one to blame but myself. I knew what I was doing."

"So you're okay with being grounded."

"I can accept the consequences, yeah. And just for the record, I haven't been completely grounded. I'm doing test flights." He lifted the glass of beer and contemplated the amber liquid before bringing it to his lips.

"But you miss combat flight."

She'd surprised him again. It was there in the way his gaze snapped up to meet hers. His mouth lifted at the corner. "I do, yes. There's nothing else like it."

"Tell me about it." She leaned forward, eager to hear him describe why he loved to fly, eager to hear him talk about anything he loved.

He set his beer down and his eyes grew distant. "If there is a heaven, I'd say streaking through the skies at Mach speed is the closest I've ever come to it. It's exhilarating and frightening at the same time. It's knowing you have the power of life and death in your control. It's the thrill of avoiding detection, of eluding radar and completing the mission, despite the danger." He laughed and shrugged. "I know, it sounds hokey, but it's the truth."

Sedona stared at him, humbled by the obvious passion in his voice, and jealous, too, knowing she'd never be able to share that part of his life with him.

"It sounds amazing." Sedona sighed, and cupped her chin

in her hand. "I've always wanted to fly in a Coyote," she admitted. "It seems so…exciting."

"Oh, it is." He quirked an odd smile at her. "Who knows? Maybe someday you'll get your chance."

Sedona snorted. "I doubt it. I'm not a celebrity, and I'm not a member of the media, and those are the only people who get free rides in a Coyote. Lowly civil servants like me don't rate."

Angel laughed. "I'm not sure I agree with you."

"Well," she said, smiling. "I'm not even sure I'd actually have the courage to do it, given the chance. I'm humbled by guys like you who do it for a living, under the most hostile conditions imaginable." She paused. "Do you think you'll ever return to combat flight?"

"Christ, I hope so." He held up a hand. "Not that I mind being a test pilot. It's just not the same as flying sorties."

"Well, if it's any consolation, I'm glad you're not flying combat missions." She grinned. "After all, we wouldn't be sitting here, making plans…"

His eyes glinted with sudden heat. Reaching into his wallet, he pulled several bills out and tossed them onto the table. "C'mon, let's get out of here."

"You don't have to pay for my meal," she ventured. "I'm on per diem while we're out here."

"Indulge me," he said, and stood up. "You've already pre-empted me on the whole seduction thing, at least give me this."

Sedona faltered. Was she being too aggressive? She knew there were guys in the office who were put off by her less-than-feminine ways. She sincerely hoped Angel wasn't going to be one of those men who couldn't treat a woman as an equal partner.

"Fine," she conceded, pushing her chair back to stand up, "but I pay tomorrow night."

He put a hand at the small of her back as he guided her out of the restaurant. "Oh, no, *mina*," he said softly into her ear, "you'll pay tonight."

His words both thrilled and infuriated her. Thrilled her with their implicit promise of hedonistic pleasure; infuriated her with the implication that he was paying for her services.

"Listen, flyboy," she said sweetly as they passed the hostess stand and stepped out into the darkness of the parking lot, "you'll get nothing from me if you don't watch your step. Paying for my meal does not instill you with any inalienable rights."

She wasn't prepared when he suddenly pushed her up against the side of the car, and followed with the long, lean heat of his own body against hers. He was pressed against her from thigh to breast, all hard, hot male. He smelled incredibly good.

"First of all, I am no boy." He dipped his head and traced his lips along the side of her throat, causing her to gasp with sensation and silently agree with him. "Second of all—" his voice was low and rough against her skin "—I don't expect anything from you that you're not fully prepared to give of your own free will. *Comprende?* If I gave you that impression, it was completely unintentional. This, however, is not."

He captured her face between his hands and claimed her lips in a kiss that was completely off the charts and seared Sedona all the way down to her toes.

She moaned.

He tasted faintly of the beer he'd been drinking. His mouth slanted hard across hers, forcing her lips apart for the intrusion of his tongue. There was nothing gentle about it; the kiss was designed to inflame and consume.

Sedona welcomed every scorching second.

She slid her hands upward, along his ribs and over his chest and curled one hand around the strong column of his neck. She found the heartbeat at the base of his throat and reveled in the feel of it pulsing strongly against her fingertips.

He feasted on her lips. He wasn't just kissing them, he was plundering. She couldn't think. If she wasn't pinned against the car by his solid, delicious weight, she'd probably slither to the ground in a boneless pile of mush. She could only feel and respond. His thumbs smoothed over her cheekbones and his fingertips soothed the sensitive skin behind her ears as he held her face in his hands.

When she slid her hand between their bodies, he eased back just enough to give her room to explore. His stomach contracted when she touched the hard ridges of flesh beneath the soft fabric of his shirt. Oh, my. The guy was layer after layer of firm muscle. When her fingertips dropped lower and encountered his belt, he stiffened and groaned, deepening his kiss.

Sedona made a soft sound of approval and slid her hand lower to cup the impressive length of him beneath his jeans. Her knees turned to Jell-O. What did he have in there, a heat-seeking missile? Even through the denim, he was hard and hot, and larger than she'd anticipated. When her fingers closed around him, he jerked reflexively. She shifted against him, uncomfortably aware of her own growing need.

He tore his lips from hers and grabbed her hand, dragging it upward. "Stop, *mina,*" he gasped. "You're killing me."

He curled her hand inside his and held it against his chest while he sucked in air. Sedona could feel the uneven thumping of his heart. She dropped her forehead against his shoulder and struggled to control her own erratic breathing. His body was big and warm and hard, and she could feel his erection pressing against her abdomen.

He chuckled softly, but there was no mistaking the rueful resignation in his voice as he gathered her closer. "Oh, man," he groaned, "I am so screwed."

8

SEDONA WAS HARDLY aware of driving back to the hotel. Her thoughts were fully occupied with the man sitting beside her, driving with ruthless speed and efficiency through the darkened streets.

He was impatient.

The realization both thrilled and terrified her. She couldn't stop staring at his hands as he drove, admiring the long, lean fingers and knowing that soon they would be touching her with the same sure confidence. It was still unbelievable to her that Angel found her attractive. Not just attractive, either. *Hot.* It was as if she'd briefly fallen asleep and woken up in some alternate universe where smart, hunky guys fell for everyday, average Janes.

Sedona's thoughts were interrupted when Angel parked the car. She found she couldn't meet his eyes as he took her elbow and steered her across the parking lot to the front entrance. The lobby seemed garishly bright after the intimate darkness of the car. Pulsing music drifted toward them from the hotel lounge.

"Christ, that guy doesn't waste any time," Angel commented.

Through the doorway of the dimly lit lounge, she could see Ken Larson. He was standing close behind a young woman wearing a microminiskirt and a tiny top. As Sedona watched, he bent his head and whispered something that made the girl throw her head back and laugh. At the same time, his hands skimmed down her sides to rest possessively on her hips as he pressed against her backside.

Sedona scowled. "He's probably looking for his next promotion," she muttered darkly.

"Are you saying she's his boss?" Angel's voice was incredulous.

"No, of course not," Sedona assured him, anxious to change the subject. "It was just a bad joke."

As if sensing her reluctance to be seen, Angel pushed her ahead of him toward the bank of elevators, using his bulk to shield her from view. Sedona was grateful for his thoughtfulness, as the last thing she wanted was an encounter with Ken Larson or any of his cronies. As far as Ken knew, she was still on board with trying to gain access to the Membership. She didn't need him jumping to conclusions if he saw her with Angel, and she definitely didn't need him making any comments about the Membership in Angel's presence. If Ken wanted to get promoted by getting busy, it had nothing to do with her.

"Elevator's here."

Angel's voice brought her abruptly out of her thoughts. With his hand lightly cupping her elbow, they stepped into the elevator. They were the only occupants, and during the short ride to the third floor, Sedona was aware of Angel watching her.

"Having second thoughts?" he asked softly.

Her eyes flew to his face. He dominated the tiny compartment with his size and presence. He hadn't touched her during the ride back to the hotel and suddenly, Sedona was unaccountably shy. They were, perhaps, minutes from engaging in the greatest intimacy two people could share, and yet she was conscious they were little more than strangers. Having second thoughts? Only every moment since they'd arrived at the hotel. What if once she got her clothes off, he no longer found her attractive? What if she couldn't please him? What if this whole thing was a huge mistake?

She drew in a fortifying breath. "Not if you aren't."

His eyes darkened perceptibly. "Not a chance, *mina*. But I'm trying really hard not to scare you. I don't trust myself to touch you until we're in your room."

The elevator jerked to a stop and the doors slid open to their floor. Heart pounding, Sedona rummaged for her key as they walked side by side down the hallway. When they reached her room, Angel didn't pause but continued past her to stop outside his own door.

"There's a connecting door between our suites," he said quietly as he eased his key card into his door. "Whenever you're ready, unlock the door from your side. I'll do the same."

"Okay." Her voice sounded breathless. Inserting her key, she pushed open her door and slipped inside. As he'd said, there was a connecting door between their rooms that she hadn't noticed earlier.

Almost immediately, she heard Angel unlocking and opening his side of the door. Once she did the same, there would be nothing to separate them.

She hesitated. Did she really have the guts to go through with this? She flipped on the overhead light in the small bathroom and studied her reflection critically. Her eyes were overly bright, her cheeks flushed. Acutely conscious of the man who waited for her on the other side of the locked door, she brushed her teeth, ran her fingers through her hair and drew in a deep breath. There was nothing more to do. She didn't own any slinky lingerie, and probably wouldn't have the courage to wear it even if she did. She consoled herself with the knowledge that at least her bra and panties were new.

After she'd left work yesterday, she'd gone straight to the mall to buy some last-minute items for her trip, and had gone into Victoria's Secret on a whim. She'd spent a shocking amount of money on underwear, including one silky thong. She hadn't been brave enough to wear it tonight, but at least she wasn't wearing granny undies.

Drawing a deep breath, she stood in front of the connecting door, and with fingers that trembled, slowly flipped the lock open and turned the knob.

ANGEL HEARD the rasp of the lock in the door. His heart thumped unevenly in his chest. Christ, he was actually nervous. He tried to relax. It was no big deal. She was just a woman, after all, and he'd had more than his share of women. He could handle this. The only reason she'd tested his self-restraint earlier was because he'd been celibate for so long. He never fraternized with female crewmates when he was aboard a carrier, and he'd been at sea for ten long months. It was just his healthy, male hormones reacting to a pretty woman, nothing more.

He'd exchanged his loafers for a pair of flip-flops, and had made sure he had a supply of condoms in the bedside table. In the few minutes before Sedona unlocked the door, he'd located a couple of single-serving bottles of wine in the minibar and put them in a bucket of ice. He'd tuned the bedside radio to a station that played soft music, and dimmed all the lights except for the one in the bathroom, and even then he'd closed the door so only a thin shaft of light fell across the carpet.

He was as ready as he was ever going to be. If seduction was what the lady wanted, he was happy to oblige. They were both adults, after all. Hell, she'd all but said it was just about the sex, so who was he to complain? He was definitely okay with it being about the sex.

But when the door opened and Sedona stepped shyly into the room, his stomach knotted with something that might have been nervous anticipation.

"Oh," she said, tipping her head, listening. "Is that Anita Baker? I love her songs, they're so romantic."

Until that moment, Angel had barely noticed the soft love song playing on the radio. "Well, then, we're off to a good start." He lifted the small wine bottle, questioning. "Care for a glass?"

Sedona came into the room and took the proffered glass, her eyes sliding over the bed and away. Angel wondered if she was imagining the two of them tangled in the bedding, skin sliding over skin. But when she tipped the wineglass back and drained the contents in one long swallow, he was concerned.

"A little false courage?" He took the empty wineglass and set it on the bedside table, smiling as she wiped her mouth with her fingertips and shuddered slightly.

"I wouldn't mind a little more." She reached for Angel's glass, standing full next to hers, but he caught her wrist.

"I think maybe we'll hold off for a bit, *mina*." He tugged her toward him, his thumb sliding over the underside of her wrist where her pulse beat frantically. "I want you conscious and at least partially sober."

She didn't protest when he drew her wrist upward and settled her arm around his neck, and drew her into the circle of his arms with his other hand at her waist. She released her breath on a soft sigh and leaned into him. Her fingers caressed the back of his neck.

"I can't believe we're actually doing this," she murmured, and pressed her lips tentatively against the base of his throat.

"You can still change your mind." As soon as the words were out of his mouth, Angel wanted to retract them. What a dumb-ass thing to say. He absolutely did not want this woman to change her mind. He'd been hard for her since he saw her in the fitness room. He wanted to spend the next eight hours doing decadent things with her. But he didn't want Sedona to be with him if she wasn't absolutely sure it was what she wanted.

"No chance, flyboy," she said, smiling against his throat. "I've spent my entire life doing things to make other people happy. This is one opportunity I am not about to pass up."

Angel breathed a silent thank-you and pulled her fully against him. "Good," he said, his voice husky, and tipped a finger beneath her chin, tilting her face upward. His eyes searched hers, and he watched as the uncertainty that lingered there was slowly replaced with something else, something languorous and heated. She moistened her lips, drawing his attention irresistibly to her mouth.

"I have to kiss you," he confessed, and dipped his head to stroke his lips across the tempting lushness of hers.

Sedona made a soft purring sound of approval and pressed closer. She parted her lips and teased him with slippery, soft strokes of her tongue against his. She caressed the back of his neck even as her other hand crept up to his rib cage and then slid around to the small of his back to draw him closer.

Angel reached down and cupped her buttocks beneath the thin fabric of the threadbare jeans, feeling her heat through the material. He lifted her, fitting himself against the cradle of her hips. She made an incoherent sound in her throat and parted her legs to allow for the intrusion of his thigh between them. She rode him, rubbing herself sinuously against the hard length of his leg even as she deepened their kiss, slanting her mouth across his for better access.

She tasted like wine and sunshine. He pressed his leg harder against her center. Heat surrounded his thigh where she covered him. His cock strained against the confines of his jeans, pulsing with need. From the small, feminine sounds she made, she was as aroused as he was. Time to end the artificial stimulation and move on to the real deal. Angel would have picked her up to deposit her on top of the bed, but she scooted out of his arms before he could get a good hold of her.

"Not so fast," she protested, but her voice was high and breathy, as if she'd just dashed up a flight of stairs. "I have a treat for you."

She caught his hand and led him to an upholstered chair in the corner of the room. She pushed him down into it, but remained standing between his legs, bracketed by his knees. Angel stared up at her.

"I've always wanted to do this," she confessed, wild color rushing into her cheeks.

Before Angel could ask what she meant, her fingers moved to the buttons on her blouse. Slowly, she began to sway her body in time with the sensuous strains of the music, gently rotating her hips so that she bumped against the framework of his legs. Her eyes never left his face.

Angel couldn't move. Couldn't think. Couldn't do anything except stare in utter fascination at the luscious woman who stood in front of him, undulating her body as she slowly began to undress. He swallowed hard and fisted his hands on his thighs.

Sedona unfastened the top two buttons of her blouse and allowed him a tantalizing glimpse of the smooth, golden flesh beneath. She cupped her breasts in her hands and then smoothed her hands down her body and over her hips. She closed her eyes, arched her neck, and slowly slid her hands back up the length of her body until she buried them in the mass of her hair, her lips parting on a sigh of pleasure.

Angel shifted uncomfortably in the soft chair. Sedona must have been aware of his rock-hard erection, but she gave no sign of relenting as she moved slowly to the seductive music. She unfastened the remaining buttons on her blouse and parted the front with devastating leisure. She wore a pale peach bra edged in lace. It was transparent. Angel could clearly see the outline of her nipples through the sheer fabric and right now they were stiff with desire. He groaned and grasped the arms of the upholstered chair, willing himself to stay seated.

Slowly, swaying her hips, Sedona turned her back to him and removed the blouse, letting it slide down the length of her arms until it spilled onto the floor in a puddle of green fabric. He held his breath as she bent her arms behind her back and deftly unhooked the fragile bra. Angel's fingers ached to trace the graceful, indented line of her spine, to smooth his hands over the narrow curve of her waist and gently bite the thrust of her shoulder blades.

He sat, immobile.

Sliding her fingers beneath the straps of the bra, she allowed it to slither from her body. She was bare from the waist up, and Angel thought he'd never seen anything as erotic as the supple line of Sedona's spine, or the feminine flare of her hips encased in the faded denim.

The music changed, became more throbbing and intense. Sedona turned sideways, allowing him a profile view of her perfect breasts. He almost swallowed his tongue when she slid her hands up her taut belly and grasped the distended nipples, rolling them between her fingertips as she threw her head back with a soft moan.

He was halfway to his feet, when she turned fully toward him and pushed him back with a fingertip in the center of his chest. She gave him a mocking shake of her head, but didn't back away. She was so close he could see the nubbed texture of her areolas and the smooth expanse of satiny skin that covered her torso, tempting him to touch, kiss and lick her. He sank back against the cushions, entranced.

Sedona smiled at him, a sultry smile full of sensual promise. She wet her lips and with her hips still rotating in slow motion, unfastened the snap on her jeans and slid the zipper down. Turning her back to him once more, she eased the denim over the roundness of her buttocks and pushed the fabric slowly down the length of her legs, shifting her weight from side to side as she did so.

Angel sucked in his breath, feeling his groin tighten even more. He wondered if he could actually die from wanting. She wore a minuscule pair of peach panties, and though they weren't exactly a thong, they didn't come close to covering the smooth mounds of her cheeks. She bent forward to pull the jeans free from her legs, thrusting her luscious bottom toward him in the process. As in the fitness room, his reaction was instantaneous.

His cock swelled even more, if that was possible, and he ached to bury himself in her delicious flesh. He wanted to consume her, to eat her alive. He couldn't help himself; he grasped her hips and drew her backward, onto his lap.

She squirmed against him, causing him untold agony. "I'm not finished," she protested breathlessly.

"Yes, you are." His voice was a rough growl. "Any more is going to kill me, *mina*. I can't wait. I have to touch you."

He pulled her completely back so that she lay sprawled on top of him, her bare back against his chest, her legs straddling his thighs, her head against his shoulder.

He nuzzled her ear, breathed in the clean fragrance of her hair. Her breathing was rapid and uneven as he trailed his tongue along the side of her neck and gently bit down on her shoulder. "Where did you learn to do that?"

"W-what?"

"The striptease, *mina*."

She gave a breathless laugh. "That was my first one. Oh!"

Angel slid his hands up over her arms and then around to her front. He cupped her breasts, kneading and caressing their firmness until Sedona gasped. He plucked at her nipples, rolled them gently between his fingers and then pinched them until she moaned and shifted restlessly on his lap.

He smoothed his hands over the soft flatness of her belly, skimmed them over her hip bones and the silken swatch of her panties, and caressed her thighs. He used his knee to nudge her legs farther apart.

"God, *mina,*" he said hoarsely, tracing his tongue around the delicate whorl of her ear, "you feel incredible. You're so responsive, so hot."

Sedona arched her neck to grant him better access, and reached behind her to draw his head down for a deep, open-mouthed kiss, her tongue seeking his with growing urgency.

He slid one hand between her legs and cupped her feminine mound, reveling in the heat that scorched him through the fragile fabric. He rubbed two fingers across her center, gently at first, until she squirmed and her breath shuddered out from between parted lips. She pushed herself help-lessly against his hand. Her panties were soaked.

"Oh my God," she gasped, dragging her mouth from his. "That feels too good. I can't—"

"Shh." He slid his fingers lower until they reached the entrance to her body, shielded by the wet silk. "Let me. I need to touch you…feel you respond to me."

He inserted one fingertip into her as far as the silk would permit. Sedona moaned softly and widened her thighs until they were draped fully across his own. Angel played with her breasts with one hand, and with the other he pushed aside the flimsy barrier and skated a finger over her slick folds, grati-fied when she sucked in her breath and jerked reflexively.

"That's it," he murmured approvingly. "You're wet for me, *mina.*" The movement of her buttocks on top of his straining cock was torture. And when he slid a finger into her drenched heat, it was almost too much for him. He wanted to stand up and bend her over, jerk her panties down and thrust himself into her from behind, again and again. He drew in a deep, controlled breath. He had to slow this down. He didn't want this to end anytime soon. Hell, he didn't want it to end ever. He wanted to take her desperately, but he wanted her primed and ready.

He inserted a second finger into her tightness and used a gentle pulsing motion that soon had her clenching her muscles around him. With his fingers still working, he located the slick rise of her clitoris and pressed his thumb against it. Sedona groaned, a deep sound of sexual pleasure, and arched her breast into his hand.

Angel swept his tongue into her mouth, even as he pumped his fingers slowly and swirled his thumb over the peak of her desire. When he withdrew his fingers, she cried out in disappointment.

"No, *mina,*" he soothed her, "I'm not finished. I've barely begun."

He stood up swiftly, sliding out from beneath her and settling her into the upholstered chair. Her head lolled against the seat back as if she didn't have the strength to hold it upright. Angel took a minute to devour the sight she made. She was sprawled gracelessly, her legs still parted, one hand draped over the arm of the chair while the other caressed her breast and toyed with the nipple. When she looked up at him, her eyes were cloudy, glazed with pleasure.

"What are you doing?" Her voice was husky.

"Just this," Angel murmured, and dropped to his knees in front of her. He slid his hands over the smooth plane of her chest until he captured both breasts in his hands. He cupped them briefly and admired the rosy nipples, before moving on to her panties.

Hooking his thumbs beneath the lace-trimmed edge, he dragged them from her body. Sedona closed her eyes and turned her face away, as if embarrassed, but lifted her hips to assist him.

Angel brushed his hands along her inner thighs and pushed her knees apart, and then sat back on his heels to admire her. She was achingly feminine, from the light cluster of damp curls atop her mons, to the lush, pink lips beneath, swollen and glistening with her desire.

"Ah, baby," he groaned, "you're so damn gorgeous down here." He settled himself more comfortably, then drew her knees up until they were draped over his shoulders. Sedona gave a mortified squeak and tried to yank her legs away, but he held them firmly in place. "No, *mina,* don't deny me this."

Then, before she could protest further, he pulled her bottom to the edge of the seat cushion, bent his head and slid his tongue along the length of her cleft.

Christ, she tasted delicious, delicately imbued with the scent of the sea. He was gratified when she whimpered softly and lifted her hips upward, straining toward him. He grasped her buttocks in his hands as he licked her with care and flicked his tongue over the most sensitive of spots. He reveled in her, thrust his tongue into her, slowly and repeatedly until she gripped his head with both hands. He swirled his tongue around the peak of her distended clitoris until she cried out. She was mewling now, soft little cries of delight as she began to rotate her hips and push against his face.

He moved one hand out from beneath her buttocks and slid two fingers into her slick heat, even as he increased the tempo and pressure of his tongue.

"Angel." She sounded desperate.

When she stiffened and her back bowed off the cushions, Angel knew she teetered on the brink. He wanted to see her come apart. He pressed his thumb against her and she gave a long, keening cry of pleasure even as her inner muscles contracted fiercely around his fingers.

Angel didn't give her any time to recover. He bent and scooped her into his arms, taking a moment to brush her lips with his own, letting her taste herself on him. She draped her arms around his neck and stared up at him with eyes that were hazy with wonder.

He tumbled them both onto the mattress. Rolling to his side, he came up on one elbow and looked down into her face, pushing her hair back with his hand.

"Tell me, *mina,*" he urged softly. "Tell me what you want."

SEDONA STARED BACK at him, amazed he couldn't read her mind.

You. Inside me.

Despite the mind-blowing orgasm he'd just given her, she ached for him. The bedspread was soft and cool beneath her bare back, in direct contrast to the man who braced himself over her prone body. His face was taut with desire, more erotic than anything she could have imagined, even in the countless sexual fantasies she'd woven around him.

"I'm thinking you have way too many clothes on," she murmured, and tugged the hem of his T-shirt from the waistband of his jeans.

He reared up on his knees and with a swift, impatient movement, dragged the fabric over his head and flung the garment away.

Sedona sucked air into her lungs. From the thrust of his powerful shoulders, down the sculpted, muscular chest, to the six-pack that rode above his belt buckle, Angel Torres was supremely, heart-stoppingly male, and so beautiful Sedona wanted to weep.

Unable to resist, she traced her finger down the deep groove that bisected his torso from collarbone to navel. His skin was smooth and tanned, but she detected a lighter band of skin just below his waistline.

She tried to speak, tried to tell him how infinitely gorgeous she found him, but couldn't find her voice, could only make an incoherent sound of need as she reached greedily for him.

"Easy, *mina,*" he gasped, when her fingers hooked into the waistband of his jeans and fumbled with his belt buckle. "Let me."

Sedona's breath hitched as he unfastened the buckle and then popped the button free. His expression was strained as he unzipped his fly and shoved both boxers and jeans down over his thighs.

Her mouth went dry and her brain ceased to function as Angel took her hands and guided them to the biggest, hardest erection she'd ever seen. Not that she'd actually seen that many, but this one topped them all. When her fingers wrapped around him, he inhaled sharply and closed his eyes.

Sedona felt her own desire kick back into full gear as she stroked him. She doubted even the high-tech control stick aboard the Coyote fighter jet, mounted so it was centered between the pilot's legs, was as responsive. The thick veins in his shaft pulsed beneath her fingers, and when she ran the tip of one finger over the engorged head, it came away slick with moisture. He threw his head back and made a deep groaning noise when she cupped his balls and lightly scored them with her fingernails. Then he moved so that he was completely over her, her nipples brushing his chest as he supported himself on his elbows.

"Enough," he rasped into her ear, "or I won't last."

His words thrilled her. She could scarcely believe that she, the pragmatic and boring engineer, had aroused this amazing guy to the point where he strained for self-control. It was a total turn-on.

She pulled him down on top of her and used her feet to push his jeans completely off until they fell to the floor. She ran her feet up and over the backs of his hard legs, feeling his erection bump against her most private spot.

"I want you so badly," she whispered, and pulled Angel's head down for a deep, openmouthed kiss. He braced himself on one hand, dragged his lips from hers and leaned down to take one of her nipples into his mouth. She gasped at the exquisite sensation

"You're so damn beautiful," he muttered against her skin. Reaching across her body, he opened the drawer of the bedside table and fished out a condom.

Sedona watched as he tore it open with his teeth and then spat the corner away. He sheathed himself with hands that trembled. Did she really have that potent an effect on him? The knowledge was heady. But when he positioned himself at the entrance to her body and began to slide into her, one exquisite inch at a time, she ceased to think.

He was large, and she hadn't had sex in a long time—longer than she'd ever admit to anyone, maybe even herself. He stretched her, filled her, eased himself into her until her buttocks were flush against his hips and there was nothing but the taste, scent, and feel of Angel, in her and surrounding her. Her entire world had reduced itself to this one room and the delicious weight of the man who pinned her against the bed.

She heard a desperate mewl of need, and was shocked to realize that it came from her.

"Mina." His voice was rough. "You're so tight… Am I hurting you?"

In answer, Sedona arched against him and drew her feet up until they rested on his firm, taut butt. The movement opened her even more, and when she shifted her hips restlessly beneath him, he moaned and buried his face in her neck.

"I can't—I don't think—" Whatever words he might have said were lost as he gave a helpless groan of surrender and reached beneath her to grasp her cheeks in his hands. "I'm sorry," he rasped hoarsely into her ear, "I don't think I can go gently."

"I don't want gentle," she breathed against his lips, and he plunged into her. The sensation of him filling her was more intense than anything she had ever experienced.

He turned his face and caught her lips in a kiss that nearly undid her. He drew on her tongue even as his pace quickened and he thrust into her with increasing urgency. Sedona felt an answering heat begin to build.

She stroked her hands over the firm mounds of his buttocks, raised her legs higher and wrapped them around his lean waist.

"Oh, yeah," he breathed. "So good…"

He raised himself up and pushed one of her legs to the side, and then reached down and slid a finger over her slick center. Sensation, pure and raw, spiraled through her, causing her to cry out and writhe beneath him.

"Come to me, *mina,*" he growled, and punctuated his words with another bone-melting thrust of his hips against hers.

Waves of pleasure coursed through her as he thrust harder, faster, and she could feel the climax beginning to throb in her clitoris. But when he lightly pinched her sex, it was her undoing, and with a choked sob, she convulsed around him as her orgasm tore through her in a blinding rush.

The intensity of her release was enough to push Angel over the edge, as well, and with a hoarse shout, he plunged into her and then stiffened as his big frame shuddered above.

He dropped his head to her shoulder, and Sedona hugged him to her. Their breathing was ragged and she could feel the heavy, uneven thumping of his heart against her chest. She wanted to hold onto this moment forever—bottle it up and savor it.

He turned his face and pressed a kiss against her neck, just at the juncture of her jaw. His breath, warm and sweet, washed over her.

"That was…amazing, *mina*." Carefully, he withdrew from her and discarded the condom, before rolling to his side, pulling her with him and tucking her back against his chest. He dipped his head and bit her shoulder gently before soothing the area with his lips and tongue, causing shivers of sensation to chase across her skin.

Sedona turned just enough so she could angle her head and look at him. His eyes were so dark she couldn't distinguish the pupil from the iris, and one dimple flirted with her as he gave her a lazy, tender smile. He stroked the damp hair back from her face before dropping a kiss onto her lips.

"I think I was wrong, you know," he murmured, pulling her tighter against the hard warmth of his body.

"How so?" God, he was so incredibly yummy. She wanted to look at him endlessly.

"I said there was no difference between flying and sex." His eyes held hers, dark and unfathomable. "But you know what? It's entirely possible that this is better than flying. In fact, I'm pretty sure it's my new favorite thing to do."

Sedona stared at him, stunned. Sex with her was better than streaking through the skies at six hundred miles an hour? Her pulse accelerated until she was certain she was going to die from sheer joy. For her, having sex with Angel Torres was the culmination of a dream come true. But to hear him say that sex with her was more intense, more thrilling, more pleasurable than being in the cockpit of his fighter jet was…well, it was pretty freaking unbelievable.

She didn't protest when he wrapped his muscular arms around her and flung a hard leg over hers, effectively trapping her within the circle of his body. He'd said being with her was better than flying.

For now, at any rate.

Even as his arms tightened around her and he pressed a drowsy kiss against her neck, she wondered how long the joyride would last. Because as a pragmatic engineer, she knew eventually—inevitably—even fighter pilots had to come back down to earth.

9

"GODDAMN. Is that guy for real?"

The words were barely more than a wondering whisper, but Sedona looked up from the documents she'd been staring blindly at to follow the other woman's gaze across the room. Angel leaned against the far wall, arms crossed over his chest. The large conference room was filled with members of the inspection team, both civilian and military, as they received the obligatory briefing.

Lieutenant Brian Palmer, the commanding officer responsible for maintaining the fleet of Coyotes, provided a slightly nasal report of the five aviation mishaps, and their own subsequent role in examining the grounded jets. He was a good-looking man in his early thirties, with thinning brown hair and sharp gray eyes that missed nothing. He'd introduced himself to Sedona as soon as she'd entered the conference room, promising full cooperation with her team.

Sedona narrowed her eyes at the maintenance technician sitting beside her. She was pretty enough, if you liked toned, muscular women who exuded raw, physical energy. The kind of woman who could no doubt spend an entire night screwing a guy blind and still wake up in the morning looking gorgeous, and ready for more.

Unlike Sedona, who was exhausted, both physically and mentally, and deliciously tender in places she'd never before imagined.

Just the memory of the previous night brought a lazy smile to her lips. She and Angel had showered together—she remembered the sensual image he'd made as he stood under the sluicing water with his hands behind his head. She'd soaped him with her bare hands—which had led to another heart-pounding interlude of erotic delights.

Later, they'd curled up in bed and flipped through the television channels until she'd made a naughty suggestion to order an adult movie. His eyes had widened in surprise, but he'd laughed and done it. In less than ten minutes, their own moans and sighs had drowned out those of the actors.

It had been nearly 4:00 a.m. when he'd finally escorted her back through the connecting doors and helped her crawl into her own bed, where she'd fallen blissfully asleep—for a whole two hours. She looked as bleary-eyed and worn-out as she felt.

She eyed the wholesome blond technician with growing dislike. The woman could have been an Olympic contender for the Swedish bust-building team with her supple body and thrusting breasts.

"Hmm…he's a pilot, too," the technician continued in a conspiratorial whisper, unaware of the daggers Sedona was throwing her way. "I hope to God I'm assigned to oversee the maintenance on his jet." She grinned. "It would be a pleasure to give him a lube job."

Shocked, Sedona blinked at her, then scowled and shifted her attention back to Angel. The connecting doors between their rooms had been closed when her alarm had finally gone off, and she hadn't seen him until she'd arrived in the briefing room of Hangar 29. But he'd only given her a benignly polite smile of greeting and continued his discussion with the inspection team's commanding officer, Captain Dawson, a severe-looking man several years Angel's senior.

Disgruntled, she'd taken a seat and tried to pretend his apparent disinterest didn't bother her. It was necessary, she knew, to maintain a professional appearance while they conducted their inspections. Still, she'd half expected to see their connecting doors open when she woke up that morning. Had hoped they might share a cup of coffee or several words at the very least, before they were required to don their mantels of indifference. She couldn't quite subdue her hurt feelings.

She sneaked another look at Angel. Somebody had dimmed the lights in the conference room to better view the overhead slides, but even in the indistinct light, she could see he was looking at her.

Watching her.

She flushed and looked quickly away. But when several minutes passed, her attention was unwillingly drawn back to him. He still watched her and then he slowly dropped one eyelid in an audacious wink. A wink that told her he, too, was recalling what they'd shared last night. It was a wink meant only for her. She blushed, covered her quick smile behind her hand and forced herself to focus on her handouts.

The maintenance technician leaned over to her. "I've gotten his attention," she whispered. "He just winked at me. Talk about hot. I'll give him something that'll fire his engines." She nudged Sedona with enough force that she almost unseated her.

Sedona cast the woman one long, baleful look, but the blonde had already turned her attention back to Angel, practically drooling as she stared at him. Dimwit. What was it like to go through life with that kind of supreme confidence, certain every man who looked your way was instantly attracted to you? Sedona wanted to lean over and tell the other woman that Angel was taken and, oh, by the way, he hadn't been winking at her.

Sedona was only distantly aware that Captain Dawson had stood up to speak. She barely heard him as he talked about the team's responsibility to gather information, establish facts and find root causes. He emphasized teamwork, safety and confidentiality. Sedona had been through the drill before. While she understood the necessity for the brief, she found she was unable to pay close attention.

Thoughts of Angel consumed her, which was not good. There would be time enough for the two of them at the end of the day. Right now, she needed to pull herself together and focus on her job. The navy depended on her expertise to ensure the safety of their grounded jets, which meant now was not the time to let herself become completely distracted. She prided herself on her professionalism and skill. There was no way she would let anything interfere with that.

Her gaze slid back to Angel and lingered on his face as he listened to the captain. His flight suit emphasized his broad shoulders and lean hips, and Sedona wondered what he wore underneath. Maybe those sexy boxer briefs he'd been so eager to get out of last night.

Slowly, she became aware that the conference room was silent and several people had turned to look expectantly at her. She dragged her thoughts back to the present and realized Captain Dawson was showing a slide that identified the various inspection teams. Her name was at the top of one of the teams, and he was staring at her as if waiting for her to say something.

"Um, sorry," she mumbled, her face flaming. "I didn't catch that. Could you repeat the question, please?"

"I asked if you could introduce the members of your team and tell the others precisely what inspection functions you'll be performing."

Captain Dawson's face reminded Sedona of her father's

when she'd insisted she wanted to study fine arts rather than engineering.

Disapproving.

Contemptuous.

For a moment, she panicked and couldn't find her voice. Her eyes flew to Angel. A slight frown furrowed his brow as he watched her.

She drew in a deep breath and quickly identified the other engineers who would be working alongside her. "My team will perform hot/cold section evaluation, as well as removal and inspection of engine system components, assessment of QEC kits and external engine components." She refused to look over at Angel. "We'll compare our findings to in-flight test data to identify anomalies or potential performance issues."

"Thank you, Miss Stewart." The commander's voice was dismissive.

Sedona sagged in her seat as Captain Dawson resumed his briefing, but it took several more minutes for her heart to slow down. She'd been caught unaware, not paying attention to her mission here at Lemoore, and all because she'd been too busy mooning over Angel. She really needed to get a grip on herself.

It was nearly an hour later when they followed Lieutenant Palmer out of the room to conduct a quick tour of the enormous hangar where the inspections would be performed.

God, she loved being around the aircraft. She loved the vaulted space inside the hangars, where swallows roosted in the shadows of the high, steel rafters. The rolling hoists and lifts, the enormous, portable tool chests, the oil containers, and the various vats of lubricants all fascinated her. She'd never admit it to anyone, but she even enjoyed the rich, acrid smell of the J-5 jet fuel.

She drifted to the back of the group, calculating how many

hours would be required to perform each inspection. There were eighty-two grounded jets that would not be cleared for flight until the inspection teams had completed their work. Realistically, Sedona's team could examine two dozen engines in the two weeks they'd been allotted. This meant they would be required to extend their stay until they'd had an opportunity to inspect all the jets, or until the navy opted to bring in additional teams.

"Hey, you okay?"

Sedona looked up to see Angel fall into step beside her. She recalled her earlier lapse in the conference room and colored hotly.

"Yes, of course. Why wouldn't I be?"

He smiled then, a slow smile that said she didn't fool him with her act of nonchalance. "You were daydreaming back there, *mina*." His voice was so low she had to strain to hear his words. "About what? I wonder."

Sedona refused to look at him. "Not what you're so obviously thinking about," she denied. "I was just going over some of the engine-calibration figures in my head and lost track of what was being discussed."

"Uh-huh." His tone said he didn't believe a word. "Shall I tell you what I was thinking about?"

"No. Please…no."

"I was thinking about you, *mina*. On top of me."

"Oh." She turned even redder as heady images of straddling him swamped her imagination. "How nice."

"You bet."

She refused to look at him. If she did, he might see how desperately she wanted him, and that wouldn't do at all. She couldn't think about that now.

"What's nice?" piped a cheerful voice, and Sedona turned to see the maintenance technician from the confer ence room striding alongside them. She radiated vitality and sensual energy.

"Nothing," Sedona mumbled.

"Actually," Angel said smoothly, "I was just telling Miss Stewart how fortunate the Navy is to have their jets in her capable hands. She comes highly recommended."

"Oh." There was no mistaking the surprise in the other woman's eyes as she raked Sedona with an appraising stare. "Lucky us, I guess." She thrust a hand out toward Angel. "I'm Petty Officer Heilmuller. You can call me Suzy." She gave him a cheeky grin. "I come highly recommended, too."

Yeah, for personal lube jobs.

Angel laughed, obviously amused by the other woman's brassy impudence as much as Sedona was annoyed by it.

"I think you'd both better pay attention to Lieutenant Palmer," Sedona said waspishly.

Anything to get Angel's attention off the other woman. Had he noticed the bosomy fräulein was a dead ringer for the St. Pauli Girl beer icon? Sedona knew her own appearance paled in comparison to Petty Officer Heilmuller's Germanic good looks.

Angel arched a brow, looking amused and seemingly undeterred by her caustic tone. "So this is where your team will be working," he said.

They had entered a section of the hanger near the massive doors that opened directly onto the flight line. Two Coyotes had already been rolled inside the hanger. They stood roped off and ready for inspection.

Sedona was always thrilled by the sight of the sleek aircraft. Standing fifteen feet off the ground, each jet was fifty-six feet long and boasted a wingspan of nearly forty feet. No matter how many times Sedona inspected a Coyote, she couldn't help but be impressed by the strength and beauty of the plane.

The rest of the inspection team had moved to the far side of the nearest jet. Lieutenant Palmer droned on about inspection protocol, about the importance of maintaining a clean work site and keeping unauthorized personnel from entering the space. She barely heard him. Nope, she was all about the aircraft. She just wished the brief and obligatory tour were over so they could get to work. She could hardly wait to get her hands on this baby's engines.

Stepping close to the Coyote, she reached up and ran an admiring hand along the nose. The metal was cool and smooth beneath her fingers. She ducked under the wing and stepped to the rear of the jet to take a peek at the engine afterburners, though she knew their configuration by heart.

"She's a beauty." Angel followed her beneath the wing. He ran a practiced eye over the plane. "There're a lot of frustrated pilots out there waiting for you to give the thumbs-up, Miss Stewart."

Sedona rolled her eyes at him, despite his words causing her imagination to surge. "You're speaking from experience, I presume?"

"What else?" He stepped closer to her, until she could smell the distinct fragrance of his soap and the underlying scent that was his alone. "I can attest to the fact that I am one frustrated pilot, *mina*."

Sedona grew warm beneath his scrutiny. She pretended to be preoccupied with the long, smooth expanse of the wing, running her fingertip along its beveled edge. "I find that difficult to believe, Lieutenant Commander Torres, considering you completed several, ah, maneuvers just last night."

"That's true." He took a step closer. "However, that was only the maiden voyage. As a test pilot conducting trials, I barely became acquainted with this new asset. I believe additional evaluation is required."

Sedona's breathing quickened at the implicit promise in his eyes and the sultry tone of his voice. She glanced under the belly of the Coyote and saw the inspection group begin to move away from the aircraft toward the open doors of the hangar.

"Additional evaluation?" she echoed faintly. "Just what kind of evaluation would that be?"

"Oh, most definitely a performance evaluation." He grinned, a wicked gleam in his eyes. "You see, while I can provide assurance that all systems are operational, and the handling qualities are superb, there is still some question as to how she'll perform under…extreme conditions."

Whew. Either it was getting hot inside the hangar, or she was starting to spike a fever. She pushed a stray tendril of hair from her damp forehead and moistened her lips, when all she really wanted to do was tear her clothes off and drag Angel to the concrete floor. She'd show him extreme. She might not be overly experienced, but she was nothing if not inventive.

"Extreme conditions," she repeated, breathless. "As in…?"

"As in how high and fast can I push her?" His voice was low and husky, the faint Spanish accent more pronounced. "What kind of thrust can she tolerate without beginning to wobble, or shudder, or, worse, fly apart completely? How hot can her engines run before the inner liner of the combustor melts down?"

Sedona slid a finger inside the prim collar of her shirt, pulling it away from her skin. "Yes, I think I'm beginning to understand, Lieutenant Commander." She swallowed hard. "But it sounds…dangerous. Are you certain you want to do this?"

He was so close, Sedona could see the individual spikes of his lashes and feel his warm breath against her cheek. He was too close. Too hot. Too completely irresistible.

"Oh yes, *mina*," he purred, "I'm absolutely certain. The only question remaining is…am I cleared to launch?"

She was a goner.

With a soft sigh of surrender, Sedona leaned forward, her lashes drifted closed and her lips parted for the inevitability of his kiss.

"Sir? Ma'am?"

Sedona's eyes flew open and she leaped back from Angel. Unfocused, she turned abruptly away and then gave a sharp cry of pain as her head connected with the horizontal stabilizer, the small wings that protruded from the tail of the jet. Her eyes smarted with tears and she swiftly bent her head to hide her confusion. How was it that when Angel was near, she lost all ability to concentrate?

A young man peered at them from beneath the underbelly of the Coyote, and his blue eyes twinkled with unmistakable amusement. "Ah, sorry to interrupt, sir. Captain Dawson is asking for you."

Angel passed a hand over his eyes and then nodded his acknowledgment. "Thank you, Ensign." His voice sounded rough. "I'll be right there."

"Yessir." The man touched his fingers to his brow. "Ma'am." Then he was gone.

Sedona listened to the ensign's footsteps fade as he sprinted toward the hangar doors, and then pressed her hands against her cheeks, appalled. She had come so close to kissing Angel, right in the middle of the hangar. Worse, they'd almost had a witness. So much for maintaining a professional distance.

"Sedona."

She drew in a shaky breath and looked at Angel. The amusement and regret in his eyes nearly undid her. "Don't you dare apologize," she warned, hating the way her voice wobbled. "Just don't—don't do it again."

She brushed past him and walked quickly toward the exit. Angel reached her before she'd gone more than a half dozen steps. He captured her arm and swung her around.

"Angel, please," she whispered. "It's bad enough—"

"Are you hurt?"

Before she could protest, he uncinched the clip that kept her hair up, causing the unruly mass to tumble around her shoulders. He drew her forward and gently worked his fingers through the loose waves, probing her scalp where she'd struck it. The sensation was cathartic.

"Mmm." The soothing pressure of his fingers was delicious, making her want to melt against him. Just as quickly, she regained her senses and shoved his hands away, horrified. "Stop that. What are you doing?"

"You banged your head pretty hard back there. Are you sure you didn't hurt yourself?"

"Quite sure. I've been told I have a very hard head." She snatched the clip from his hands and turned away from him. It seemed when Angel was near, the only thing she could think about was him. She couldn't remember feeling like this about any other guy. Ever. He overwhelmed her, made her realize again just how completely out of her league she was.

Angel fell into step beside her as they walked through the hangar. He watched as she scooped her hair up and coiled it neatly before clamping it securely to the back of her head.

"Why do you wear it like that?" he asked. "I prefer your hair down."

"It's easier like this. Besides, I can't wear it down if I'm working near moving parts." She thought of Petty Officer Heilmuller and her short crop of spiky blond hair. The technician managed to ooze sex appeal despite her olive-drab coverall and steel-toed boots. "Maybe one of these days I'll just get it all cut off and be done with it."

"That would be a shame, *mina,* considering how much I enjoy your hair spilled across my pillow." He gave her a roguish grin.

Sedona's stomach flipped and a peculiar heaviness descended into her pelvic region. She closed her eyes briefly against the images his words conjured. She needed to put some space between herself and Angel before she did something completely unacceptable in a military-aircraft hangar. She pictured Captain Dawson's reaction if he came across her clinging to Angel's neck with her legs wrapped around his waist and her tongue down his throat. She almost smiled. Nope, definitely not the way to get on the captain's good side.

She stepped outside into the brilliant sunshine of a cloudless day. Overhead, two low-altitude Coyotes rocketed through the skies in formation, and Sedona's entire body vibrated to the thunderous roar of their engines. Shielding her eyes, she watched them streak across the heavens until they disappeared on the horizon.

"Looks like they've already begun to conduct test flights," she commented. Lowering her hand, she arched an amused brow at Angel. "You're late, flyboy."

He grinned ruefully. "Actually, I was down on the flight line at 0500 hours." Seeing her look of dismay, he shrugged. "Must be the time difference. I couldn't sleep. I told the flight captain I'd report in later this morning, after the brief."

Sedona stared at him. "You could already be in the air, and yet you chose to come to this? Why?"

He gave her a quick smile. "Why else? Because you're here."

Without waiting for her response, he strode across the tarmac toward the assembled inspection teams, leaving Sedona to gape after him. He had voluntarily subjected himself to the painfully boring brief in order to see her? She blinked, then smiled. Oh, yeah. He'd definitely gone above and beyond the call of duty. She conjured up delicious images of just how she would reward him for his sacrifice.

10

"HEY, STEWART! You staying here all night, or what?"

Sedona hunched her shoulders and ignored Ken Larson. She couldn't leave the engine test cell, located in a concrete building next to the Coyote hangar, until she'd assured herself the tests they'd run that day were accurate.

"You know, it's okay to get out and party at least a little while you're here." His voice was friendly. Persuasive.

With a deliberate, long-suffering sigh, she swiveled in her chair to face him as he leaned against the doorjamb of the dimly lit calibration room. "Not all of us are here to screw around, Ken." *Well, at least not much.* "Some of us actually take our jobs seriously."

So seriously, she hadn't gotten back to her hotel room before ten o'clock for the past three nights, and hadn't seen Angel since that first morning at the briefing.

Undeterred, Ken glanced at his watch. "Yeah, well, it's almost eight o'clock, and all work and no play makes you a very dull girl." He grinned at her. "Why don't you go back to your room, get out of that jumpsuit and let me buy you a drink downstairs."

Sedona arched a brow at him. Was it possible he was hitting on her? She coughed indelicately and turned her back on him to resume her study of the test results. "What's wrong, Ken? Striking out with the babes at the hotel bar? Afraid if you don't get somebody to sleep with you, you'll miss out on the next big promotion?"

She didn't hear him enter the room, didn't know he was close until suddenly, his face was next to hers as he leaned over her shoulder and spoke softly into her ear.

"Actually, Sedona, I was hoping we could come to some kind of…arrangement. After all, you said you wanted to join the club." She stiffened when he took a loose tendril of her hair in his hand and rubbed it slowly between his finger and thumb. His voice was low and silky. "I was thinking we could kill two birds with one stone. We could have a great time together, you know. We could get naked, take a few photos, and maybe both get promoted."

As Sedona sat rigid with surprise, he turned his face fractionally and inhaled. "Mmm, you smell good. I wonder if you taste as sweet." His face moved toward hers.

She shot to her feet so fast the chair skittered out from beneath her and Ken took a hasty step back to avoid hitting his chin on her shoulder. Her heart slammed in her chest and her blood pulsed in her ears.

They stared at each other for a long moment until finally, Ken laughed softly and stepped back. "Think about it, Sedona. I haven't had any complaints about my performance, and I wouldn't expect our relationship to continue once we get back to the office." He grinned as he looked her over. "But we sure could have a hell of a time while we're here."

"Somehow," she finally managed to say, "I don't think so. I—I've changed my mind about the whole thing. But thanks for the offer."

He backed away slowly, his grin never wavering. "Well, okay, if that's how you feel about it. But if you change your mind, you just let me know."

"I'll do that." *When hell freezes over.*

She heard him whistling as he made his way down the narrow flight of stairs and out the building. She rubbed a trembling hand across her eyes, and reminded herself that if Ken thought she was up for a little casual sex, she had no one to blame but herself. She'd all but begged the Membership to let her prove she, too, could have meaningless sex with a stranger. He probably thought he was doing her a favor by offering himself up as stud. Just thinking about sex with Ken Larson made her shudder. How was she going to work with the guy for the next week and a half?

They were only into their third day, but it felt more like three weeks. Each day, the routine was the same. Under Sedona's watchful eye, a team of navy technicians pulled the engines from each of the hangared aircraft and brought them into four separate test cells. With four engineers on her team, including herself and Ken Larson, they each tested one engine per day.

Sedona examined the records for each engine prior to the engine teardown. During the disassembly, the team recorded torque values and then inspected each component for damage, wear or erosion. The engine components were also boroscoped for cracking.

Sedona spent the entire day behind a window of tempered glass, seated at a control panel that glowed with a multitude of lights, levers and illuminated displays, while she conducted calibration and performance testing on her engine.

While the work wasn't physically demanding, it was mentally exhausting. Worse, the room reeked of the jet fuel they'd guzzled their way through during the tests. Normally, she didn't mind the smell, but today it made her feel queasy.

She'd run several of the tests more than once, had painstakingly compared her findings to the model specifications and, to her relief, everything she'd tested thus far had come up negative. Long after the other engineers and the team of navy technicians had packed away their tools and returned to their hotel or billets, Sedona remained in the calibration room to pore over the test results for those engines she hadn't personally tested.

She didn't want to miss anything vital. There was no way she'd let Angel fly with a compromised engine. She needed to assure herself they were in perfect condition before she allowed them to be reinstalled on the jets.

If she'd known Ken Larson was going to come back down to check on her, she'd have left long ago. She hated to admit it, but the calibration lab made her nervous after hours. It was dark and isolated, and eerily quiet without the residual noise that came with running the engines.

She tore the sheet of paper from the readout machine and stared blindly at the numbers recorded there. A dark thought occurred to her. Did Ken make the offer out of sympathy because he didn't think she could attract a guy on her own? She might not have a body like Petty Officer Heilmuller, but Angel hadn't had any complaints.

Of course, Angel hadn't sought her out since that first morning in the Coyote hangar, either. She didn't think he was avoiding her, but she couldn't help feeling a little bit hurt that he hadn't made an effort to see her again. It didn't help telling herself he was as busy as she was. In addition to conducting the flight tests, the pilots spent hours briefing the rear admiral and his staff on their findings at the end of each day. Combined with her own long days, she'd be lucky if they managed to connect even one more time during the course of their stay.

The thought was completely depressing.

What if it was true? What if the one night she'd had with Angel was all she was ever going to have? She'd thought it would be enough. Hell, less than a week ago she'd have given her left arm for just one night with him.

Crumpling the paper in her hands, she realized it wasn't enough. She wanted more. Wanted to hear his seductive voice enticing her to do things she'd only ever dreamed about. She wanted to see his face tauten with desire, see the muscles tighten in his jaw, neck and shoulders as he fought to retain control.

She hadn't stopped thinking about him since that night. She tried not to wonder why he hadn't contacted her. Because she was weak, she avoided going back to her room, worried that she might throw open the connecting doors and fling herself at him. Only pride kept her from completely humiliating herself.

However, it hadn't prevented her from pressing her ear to the door each night for some sign of activity. Some indication that he was there, yet apparently not interested enough to turn the knob and invite her in. In his defense, his room had been completely silent each night. It seemed no matter what time she returned, he returned later. It was clear that unless she took some drastic action, the likelihood of engaging Angel in another night of bliss was remote, at best.

Throwing the crumpled paper into the wastebasket, she leaned over the test console to shut the power down. She wasn't going to accomplish much more tonight, anyway. Tomorrow, the technicians would reinstall the engines they'd tested today and roll the aircraft back onto the flight line. Then they would bring four more aircraft in, and the process would start all over again. She'd have at least a few hours in the morning to rerun the printouts. She didn't need to stay in the calibration room any longer.

She drew the door closed behind her and locked it, before making her way down the stairwell. Outside, the night was dark and cool. A partial moon helped to illuminate the walkway that led toward the parking lot. The stars over the desert were breathtaking, and Sedona stood for a moment, admiring them.

She was turning toward the parking lot when she noticed a movement beneath one of the jets in the flight line. Was that an animal of some kind? She'd heard that wild coyotes sometimes wandered onto the base, and she sincerely hoped this wasn't one of them. How far away was it? A hundred yards? If the animal decided it wanted to eat her, could she outrun it?

She was debating whether to slip back into the building or make a dash for her car, when the figure shifted. As she watched, it unfolded and stretched upright, and she sagged with relief when she realized it was a man.

Who was he, and why was he out on the flight line at this time of night? Even as it occurred to her that the man might not be authorized to be there, he turned and began walking toward her. A frisson of fear feathered its way along her neck. Just as she was debating whether or not to run, she recognized the man as Lieutenant Palmer, the maintenance officer in charge of the Coyotes.

"Miss Stewart?" There was no mistaking the surprise in his voice.

Sedona expelled a shaky laugh of relief. "Oh my God, you scared me. I thought at first you were a coyote. You know, the four-legged kind."

He stepped closer, and Sedona could see he was wearing civilian clothing. It was strange to see him out of uniform.

"I'm sorry." He smiled. "I didn't mean to make you nervous." He gestured toward the aircraft. "I was, uh, just doing my final check of the jets before calling it a night." He peered at her. "What are you still doing here?"

"Oh, I was in the calibration room going over some results on the last engine we tested." She laughed. "I won't do that again. This place totally creeps me out after dark."

"Can I walk you to your car?"

"Thanks, no. I'm fine, now that I know you're not some wild animal or escaped lunatic." She didn't miss how his eyebrows shot up. "That was a joke."

"Well, good night, then."

"Bye." Sedona made her way to the parking lot. Halfway down the walkway, she couldn't resist peeking back over her shoulder, mildly disconcerted to see the lieutenant standing where she'd left him, watching her.

She was still thinking about him as she slid into her rental car and began the drive back to the hotel. Was it normal for a maintenance officer to perform checks on the aircraft so late at night? And if he was on duty, why was he out of uniform? She made a mental note to mention the incident to Angel when she saw him.

If she saw him.

Since that first night with Angel, she'd kept her own side of the connecting doors unlocked and open. She didn't even want to think about why Angel had left his door firmly closed. She hadn't had the nerve to try to open it, and the whole thing was beginning to make her crazy. She needed advice, and she needed it now.

As she drove, she rummaged through her backpack and dug out her cell phone, biting her lip as she punched in her sister's cell-phone number. She didn't know if Ana was working tonight or not, but knew her shift wouldn't start until later. Ana's workday kicked into full gear about the same time Sedona's ended.

"Sedona? Hey, this is unbelievable! I was just thinking about you. Really!"

Sedona couldn't help but smile as she heard Ana's voice. Always cheerful, always upbeat, Ana was the epitome of the free spirit. Sometimes Sedona envied her ability to do as she pleased, without regard for what anyone else thought.

"Hey, sis. I was thinking about you, too."

"So what's up? You never call unless there's a problem."

Was that true? Surely she'd called Ana just to tell her she missed her, or to ask how her life was going. But, try as she might, she couldn't recall the last time she'd done that.

"No, everything is good. I mean, Mom is fine and Allison is fine. I just, um, had something I needed to ask you. You know—" she cringed inwardly "—a girl thing."

There was a momentary, stunned silence. "Oh my freaking God. You've met someone."

Sedona laughed. "Yeah, something like that."

"You've met a guy? Oh, Sedona, that's great!"

Sedona laughed again, this time at the unabashed relief and sincere joy in Ana's voice. "Yeah, it is pretty great. He's…" She paused. "He's the most amazing guy I've ever met and…Ana?"

"Yes?"

"He's incredible in bed."

There was a shrill squeal of delight. "You slept with him! Oh my God! This is so unbelievable! Tell me everything!"

Sedona did, leaving nothing out, not even the striptease she'd performed for Angel, or the adult movie they'd watched for all of eight minutes before he'd rolled her beneath him. She told Ana everything she knew about him, including the fact she'd had a serious crush on the guy for over a year.

The only thing she didn't tell Ana was her discovery of the secret club that promoted men based on their sexual activities. Nor could she bring herself to talk about Ken Larson and his repugnant offer to get them both promoted by engaging in an affair.

"Anyway," she sighed, "I haven't seen Angel since Wednesday morning, and I'm trying not to freak out about it, but what if he's not interested anymore? What if it really was just a one-nighter?"

"Okay, listen," soothed Ana, "this is what you do. Trust me in this, sweetie. There isn't a guy out there who won't roll over and beg at the sight of a beautiful woman, naked and primed, in his bed."

"I am *not* beautiful," Sedona protested with a self-conscious laugh. "You got the looks and I got the brains, remember?"

Ana snorted. "All I remember is you wanting to do everything in your power to make Dad happy, including being the son he never had."

Sedona frowned. "Is that really what you think?"

"It doesn't matter. It's water long under the bridge, and Dad's probably beaming down at you for fulfilling every dream he ever had."

"But not you," Sedona mused aloud, turning in to the parking lot of the hotel. "You thumbed your nose at him and took off for the West Coast."

Ana laughed. "If you say so, sis. I think you missed a lot of what really happened. You were in college by then, remember."

Sedona sighed as she parked the car and turned off the ignition. She didn't really want to remember. Too many of those memories were colored by resentment and unhappiness. What Ana said was true; it was water under the bridge.

"You're right. So tell me what I should do now. I mean, there's always the possibility Angel is avoiding me. I don't want to set myself up for a big fat rejection."

"Honey," Ana drawled, "what I have in mind is absolutely, one hundred percent rejection-proof."

And as she outlined her simple plan for seduction, Sedona had to agree; it sounded pretty foolproof. Daring? Yes. Audacious? Definitely. Designed to bring a guy to his knees? She certainly hoped so.

Fifteen minutes later, she let herself into her room. Unzipping her Navy-issue jumpsuit, she crossed to the connecting doors. With one ear pressed against the panels, she hopped first on one foot and then the other as she pulled her shoes off.

Nothing but silence.

Quickly, without turning on any interior lights, Sedona crept out onto her balcony and peered over the railing at the room next to hers. It was completely dark. Angel had not yet returned to the hotel. Or if he had, he'd left again.

Slipping back into the room, she sprinted to the bathroom for the fastest shower of her life. He could come back at any moment. She had to be ready. She stood under the shower and let the hard spray of water loosen the knots of uncertainty in her neck and shoulders. This would work. She refused to be a victim of her own self-doubts. She was desirable. She was feminine.

Or she could be.

She just had to let herself go. At least, that's what Ana had said. She only hoped she had the courage to do what Ana recommended.

Stepping out of the shower, she wrapped her hair in a towel and scrubbed herself dry before wrapping a second towel around her body. She rubbed her hand over the condensation on the bathroom mirror and leaned forward to examine her face.

Her pupils were huge, drowning out the green irises. She bit some color into her lips and pinched her cheeks, wishing she owned some cosmetics to even out her complexion. She yanked the towel from her hair and scrubbed it vigorously. She rarely used a blow-dryer as it only made her hair frizzy. Better to let it dry naturally into the thick waves that defied styling.

With the towel still wrapped around her body, she crept

back to the connecting doors and pressed her ear once more
against the panels. Still nothing.

Biting her lip, she tried the knob and her heart leaped
when it turned effortlessly beneath her fingers. That had been
the one unknown variable in the equation. According to Ana,
if the door was unlocked then Angel definitely wanted more
action, even if he didn't realize it.

The adjoining room was dark and quiet. As she stepped
inside, she caught a subtle whiff of Angel's aftershave and
froze, half expecting him to materialize from the shadows.
When all remained quiet, she drew a fortifying breath and
switched on the bedside lamp. She yanked the brightly
flowered bedspread down to the foot of the bed and plumped
the pillows invitingly. She tuned the bedside radio to an easy-
listening station.

Then she dropped the towel, stretched herself out on
Angel's bed and waited.

GOD, HE WAS TIRED. Angel scrubbed a hand over his eyes as
he rode the elevator to the third floor of the hotel. He'd conducted two flight tests that day, pushing the aircraft through
their paces in a punishing routine guaranteed to root out any
performance issues.

The jets had performed flawlessly.

Afterward, he and the other test pilots had completed the
reams of paperwork required to document the tests, and had
spent several long hours in the admiral's conference room,
bringing the senior brass up to date. He was completely fried.

The elevator doors slid open and he drew his key card out
of his wallet as he walked to his room. He paused briefly
outside Sedona's door and checked his watch. It was barely
nine o'clock. Had she returned? Or was she still in the calibration room, poring over the test results? He raised his hand

to knock, then hesitated. He doubted Sedona would thank him for showing up smelling of jet fuel and sweat. He could really use a shower.

He let his hand fall back to his side.

He'd hoped to hook up with her tonight, either for dinner or something a little more intimate, but had been roped into going to the officers' club for a quick bite with the other pilots, instead. He'd tried to call Sedona on her cell phone, and was frustrated when he hadn't been able to get through to her.

But he'd been unable to stop thinking about her, and when his buddies said they were going to finish the evening at a local strip club, he'd declined and headed back to the hotel. If Sedona returned to her room before ten o'clock, he intended to keep her fully occupied for several hours, at least. But a shower was definitely in order. Reluctantly, he turned away from her door.

Inserting the key card into his own door, he pushed it open and then stopped dead in his tracks, speechless. Lying on top of his bed, looking like every erotic fantasy he'd ever had, was Sedona.

Naked.

Smiling.

Waiting for him.

Every cell in his body snapped to attention.

Her pale golden skin seemed to gleam in the soft light. Her hair tumbled in an enticing mass around her face, and the bedside lamp cast intriguing shadows across the curves and contours of her luscious body.

She lay on her side with her head propped on one hand, and as he watched, she bent her top leg and slid it upward until her knee hid the enticing juncture of her thighs from view. He drank in the graceful dip of her waist, the rounded curve of hip and thigh, and the pale globes of her breasts, full and begging for his touch.

She reached up and twirled a tendril of hair lazily around one finger as her smiled widened. "So, flyboy," she murmured in a sultry voice, "you going to shut the door, or stand there until you draw a crowd?"

With a start, Angel realized he was still standing with the door open, his hand on the knob. Shock, and then pure, unadulterated delight had rendered him momentarily incapable of movement. He stepped into the room, dropped his flight bag onto the floor and let the door close with a click behind him. He didn't take his eyes off Sedona as he flipped the dead bolt and slid the security chain into place. No way would he allow anyone to interrupt this.

"So, flyboy," she crooned, sliding her legs sinuously against each other and allowing him a brief, alluring glimpse of the dark patch of curls between her legs, "how was your day?"

He grinned as his body responded with wholehearted enthusiasm to the visual stimulation she provided. "Much better now," he assured her, and stood at the edge of the bed and looked at her. He didn't dare let himself touch her. He just looked, and as he did so, her body slowly flushed with color.

Sedona released the tendril of hair and artfully ran a hand over the curve of hip and thigh. "I couldn't stop thinking about you," she said in a husky voice. "The more I thought about you, the hornier I got."

O-kay. This was unexpected. His grin faltered for a moment as he tried to decide if she was teasing him. "Really."

"Mmm." She sent him an inviting look from beneath her eyelashes. "I've been waiting for such a long time for you to…come."

Her words sent a bolt of liquid heat straight to his groin.

He couldn't help himself. He leaned over her to capture her lips. It had been too long since he'd tasted her. But before he could kiss her, she turned her face to the side and pushed him back with a surprisingly forceful hand against his chest.

"Not so fast," she purred.

He straightened and frowned down at her, his body already pulsing with need. What game was she playing? "Christ, *mina,*" he said on a half laugh, "don't torture me, okay?"

In answer, she rolled fully onto her back and bent one arm gracefully over her head. The movement pulled her breasts higher and tautened the slender line of her waist. She skated the fingers of her free hand over her body, finally settling on her breast.

"Why not?" she asked, all innocence. "After all, you've tortured me for the past three days."

Angel swallowed, riveted by the delicate play of her fingers against her nipple. As he watched, it tightened into a small bud. He dragged his attention upward, to her face. She studied him from beneath her lashes, and her breath quickened.

"Oh, yes," she breathed. "Every time I thought of you, it was torture. I thought of you doing this."

Angel's body tightened as she arched her back and cupped both breasts in her hands. She alternately squeezed and pinched them, and her hips shifted restlessly against the sheets.

"Okay, *mina,*" he finally rasped. "I think I understand. You're feeling neglected, but if you'll just let me—"

He unzipped his flight suit with lightning speed, and peeled it from his shoulders and arms until it hung around his waist. He yanked his T-shirt over his head and sent it sailing, but when he would have unzipped his flight suit farther, she put out a hand and restrained him.

"Wait."

She twisted around and plumped the pillows up behind her. Then reclined back in a half-sitting position. Her knees fell slightly apart and Angel just about wept when he glimpsed her feminine folds. He wanted so badly to touch her. Taste her. Take her.

"Mina," he groaned, "have mercy."

"I want you to watch," she said breathlessly. "I want you to watch what happens to my body when I think about you."

Slowly, then, with her eyes caressing him, she began to tease her breasts with both hands. Then, as a flush deepened on her neck and face, she slid the palm of one hand down over her abdomen until she cupped herself. "Oh," she sighed, "I'm so hot. And wet. And that's just from looking at you."

Angel groaned. Mesmerized, he reached over and hauled the hard-backed chair from the desk closer, until he could sit and watch. His heart thudded hard enough that he was sure she would hear it, and the instant her hand dropped low on her body, he broke out in a fine sweat.

His breathing quickened as she used two fingers to open herself, and he swiftly adjusted his seat for an unobstructed view. She obliged by spreading her legs wider.

"Oh, yes," she breathed, and dipped a finger ever so slightly into herself. It came away glistening, and she touched the moisture to her clitoris. "Oh, that feels good."

Her folds were pale pink and smooth, and Angel longed to touch his tongue to them. He shifted uncomfortably in his seat, helpless to look away. She swirled her finger over the spot where he knew she felt the most intense pleasure, drawing her clitoris from its secret fold until it began to blossom.

Angel stared, transfixed by the changes he witnessed. Her gorgeous sex changed, grew flushed and engorged as her desire increased. The sight of Sedona pleasuring herself was the most erotic thing he'd ever seen. His balls ached, and his cock throbbed painfully within the confines of the jumpsuit. It took every ounce of self-restraint not to free himself and take over what she was doing.

"Please," he groaned, and moved to sit on the edge of the bed near her feet, "I need to touch you."

"No," she gasped, her hips gyrating, "you just need to watch."

She inserted a second finger alongside the first, and her head fell back as she let out a soft moan. Then she slid her free hand down her body until both hands were seductively engaged between her thighs. As she pumped two fingers into herself, she used the other hand to caress and stroke her clitoris, sliding a finger down either side of it until it stood out, flushed and swollen, against her tender flesh.

It took all of Angel's hard-won discipline not to reach out and touch her. He pressed the palm of his hand hard against the base of his swollen cock and willed himself not to come. But when he realized Sedona watched him through half-closed eyes, her mouth moist and parted, he was done.

With a subdued growl, he stood up and stripped the flight suit down his legs, pushing his briefs down with it until his erection sprang free. He reached over and grabbed a condom from the bedside table and, in one deft movement, covered himself.

"I'm sorry, *mina*," he said huskily, and with his flight suit still bunched around his ankles, he propped himself above her. "You make me crazy, you know that."

Poised at the entrance to her body, he braced himself with his hands on either side of her and stared down at her flushed face. She had stopped touching herself, mercifully, but she still writhed her hips in a manner that made him groan with lust.

"Come into me," she breathed. Her green eyes were cloudy with desire as she gazed up at him. "Let's see how my body reacts when I do more than just think about you, when I join myself with you…"

Her words were like a catalyst, crumbling the last remaining fragments of his self-control. With a ragged sigh of surrender, he buried himself in her tightness. She came immediately, crying out with pleasure as her flesh contracted around his length.

Angel watched her face, enthralled, as she climaxed. His chest tightened. It was incredible to watch. The combination of the visual and the physical stimulation was too much, and with a harsh cry, he exploded in a white-hot rush of pleasure that caused his eyes to roll back in his head and his back to arch.

Long minutes later, when he could breathe again, he rolled to his side, pulling Sedona with him. "Damn," he gasped. "Where did you learn to do that?"

Sedona laughed softly and curled her body against his. "Years of practice. But," she added almost shyly, "this is the first time I've had an audience."

He raised his head and looked down at her, stunned. "You're kidding."

"What? You think I do this for a living?"

"No, that's not what I meant." He blew out his breath and lay back against the pillows. He tightened his arm around her. "I'm just thinking what an incredible turn-on that was." And how goddamn sorry he was for every guy who'd never get the chance to experience it firsthand. Just the thought of any other guy watching Sedona do *that* caused a surge of jealousy so intense it startled him.

Sliding his arm out from beneath Sedona, he swung his legs over the side of the bed and sat up. He discreetly disposed of the condom, surprised to see he still wore his flight boots. The mattress shifted behind him as Sedona came up on her knees and pressed herself against his back. She wound her arms around his neck and planted a moist kiss against his jaw.

"Hey," she murmured in his ear. "You okay?"

"Yeah." He didn't dare look at her, afraid she might see the conflicting emotions churning inside him. Jealousy. Need. And, unbelievably, desire. He bent over and unlaced his boots and kicked them to the floor, then pushed the rest of his clothing off. "I, uh, was going to knock on your door tonight," he finally admitted.

"Oh. I guess I sort of preempted you again, huh? Sorry."

She sounded anything but sorry as she caressed his chest. Could she feel his heart beating hard beneath her fingers? He shivered when she feathered a kiss along the nape of his neck.

"Mmm," she murmured, "you smell good."

Angel arched a brow in disbelief. "I smell like jet fuel. In fact, I was headed into the shower before I knocked on your door."

"Didn't I tell you?" She caught his earlobe gently between her teeth and then swirled her tongue against the sensitive skin. "Jet fuel is my new favorite scent. But a shower sounds…interesting. I could wash your back. Or something."

Her voice was sweetly seductive and Angel almost groaned aloud as he recalled their last shower together. It gave a whole new meaning to the term *oral hygiene.* Just thinking about that intimate exchange, combined with the moist heat of her tongue in his ear, had him growing hard again.

He laughed ruefully and disentangled himself from her arms before standing up to let her see the proof of his need.

"Oh." Her eyes widened when she saw he was ready for her again. She uncurled her legs from beneath her, scooted to the edge of the mattress and grasped his hips, drawing him into the vee of her legs. "Oh, my."

But when she would have reached for him, he forestalled her, grabbing both her hands in his and tugging her to her feet. "Oh, no you don't," he growled down at her. "If you touch me, I'm toast, and since I plan on spending the next—" he glanced at his wristwatch "—six hours loving you, long and slow, let's see if you can manage to keep your hands to yourself for a while."

Sedona laughed and fell back onto the bed, throwing her arms outward in a sign of surrender. "I'm all yours, flyboy."

She watched him through heavily lidded eyes, but the uneven rise and fall of her chest let Angel know she wasn't nearly as unaffected as she let on. He eased himself down on one elbow beside her, letting his gaze travel over her.

He traced a finger over her pale hip bone and admired the whorl of her navel. He pressed his palm against her rib cage, just beneath her breast. Her heart beat fast under his fingers. Leaning over her, he pressed a kiss to the spot.

"God," he sighed, his breath tickling her soft flesh, "I want you again. Unbelievable."

Her tummy contracted as she chuckled. "And here I thought you weren't letting me touch you because you didn't like me."

Angel raised his head and looked at her over the enticing mounds of her breasts. "I think we both know that's not the problem," he said hoarsely, and slowly worked his way upward to her mouth.

Man, oh man, the woman could kiss. The problem had nothing to do with not liking her, he thought as he pulled her closer, and everything to do with liking her way too much.

11

"I CAN'T FIND anything wrong with any of them. They all seem pretty perfect to me." Sedona stood at the edge of the sun-baked flight line and watched as a dozen or more maintenance officers, each clad in a bright-red T-shirt and camouflage pants, prepared to roll two more Coyote jets into the hangar for inspection.

"Oh, yeah," purred Petty Officer Heilmuller beside her. "No argument there, ma'am. They're all prime cuts."

Turning to the other woman, Sedona made a sound of exasperation. "I was talking about the jet engines."

To her amazement, Petty Officer Heilmuller gave her a broad wink. "Sure you were. Ma'am."

Sedona watched the other woman saunter back toward the hangar, idly swinging a long wrench from one hand. It was just her luck the attractive petty officer had been assigned to her inspection team. Although, to her credit, she was an accomplished mechanic, despite her sometimes ribald sense of humor. On top of that, the other woman was right; Sedona couldn't remember the last time she'd been surrounded by so many young, virile, good-looking guys. Not that it mattered to her, of course. Next to Angel Torres, they were merely boys.

Shading her eyes, she peered farther down the fight line to where two pilots were conducting a visual inspection of a pair of Coyotes in preparation for a test flight. She didn't have to see his face to know one of the pilots was Angel. His tall, broad-shouldered physique was difficult to mistake.

She thought again of the previous night, and couldn't stop smiling at the memories of what they'd done together. The guy was beyond amazing. He hadn't walked her back to her own room in the wee hours of the morning as he'd done their first night together. Instead, she'd stayed wrapped around him until the alarm clock on his wristwatch went off at 4:30 a.m. He'd kissed her and left her in his bed while he took a shower. She'd curled up on the edge of the mattress and watched him as he dressed.

"Sleep in this morning," he'd said as he knelt next to the bed and smoothed her hair back from her face. "I'll send a message over to the inspection team that you had a conference call with Joe or something."

"That's okay," she murmured, smiling up at him. His hair gleamed, sleek as a seal's, from his shower and he smelled delicious. His flight suit was open at the throat, revealing the drab olive-colored T-shirt beneath. "If you can get up this early, so can I."

"Okay." He leaned forward and kissed her so sweetly she'd been tempted to pull him back into bed. "I'll try and get back early tonight, okay? Wait for me?"

Wait for him? Was he kidding? She'd been waiting for him her whole life.

"I'll be right here," she'd responded with a smile. "Well, maybe not right here, exactly. But next door."

She longed for the day to be over. She still had the sense that she was part of a surreal dream, and any moment she'd wake up to find herself back in the unexciting, predictable reality of her plain-Jane life. She didn't want to think too much about what it was that Angel saw in her. She wasn't superstitious, but there was a small part of her that prescribed to the theory of self-fulfilling prophecy. If she couldn't understand why Angel was with her, eventually he'd begin to wonder why, as well. She wasn't naive enough to believe their relationship could possibly last, but she wouldn't do anything to jeopardize it, either.

"Hey, Stewart, want to take a walk with me?"

Sedona turned away from watching Angel, to see Ken Larson striding across the tarmac toward her. She shoved her hands into her pockets. "Not particularly."

"I think you might want to reconsider." He was wearing aviator sunglasses with mirrored lenses, and Sedona couldn't read the expression in his blue eyes.

"Why?"

He jerked his head in the direction of the hangar. "They just brought in the two Coyotes that experienced in-flight engine failures. They're over in Hangar 74. The Navy investigation team responsible for inspecting the damaged aircraft is going over them with a fine-tooth comb, but I thought it would be a good opportunity to see what kind of damage the engines sustained. Maybe it'll provide clues as to what we should be looking for."

"Are you kidding?" Sedona's excitement level kicked into high gear. "What are we doing standing here? Let's go."

Finally, something that might provide a hint as to why the Coyotes had crashed. Nearly a week of inspections had turned up nothing. All systems were fully operational and showed no signs of damage or malfunction. She had wondered about the jets that had suffered mishaps, but she hadn't hoped to actually see any of them.

"So," Ken said as they followed the road that led along the flight line to Hangar 74, "what'd you do last night? I sort of hoped to see you downstairs in the lounge, but you never showed."

Sedona gave a sidelong look. "Why would I?"

He spread his hands. "Hey, my offer still stands. I mean, think about it. We're friends, right?"

"I guess," Sedona said warily.

"Well, we could be friends with benefits." He swept her body with an appreciative glance. "We could get wild together, take a couple of photos, then give the evidence to the Membership and get promoted, right?"

Sedona stopped walking and stared at him, mortified. "Ken," she began, "I'm flattered by your interest, but I already told you—" She broke off with a laugh. "I'm no longer interested in being part of the Membership. In truth, there's no way I'd *ever* sleep with somebody just to get ahead in my job. So the answer isn't just *no*, it's *hell no*."

"You know what your problem is, Stewart?" Ken's voice had turned hard and cold. "You think you're better than everyone else. I know your kind. I've had to deal with bitches like you my entire life. If a guy doesn't meet your exacting standards, he's beneath your notice."

What the…? Sedona couldn't keep the astonishment out of her voice. "What is your problem, Larson? That I won't sleep with you?" She stared at him incredulously. "Get over it. I don't sleep with coworkers."

Ken jerked his sunglasses off. His face was flushed and his eyes simmered with anger at whatever old memories still haunted him. Sedona watched as he visibly struggled with his emotions. Finally, he gave a grim parody of a smile.

"Oh, yeah? Well, here's a news flash for you, Stewart." He leaned slightly forward, until his face was so close, Sedona could see the individual pores of his skin. "There's only one way to get a promotion in this place and you'll never see one."

Sedona watched through narrowed eyes as he strode away, telling herself it didn't matter what he thought.

"Because you don't have what it takes, Stewart," he called back over his shoulder, "in business or in bed."

She shook her head in bemusement as she watched him go. Why had she never realized what a jerk Ken was? She'd been so duped by his easygoing, friendly manner that she hadn't seen he was really no better than Mike "Hound Dog" Sullivan. She told herself his insults couldn't truly hurt her. After all, she was heading up the engine inspection team and sharing bed space with the most perfect guy she'd ever known. All things considered, she'd say she definitely had what it took, both in business and in bed.

SEDONA LEANED OVER Senior Chief Hamlin's shoulder for a closer look at the damaged engine. She and Ken had been permitted to come into the hangar to view the jets, but only after they'd promised not to touch anything. While Sedona looked at the first engine, Ken had deliberately moved away from her to look at the second of the two engines. Fine. She didn't want him hanging over her shoulder.

The engines had been removed from the aircraft and hung suspended from two enormous rolling hoists. Portable workbenches positioned around the first of the crippled Coyotes were littered with boxes of parts that had been tagged and labeled. The smell of oil and grease hung heavy on the air, and the metallic clang of tools contrasted with the high-pitched whine of electric drills and pneumatic wrenches.

"Check out the blades on this blisk," Sedona observed, circling the engine to get a better view of the fan blades. The ends were bent and mangled, as if something small and hard had been sucked through at high speed.

"Yes, ma'am," answered the maintenance officer. "We found a loose ball bearing in the HPC module. If the pilot hadn't shut down the engine when he did, it would have blown out the back and we'd probably never know what caused the damage."

"But how—"

The senior chief shrugged. "Ball bearings are an integral part of the engine components, ma'am. There are several dozen of them throughout. Could've been any one of them that came loose."

"Hmm. I suppose it's possible," Sedona conceded, but inwardly she had her doubts. Without exception, the ball bearings were encased within a titanium or Kevlar housing to prevent them from coming loose. Foreign-object damage was a prime cause of engine failure. To have a ball bearing come loose during engine operation could have catastrophic consequences.

"What about the other Coyote? Have her engines been removed yet? Have you determined if the damage is similar?"

The senior chief glanced up at her with an amused smile. "We're working on it, ma'am. At this point, nothing has been determined. After all, the Coyotes only arrived this morning."

Sedona nodded, embarrassed. "Right. Well, I'd be very interested in your findings." She tilted her head, surveying the bent and twisted fan blades with pursed lips. "These Coyotes are originally from Lemoore, right?"

"Yes, ma'am," he replied. "They all launched from that flight line, right out there." He jerked his thumb in the direction of the hangar doors. "All within twenty-four hours of each other. Coincidence?"

Sedona arched a brow at him. "What do you think?"

"I think you'd better check the remaining birds very carefully, that's what I think."

Sedona turned to look at the flight line. Angel was flying one of those jets right now. The thought of him encountering a problem with the engines midair caused her stomach to clench.

"Who oversees the flight tests?" she asked.

"That'd be Captain Dawson, ma'am," the senior chief replied. "He's got an office over at command headquarters, but I think he's been working out of Building 281 while the investigation is going on."

Sedona sighed inwardly. The thought of having to deal with Captain Dawson made her temples throb. He reminded her too much of her father.

"Is there somebody else—a lieutenant or somebody—who coordinates the flight tests? I mean, Captain Dawson has to have someone else doing the bulk of the work for him, right?"

"Yes, ma'am. Lieutenant Palmer oversees the plane captains. There're a dozen or more of them on the flight line. They control the flight plans and perform the final inspections before the jets actually leave the ground."

His words reminded Sedona of the previous night when she had seen Lieutenant Palmer on the flight line. She'd completely forgotten to mention it to Angel.

"Does Lieutenant Palmer also perform inspections?" she asked.

"Sure. He knows more about those jets than most of the plane captains. Hell," the chief continued, "he's spent more time learning how to fly them than anyone I know."

"Lieutenant Palmer is a Coyote pilot?"

"Nah. He went through the training a couple of times, but couldn't get through the final stage of the flight program. Some kind of medical problem is what I heard." The senior chief shrugged. "But man, it takes balls to go through that program once, never mind three times, and still not make the cut."

"Wow, what a shame."

"You bet. I heard he was pretty torn up about it."

"So where would I find one of these plane captains?"

The senior chief nodded toward the flight line. "That might be a couple of them over there. Too far to tell for sure, but one of them looks like Wheeler, and I think the one on the left is Airman Laudano. He's an aviation machinist's mate."

Sedona flashed him a quick smile. "Thanks very much. And you'll let me know what you find on the other engines, right?"

The senior chief saluted. "Yes, ma'am."

Leaving the hangar, she made her way across the tarmac to where the fleet of Coyotes were lined up, dull pewter beneath the blue sky. She noted with approval that the jets had been separated into two groups—those that had been inspected and those that had not.

As she drew closer, she saw three men standing close together, reviewing some kind of paperwork. They each wore a helmet equipped with ear protectors and a microphone. Dark goggles were pushed up onto the top of the helmets, and one man had two bright-orange flight sticks shoved in his back pocket.

"Excuse me," she called. "Airman Laudano?"

The three men lifted their heads. The one nearest her looked like an advertisement for the all-American boy next door. Sedona glanced at his name patch. Ryan Wheeler, aviation machinist's mate. He gave her a shy smile and nodded toward the man next to him, who stepped away from the others, toward her.

God, when did they start enlisting babies? The boy couldn't be more than fourteen. Okay, maybe sixteen.

"I'm Laudano," he said warily, peering at the badge she wore around her neck. "Can I help you?"

He was a handsome kid with dark eyes, but his good looks were marred by a sullen expression. He wore camouflage combat pants, boots, a brown shirt and a camouflage vest. He kept his hands shoved in his pockets.

"I hope so," Sedona answered. "I'm Sedona Stewart. I'm part of the Coyote inspection team working over in Hangar 29. I oversee the engine inspections."

He shrugged. "So?"

Sedona raised her eyebrows. "So, I want to ask you a few questions."

He started to turn away. "I already filed a report with the Aircraft Mishap Board. I told them everything I know. I got nothing else to say."

"Hey, wait a minute." Sedona fell into step beside him. "You don't even know what I'm going to ask you."

Resentment sparked in his eyes. "I got a good idea. I'm a plane captain. You think because we're the last ones to inspect the jets before they launch, we must somehow be responsible, right?"

Sedona frowned. "No. Of course not. Why would I think that?"

"Because that's what they all think."

Sedona spread her hands. "Well, not me. Look, I'm not here to interrogate you. I'm just trying to get an understanding of the whole process, and wanted to ask what it is plane captains do before a jet launches. You know, what kinds of safety checks you perform."

He stopped and narrowed his eyes at her. "Why?"

Okay, the kid was beginning to irritate her. "Because I happen to have a…good friend test-flying these jets, and it sure as hell would make me feel better to know you and the other guys are doing everything you can to keep him safe."

He stopped, hands braced on his hips, and stared at her, and suddenly he looked weary and resigned, and much older than she'd originally thought.

"Look, it's a tough job. We work long days, sometimes sixteen-hour shifts. We're each assigned our own aircraft, and it's our job to make sure they're safe to fly."

"So you perform inspections?" Sedona prompted.

He squinted up at the sky and then back at her face. "Yeah. We do constant inspections. We check fluid levels, prepare the cockpit for flight and make sure there's no FOD, stuff like that."

"FOD? As in foreign object damage?"

He gave her a look that said he knew she was fishing. "Yes. Exactly like that."

Sedona refused to be intimidated. "So you would notice if a ball bearing, for example, was rolling around inside the engine compartment?"

Airman Laudano compressed his lips. "Yes, ma'am. I would. I'm the final set of eyes for the aircraft. The safety net, so to speak. The plane, the pilot and the mission rest solely on how well I do my job." He practically bit each word out.

"And do you do your job well, Airman?"

He gave her one long, contemptuous look and then turned on his heel and began walking away. "Speak to my XO. Ma'am."

XO? Ah, military-speak for commanding officer.

"I may just do that," she murmured.

As she turned thoughtfully away, she saw two men standing outside the Coyote hangar. Even from a distance, she recognized one of them as Captain Dawson. She squared her shoulders. He might intimidate her, but it wouldn't prevent her from asking about Airman Laudano's competency as a plane captain. Even as she made up her mind to do so, Captain Dawson turned away and entered the hangar. As she walked across the tarmac, Sedona recognized the second man.

"Excuse me, Lieutenant Palmer?"

He turned toward her with a smile. "Miss Stewart. We

meet again." The surprise in his voice was unmistakable. "What brings you over to this part of the base? I'd think the engine inspections would keep you busy enough."

Sedona laughed. "Oh, they do. I was actually taking a look at the two compromised Coyotes that just came in."

His smile grew quizzical. "Were they helpful to you?"

"Yes, actually, they were." She hesitated. "I was just curious as to which of your plane captains were responsible for overseeing the jets that crashed or had in-flight problems."

"Miss Stewart," he began, but Sedona cut him off.

"Please, Lieutenant, I'm not jumping to any conclusions. I just thought…" She paused, and then plunged ahead. "I just thought Airman Laudano seemed a little…well, hostile, when I spoke to him."

Lieutenant Palmer's eyebrows shot up. "You spoke to my guys?"

Sedona frowned. "Is there a problem with that?"

"I guess not. It's just that…well, the kid's been under a lot of pressure, there's no question about it." He removed his hat and rubbed the back of his head. "Airman Laudano is one of our best plane captains. Unfortunately, he's dealing with some personal issues. So if he seems a little unfriendly, please try to understand."

"Can I ask what those personal issues are?"

The officer held her gaze. "I'm not at liberty to discuss it."

"Wow. It must be pretty serious, then. What is it? Drugs?"

Lieutenant Palmer frowned, pinched the bridge of his nose, and looked away, not answering.

Sedona gaped at him. "That's it, isn't it? Why is he still working on your flight line?"

"He hasn't been convicted, and his blood tests came back clean." The lieutenant's voice was soft, but had a steely edge. "His performance since the incident has been exemplary, and when he's not on duty, he's confined to quarters. It's not a problem."

"Not a problem? I can't believe your pilots are willing to have somebody under suspicion of drug possession oversee their aircraft." Hello! When had the Navy surrendered its common sense? With guys like Airman Laudano on the flight line, who needed al-Qaeda?

"Look, maybe it's better if you just stay away from my guys, okay? The last I heard, your job was to inspect the engines on the grounded jets, not act like some CSI investigator." Lieutenant Palmer stared with hard eyes over her shoulder toward the flight line, where even now the airman was performing a wing inspection on one of the Coyotes. "Airman Laudano is one of our best plane captains." He shifted his gaze to Sedona. "And just for the record, none of the planes that experienced problems were under his jurisdiction."

He turned to walk away, and Sedona only just prevented herself from grabbing his arm to stop him. "So whose planes were they, Lieutenant?" she called after his retreating back.

Lieutenant Palmer kept walking, but gave her a warning look over his shoulder. "Stay away from my men, Miss Stewart."

She stood for a moment, debating what to do. She couldn't very well demand information from Captain Dawson, but somehow she would find out whose jets were being compromised. She didn't know whether it was sheer coincidence that all the affected jets originated here at Lemoore, or something more ominous, but until she figured out what was going on, there was no way Angel was going up in one of Airman Laudano's jets.

12

ANGEL STOOD beside the Coyote and stared across the tarmac toward the row of buildings and hangars that bordered the flight line. Even from a distance, he recognized the woman who stood on the walkway, hands on her hips, talking with Ken Larson. If the brightness of her hair hadn't given her away, her long-legged, straight-backed stance would have.

"Sir!"

Angel dragged his gaze away from Sedona and Ken and looked at his plane captain, a kid named Wheeler.

"She's ready, sir!" The kid had to shout over the whine of the engines from two nearby Coyotes, fired up and ready to roll.

Angel had just completed his walk-around, visual inspection of the jet he was preparing to test-fly when he'd spotted Sedona striding along the flight line with Larson. She'd said they were nothing more than coworkers, but as he watched, they stopped walking and Larson moved closer to her.

What the hell was going on? Their faces were scant inches apart. They were arguing about something. The hostile body language was unmistakable. But when Larson shoved a finger in Sedona's face, Angel saw red. He shoved his flight book at the plane captain.

"This'll just take a minute," he growled, but hadn't gone more than two steps when Wheeler caught his arm.

"Sir?"

"Let go, Wheeler," he commanded, his voice low and tight. It'd take no more than five minutes to sprint across the tarmac that separated him from Sedona. He could almost feel the satisfaction of smashing a fist into the other man's face.

"*Sir.*" Wheeler's tone was urgent, breaking through the haze of anger that clouded his mind. "The jet's ready to go. You'll miss your window."

Angel knew the kid was right. He had a flight test to conduct, and walking over to kick Larson's ass would not only put him behind schedule, it would raise red flags all over the command. The last thing he needed was to attract negative attention from top brass. They'd stick him in a cubicle somewhere and he'd spend the rest of his military career pushing paper. No thanks.

As he watched, Larson turned away from Sedona and continued walking. After a moment, she followed.

Angel spun on his heel toward his jet. "All right, fine," he muttered. "I'll take care of it later. Let's roll."

Whatever was going on between Sedona and Ken Larson would have to wait until he returned to the hotel. But it sure as hell looked to be more than a difference of opinion between coworkers. If Angel didn't know better, he'd think the guy had a thing for her.

Had Sedona lied to him? She'd admitted to traveling with Larson before. Maybe the last time she'd traveled with him he'd been the one she'd performed private strip dances for. Hell, for all he knew, she made a habit of screwing different men each time she went on business travel. He might be nothing more than her latest conquest. Just the thought made his chest tighten and his hands curl into fists.

The only thing he knew for sure was that something was definitely going on between Sedona and Larson, and he would find out what. Frustrated, he jerked his helmet on and fastened it. Right now he needed to concentrate on doing his job.

It took all his discipline to climb into the cockpit, fasten his seat belt and focus on performing his flight-readiness checks. Even so, he found it impossible to put Sedona completely out of his mind.

He loved takeoffs. Craved the dizzying speed of accelerating down the runway until that final instant when his wheels left the ground and he wasn't just airborne—he was flying. But as the earth fell away beneath him and he shot upward through the drifts of clouds, he couldn't fully appreciate the beauty that surrounded him.

Damned if he wouldn't rather be on the ground.

He looked down at the tiny patch of earth that was Lemoore Naval Air Station. Where was Sedona right now? Was she with Larson? Images of the two of them together swamped his imagination. He pictured Sedona clinging to the other man, making needful little noises as he pleasured her. His hands tightened on the throttle and he banked sharply, pushing the aircraft through her paces.

He glanced down at his gauges, noting the numbers on the tiny digital clock rapidly rolling away the microseconds. The entire test flight would take no more than two hours. He'd spend several more hours completing paperwork and briefing the admiral. It was still early afternoon. With luck, he'd be back at the hotel by supper time.

It couldn't be soon enough for him.

It was almost ten o'clock when Angel set his empty beer mug down on the bar and pushed his stool back. He hadn't wanted to go out with the guys again, but having already turned them down the last two times, he couldn't do it a third.

He'd used the base facilities to shower and change his clothes, and had gone along to their favorite club, the 4-Play. But he hadn't been able to relax and after an hour or so, gave up the pretense.

"Sorry, but I'm calling it a night," he said, pulling several bills from his wallet and tossing them on the bar. "But you guys hang around. The next one's on me."

"Hey, man, why you leaving? Got a hot babe waiting for you, Diablo?"

Angel glanced at the man next to him, a fighter pilot he'd trained with nearly twelve years ago. Steve Platt, call sign "Splatt," grinned at him.

"Yeah, something like that," he answered, unwilling to share anything about Sedona with them. They'd use it against him, and even if their ribbing was meant good-naturedly, it would only come back to bite him in the ass. He might not know Sedona as well as he'd like to, but he knew her well enough to guess what her reaction would be to a squadron of Coyote fighter pilots knowing she was intimately involved with him. She'd completely freak. Then she'd unload him like yesterday's trash.

"Hey, Diablo! Where you going?"

Angel looked at his friend, Tony Gregory, call sign Tuna. It stood for the The Ugliest Naval Aviator.

His own call sign, Diablo, or devil, was one he'd grown accustomed to, whether he liked it or not. It was a tribute to his Spanish heritage, and a deliberate play on his name. Call signs weren't something you got to choose. You just hoped you got one you could live with, especially since they were often derogatory and cruel approximations of physical limitations or sexual inadequacies.

No one could ever call the Navy overly cerebral with the selection of call signs. With his beaky nose and oversize ears,

Tuna might be a homely man, but he was an expert pilot, and had been Angel's wingman on several sorties off the deck of the USS *Abraham Lincoln*.

"I have a morning test flight, so I'm bugging out early."

"Man, no wonder the top brass is always on your ass," Splatt commented. "Don't you know this is considered a team-building experience? Don't you want to show them you're not really a lone wolf? That you can follow direction and be a team player? C'mon, man, don't be such an asshole."

"Don't forget," called Tuna, "twelve hours from bottle to throttle!" He lifted his own beer bottle in a mock salute. "That's why we're not on the books until tomorrow afternoon."

He waved away the good-natured protests and ribald comments and worked his way through the crowded bar. Two attractive young women sat at a small table near the door and eyeballed him as he drew closer. When one of them gave him a flirtatious wink and shifted on her bar stool to reveal a slim length of bare leg clad in minuscule shorts, he just smiled at them.

They were young and pretty and obviously looking for some action, but Angel wanted more. With a sense of shock, he realized it was true. Generally speaking, he had no problem with one-night stands. But now he wanted more than just a night of hot sex with a stranger, no matter how beautiful she might be.

He wanted a woman with substance. He wanted an intelligent, self-confident woman who could hold her own in a discussion that involved something besides superficial nonsense. A woman who was self-absorbed and demanding didn't interest him. He wanted a woman who wouldn't exploit her femininity or compromise her identity to get ahead. He wanted a woman who made him laugh. A woman who made him burn.

A woman like Sedona.

He couldn't stop thinking about her. The afternoon brief-
ings had dragged on and on until Angel thought he'd howl
with frustration. When they had finally finished for the day,
he'd called Sedona's room but she hadn't answered. Where
was she? She'd said she'd be back at the hotel by six o'clock.

She'd said she would wait for him, but he hadn't planned
on being out this late. While he didn't expect her to just sit
around and twiddle her thumbs until he showed up, he
couldn't imagine where she might be.

Angel caught a cab the short distance from the bar to the
hotel. The vehicle pulled up to the front doors and he paid the
driver. Then he glanced at his watch. It was nearly 10:30. Would
she still be awake? Did he dare wake her up if she wasn't?

Hell, yes.

He'd thought about nothing else the entire day. He strode
through the hotel lobby, ignoring the loud music and voices
that drifted toward him from the lounge, which was in full
swing at this time of night. As he rode the elevator to the third
floor, he blew out his breath. He was nervous, which was
completely ridiculous. Of course she'd be there.

He half expected Sedona to be stretched out on his bed,
waiting for him, but when he finally entered his room it was
dark and quiet. Pushing down his disappointment, he dropped
his flight bag onto the bed and flipped on the lights. The connecting door was closed. The message waiting light on the
bedside phone was dark. No messages.

Okay. No problem. He'd just open the door and tell her he
had to see her. If she was asleep, he'd wake her up. If she was
grumpy, he'd make it up to her.

But when he opened the door, it was to find her side of the
connecting doors closed. What the hell? Hadn't she said just
that morning that she'd keep her door open for him? Frown-

ing, he turned the knob, relieved when the door pushed open beneath his hand. At least she hadn't locked it. That was a good sign, right?

Cautiously he stepped into her room. The bedside light was on, but he knew immediately she wasn't there. The alarm clock radio played softly in the background. A pair of pajama bottoms lay crumpled on the floor beside the bed, and the matching top had been tossed carelessly on top of the blankets. The room still bore the light, floral fragrance that he'd come to associate with Sedona.

The bed looked as if it had recently been occupied. The covers were thrown back and the pillows were stacked on top of each other and pushed against the headboard. A book lay open and facedown on the sheets with an odd-looking, flat-edged pencil next to it.

Curious, he picked it up. It looked like a drawing pencil. He turned the book over and saw it was a hardbound sketch-book. He stared at the drawing on the open page, and his heart skipped a beat.

It was a picture of his face, captured in amazingly life-like detail. He wore a small smile, and he thought if he touched his fingers to the paper, he might actually feel the indents of his own dimples. In the background of the picture, she'd drawn an F/A-44 Coyote jet, sitting on the deck of an aircraft carrier. The picture was incredibly realistic. From a distance, he might have believed it was a photograph.

Amazed, he flipped through the book. A scrap of paper fluttered out from between the pages and landed on the bed. Picking it up, he saw it was a photo of himself. He recognized it as a clipping from a Navy magazine. The Public Affairs office had done a brief story about the pilots who served aboard the USS *Abraham Lincoln,* and accompanied the story with a group photo of the pilots. It wasn't a great picture of him, and the quality was poor.

Replacing the clipping, he realized there were more sketches of him. In one, he stood in the doorway of an aircraft hangar with his head bent, while an unseen breeze rippled the fabric of his flight suit.

The last picture was of him from the waist up, nude. She'd drawn the texture of his skin so that it gleamed, as if he'd just been sluiced with water. He had his arms bent behind his head, and she'd sculpted the muscles of his stomach, chest and arms with unerring accuracy. The image of him looked out of the picture, directly at the artist. His lips were tilted in the slightest of smiles, so that only a hint of his dimples showed. She'd stopped the drawing low on his hips, just shy of actually showing his credentials, but there was no mistaking the barest hint of his pubic hair.

The picture was alluring. Erotic.

There were more than a dozen pictures of him, each crafted with infinite detail and obvious care. He'd guess some of them had been done months ago, maybe even before he'd been deployed aboard the *Lincoln*.

Had she been that aware of him back then? During those six months that he'd first worked with the Defense Procurement Agency, he'd hardly known she existed. The thought was completely humbling, even as alarm bells jangled in his head.

Sedona had obviously harbored a huge crush on him. What were her feelings now? If her most recent drawings of him were any indication, they definitely hadn't waned. Any idiot could tell how she felt about him just by looking at her artwork.

Christ, he needed a drink.

He placed the sketchbook carefully back where he'd found it and returned to his room. Opening the small fridge, he saw it contained soda, a small bottle of wine and a couple nip-size bottles of sweet liqueur. He definitely needed something stronger. He needed a double shot of bourbon.

He headed down to the hotel bar. He'd have one drink, and then go back upstairs and wait for Sedona to return. He crossed the lobby; the music and noise of the lounge area was raucous. In the short time they'd been at the hotel, he hadn't been to the bar, and he stood for a moment just inside the entrance to get his bearings and let his eyes adjust to the dim lighting.

As he wove his way through the small tables, he recognized several of the patrons as members of the inspection team. But it wasn't until he was almost to the bar that he saw her.

Sedona stood at one end of the bar, near the waitress station. She wore a T-shirt and jeans, and her hair was pulled back into a ponytail. She held a drink in one hand, and she was talking to Ken Larson.

At first glance, they looked to be having a friendly conversation, but Angel didn't miss the rigid set of Sedona's shoulders, or how she held her drink carefully between her and Larson, like a barrier. She was smiling, but the expression in her eyes was less than friendly.

Frowning, Angel began weaving his way through the cluster of tables. When he was about twenty feet away he saw Larson take Sedona's drink and set it down on the bar, then grab her by the arm and pull her toward a side exit.

A cocktail waitress carrying a drink-laden tray stepped directly into Angel's path, effectively preventing him from chasing after them. As he waited impatiently for the woman to move, Ken opened the rear-exit door and stepped into a hotel corridor, pulling Sedona behind him.

Angel felt a flare of white-hot jealousy. He pushed his way

past the waitress, muttering an apology when she threw him a disgusted look. He'd suspected Larson had a thing for Sedona, but he couldn't understand why she'd gone with him so easily. She hadn't appeared to even object. How could he have misread her so completely? Just the thought of her with another guy ate at his gut.

With a low growl of anger, Angel reached the rear door and threw it forcibly open. He glanced swiftly down the length of the corridor, but there was no sign of them. But when the door shut behind him, muting the sound of the lounge, he thought he heard Sedona's voice. He walked in that direction with long, determined strides.

As he rounded the corner, he saw Larson gripping Sedona by the upper arms. Before he could reach them, Sedona gave Larson a shove backward. The other man staggered once before he regained his balance and then advanced on Sedona. Angel saw red.

"Larson."

Larson's expression of astonishment gave Angel a brief second of satisfaction, but not nearly as much as when he grabbed the bastard and jerked him away from Sedona.

"Angel!" Sedona's voice was low and shocked.

Surprised to see me, baby? I'll bet. He had Larson by the collar of his shirt, and the little puke's eyes were about bugging out of his head. He glanced over at Sedona, who was watching them with a mixture of horror and relief in her green eyes. Then his gaze fell on her arms, where Larson's fingers had left reddish marks on her pale skin.

It was enough to snap the last bit of sanity he still clung to. Without a word, he pushed Larson slightly away and then followed with a hard right to the guy's jaw. Larson staggered and fell heavily against the wall.

"Angel, oh my God…"

Sedona took a step toward Larson, arms outstretched as if to catch him, as he staggered and tried to regain his balance. With an incoherent sound of fury, he pushed her away.

"Stay away from me," he spat.

"No, Larson," Angel growled, "you stay away from her." Reaching out, he caught Sedona by the arm and propelled her through the corridor toward the elevators.

"Angel," she gasped, jogging to keep up with his long strides, "I can explain."

He glanced sideways at her. Her face twisted as if she might cry.

"Please," she said, her voice trembling, "I can't keep up with you."

Angel stopped and turned to face her. "No, *mina,*" he bit out, "it seems I can't keep up with you." He raked a hand over his hair. "Jesus." He laughed humorlessly. "When I think I came back here hoping you might actually be waiting for me…"

"I did wait for you!"

"Oh, yeah?" Angel stared down at her. "And then what? You just couldn't wait anymore? You had to go down to the bar and snag the first available guy?"

Her eyes widened. "Is that what you think? Did it really look to you like I was interested in Ken Larson?"

Angel recalled the hard shove she'd given the other man, but right now he was still too pissed off to listen to reason. He raised his hands and turned around to continue walking. He didn't want to see her eyes filling up with tears. Didn't want to hear her excuses.

"Forget it, okay? I don't really want to hear it, anyway." But he hadn't taken more than a step when he found his path blocked by Sedona. Her face was blotchy with suppressed emotion, but she was determined. She glared up at him, hands on her hips.

"Too bad, flyboy," she said, and despite the tears in her eyes, her voice no longer wobbled. "You'll stand there and listen to what I have to say, and then if you still want to walk away…well, that'll be your choice."

Angel blew out his breath in resignation. He was behaving like an ass, and he knew it. He'd seen how Sedona had shoved Ken away and knew whatever had transpired, she hadn't been a willing player. But seeing them together had caused something inside him to bend, and then snap. He'd felt a little rabid. Had wanted to tear into someone.

But not Sedona.

"Okay," he conceded grudgingly. "I'm listening."

Sedona blew her breath out. "I was waiting for you. I was in bed…reading. I was thirsty and wanted something cold to drink, but the icemaker on our floor isn't working. I put some clothes on and came down to get a soda."

Okay, so far what she said agreed with everything he'd seen in her room. Except the part about reading. He shrugged. "So you needed a cold drink because you were, what…hot? So hot you had to run down to the bar and see who was available?"

"No, and if that's what you believe then you don't know me." She crossed her arms and hugged herself, looking miserable.

"Then enlighten me." Angel knew his voice sounded hard and cold.

She gave a small huff of laughter, but Angel thought it had a nervous edge to it. "It sounds so…stupid when I try to put it into words."

He gave her an encouraging squeeze. "Try."

She blew out her breath. "It's just that—" She broke off and groaned in frustration. "You're not going to believe me. I can hardly believe it myself."

Angel gave her a tolerant look.

"Okay," she continued, "I'll just say it." She turned solemn eyes to him. "I found out there's a group of guys at the agency who started a club, where promotions are based on having a fling while on business travel."

"What?"

"It's the truth," she insisted. "And initially, I thought I could expose them, put an end to the whole thing, but they think I want to become a member, and I don't. Ken Larson doesn't get that, though, and he's a member so now he thinks that if he and I have a wild fling while we're out here, we'll both get promoted." The words tumbled out while her eyes sought his with something like desperation.

Angel just stared at her.

Finally, dumbfounded, he raked a hand over his head, and turned away, then spun back to her. "Are you serious?"

"Completely." She bit her lip and watched him. "I'm sorry. I didn't think he'd be so persistent, but I guess he really wants that promotion." She smiled weakly.

His brain was spinning. He'd heard some vague rumors on the flight line about an exclusive club of engineers, but hell, he'd figured it was more along the lines of a math club, not a sex club. "Jesus," he breathed, and shook his head. "I can't freaking believe it. A bunch of Poindexters, starting a sex club?"

"I know, it's pretty disgusting."

"So is that why you…wanted to get together with me? Because you want a promotion?"

Her face paled, and the genuine distress he saw in her eyes said he couldn't be further from the truth. "What? *No.* I already told you, I don't want anything to do with the club! I've told Larson I'm not interested, but he won't leave it alone."

Angel closed the distance between them in one step and jerked her into his arms. "I believe you," he said roughly, knowing it was the truth. "When I saw you leave with him, I thought—" He couldn't finish. "Let's just say I thought the worst."

She tipped her face up and gave him a trembling smile. "I only left with him because I thought he'd found out about the two of us, and I was afraid he'd make a scene right there in the bar."

Angel gave her a quizzical look.

"I don't know how the Navy feels about their officers engaging in…" She blushed furiously and averted her eyes. "I just didn't want you to get in trouble, so I went outside to try and reason with him."

Angel tightened his arms around her, breathing in the fragrance of her hair. "I don't care who knows about us," he said. "Even Larson. Especially Larson."

Sedona lifted her face to his. "You thought I was involved with him?" She slid her arms around him and pressed herself closer. "How could I even think about anyone else when I have you, my own real-life fantasy, right here?"

"Is that what I am? Your fantasy?" He cupped her face in his hands, smoothing his fingers over her jaw.

"Oh, yeah," she whispered, and lifted her face to his, her spiky, wet lashes drifting down to her cheeks.

With a groan, Angel kissed her, sweeping his tongue past her lips and claiming her with an urgency bred of fierce relief and hunger.

When he finally lifted his head, Sedona's mouth was swollen and damp. "Jesus," he groaned, fitting his hips against hers, he let her feel the effect she had on him. "I want you, Sedona, right now." He rested his forehead against hers. "When I thought you might be getting it on with Larson…"

He didn't finish the sentence, but when he'd thought she was involved with Larson, he'd wanted to kill somebody.

When he had seen her leave with him, he'd been consumed by a surge of jealousy and rage, sure. But there'd been more. He'd felt as if someone had ripped his heart out.

"C'mon," Sedona whispered to him, her fingers caressing his back and neck. "Let's go back to my room."

Angel growled softly and crushed her lips with his. "I thought you'd never ask, *mina.*"

He guided her swiftly toward the elevators, unable to rationalize the crushing relief he felt at knowing she hadn't sought out another man. He'd been crazy to think she was capable of it.

After all, he'd seen her sketchbook, and there hadn't been one picture of Larson in it. Nearly every picture had been of him, rendered by a woman who was obviously infatuated with him.

Maybe even in love with him.

13
___

SEDONA DUCKED into her room, knowing she had about two seconds to scoop the incriminating sketchbook off the bed and tuck it safely away before Angel opened the connecting doors between their rooms. She'd have a tough time explaining that to him.

She snatched up the pad and looked around for a quick hiding spot. When she heard Angel turning the knob of the connecting door, she made a beeline for the bathroom, the only place she could think of where he wouldn't follow her.

"I'll be right out," she called, and closed the door, locking it behind her. The bathroom didn't yield any drawers or cupboards in which to stash the sketchbook, so she slid it between the folded towels on the chrome rack next to the shower enclosure.

Glancing into the mirror, she gasped. God, she looked awful. Her hair had come slightly free of the ponytail and hung in disarray around her face, which was pale except for two bright spots of color high on her cheeks. She'd come so close to crying back there when Angel had turned and walked away.

She felt a huge sense of relief at having told him about the Membership. He'd been shocked, but he'd believed her. She hadn't told him she would be leaving the agency once their inspection of the Coyotes was over, but there would be time for that later. It probably wouldn't even be an issue, since they'd already agreed their relationship wouldn't continue once they returned to the East Coast. For all she knew, he'd breathe a sigh of relief to discover she wouldn't be a potential burden or embarrassment to him. But for now...

She yanked the elastic band out of her hair and combed her fingers through the unruly mass. She hadn't anticipated running into Angel down in the bar, or she'd never have been caught dead in the T-shirt and jeans she now wore. She'd owned both for more years than she cared to admit, and it showed. But her pajamas were still on the bed in the other room.

What was it her sister had told her? The one thing a guy couldn't resist was a naked woman? Pushing aside her inhibitions, she peeled off her clothing and wrapped a towel around her nudity. Then drawing a deep breath, she stepped out of the bathroom.

And stopped dead in her tracks.

She swallowed. Hard.

Angel sprawled indolently on top of her bed, wearing nothing but a pair of loose pajama bottoms and a wicked smile. The light on the bedside table cast intriguing shadows over the dips and angles of his body. He'd pulled the bedspread down to the foot of the bed, and against the pristine white of the cotton sheets, he looked dark and exotic.

He held her sensible cotton pajama top and bottoms in one hand. His grin widened as his dark gaze swept over her, and with one lazy motion, he tossed her pajamas over his shoulder.

"Well," he drawled, "you won't be needing these." He bent one arm beneath his head and patted the mattress with his other hand. "Come here."

Talk about Christmas in July! Seeing him stretched out on her bed, tempting her with all that bare, tanned skin, was like another of her fantasies come true. She put a hand to her hair, suddenly self-conscious.

"I look terrible."

His eyes grew darker, hotter. "You look incredible. I've been dying to get my hands on you all day, *mina*. Don't make me come get you."

He sat up and swung his long legs over the edge of the bed. She noticed how, even in a sitting position, his pajama bottoms tented over his arousal. Her stomach knotted in anticipation and a languorous heat began to build between her legs. She longed to run her hands over all that wonderfully smooth, bronzed skin. His shoulders bunched as he pressed his hands against the mattress and prepared to rise.

Slowly, her face flaming and her heart thudding with expectation, she loosened the towel from where it was knotted over her breasts, but found she couldn't quite release it. She held a corner of it bunched in her hand and let it hang in front of her, partially obscuring her body from his view. Instinct made her clutch it tightly against her breasts, which was crazy. Angel had already seen her. Every bit of her. She had no reason to feel so self-conscious. Especially not when he eyed her the way a kid would eye a free ice-cream cone.

Heat flared in his eyes, and Sedona didn't miss the way his fingers curled into the bedding.

She dropped the towel onto the floor.

He groaned.

Emboldened, she stepped slowly toward him until she stood within arm's reach. "So…here I am, flyboy."

His gaze slid down the length of her body and he swallowed. Hard. "Jesus, *mina*," he rasped. "I'd forgotten…"

She stepped into the opening between his legs and laid her palms on his shoulders, reveling in the satiny heat of his skin. "What did you forget?" Her words were no more than a whisper.

He tipped his head back to look at her, then grasped her hips in his hands and drew her forward until her legs bumped against the edge of the mattress. "How damn hot you are, and how much I want to do this."

His husky confession caused a liquid heat to slip along the underside of her skin, and her pulse began a heavy, sweet thudding. Still watching her face, he slid his hands up over her belly and filled his palms with her breasts. He cupped them, caressed them until she gasped softly. Then he bent his head and drew one breast into his mouth, gently laving the nipple with his tongue.

Sedona's breath caught and she brought her hands up to stroke his cropped hair, enjoying the rough velvet texture.

"Oh, God," she sighed. "That feels too good."

Angel wrapped his big arms completely around her and buried his face between her breasts. He inhaled deeply. "You smell good."

"I missed you today," she admitted, and rubbed her cheek against the top of his head. It was true. She had missed him. When he wasn't around, she missed his easy confidence and his quiet capability. She missed the way his eyes heated when he looked at her. She missed how he made her feel—feminine, and safe.

"Mmm," he mumbled against her sensitized skin. "I missed you, too. I couldn't believe it when you weren't in your room tonight. I'm sorry about what happened, *mina*. Earlier, with Larson. I jumped to conclusions and behaved badly."

Sedona pulled back slightly and looked at him. "I'm glad you showed up when you did." She shivered. "I mean, I could have handled Ken, but I'm glad I didn't have to."

Angel's arms tightened around her. "You don't need to think about him again. All you need to think about is this."

He ran his hands down over her hips, grasped her buttocks and squeezed gently. "I love your ass."

Sedona laughed and couldn't resist caressing his jaw with her fingers, enjoying the texture of shadowed stubble. "The Navy actually lets you fly their jets? Your eyesight is obviously impaired, or you'd see my butt is huge."

He growled playfully and fell backward onto the bed, dragging her over him with his hands cupping her buttocks. His eyes gleamed with devilry. "That's crazy. Feel how you fit perfectly into my hands."

Her breasts were flattened against the broad planes of his chest, and his erection pressed on her belly. Only the thin material of his pajama pants separated them. When he squeezed her bottom, and slid a finger deftly between her legs and stroked her cleft, desire licked its way through her. Molten heat pooled at her center, and her breasts ached for his touch.

She braced herself on her elbows and stared down at his face, mesmerized by the endless depths of his dark eyes. Her gaze drifted lower, to the tantalizing fullness of his lower lip. He smiled, bringing his dimples briefly into play, and it was all over for her.

"Yeah, we're a perfect fit," she finally breathed in response, her lips scant millimeters from his, "Angel…" She covered his lips with hers, putting everything she had into the kiss. She reached down and stroked him through his pajamas, loving the hot, thick feel of him against her hand, loving how he moaned and thrust himself helplessly into her palm.

"You feel so good." She slid her hand inside the waistband of his pants and closed her fingers around him. She squeezed him, then moved her hand up his impressive length to swirl her thumb over the swollen head.

"Mina," he choked, "stop."

Sedona smiled against his mouth. "Why? Don't you like it?"

He made a noise that was part laugh, part groan. "I'm trying really hard not to lose it right now. But if you keep that up, I'm not going to last."

In one smooth movement, he rolled her beneath him, dragging her hand from him in the process. Sedona gave a small cry of surprise and clutched at his broad shoulders for support.

For a moment, they stared at each other. When Angel finally bent his head to hers, it was to cover her lips in a kiss that was incredibly sweet. Sedona made a small sound of approval and arched against him, rubbing her breasts against the firmness of his chest. At the same time, she pushed his pajama bottoms down over his thighs and used her feet to free him completely from the soft fabric.

Dragging her mouth from his, she scooted herself partway up the mattress, until her head bumped the pillows mounded in front of the headboard. Pushing them beneath her head, she used her hands to urge Angel higher.

He looked down at her, bemused. "What…?"

"Kneel above me," she urged softly, and grasped his hips to show him what she wanted. But it wasn't until he straddled her waist and she pushed herself up onto her elbows, that he finally understood her intent.

"Mina," he said with an astonished laugh, "you don't have to do this."

"Are you kidding?" she asked, eye level now with his amazing erection. "I've been wanting to do this for a long time."

The thick shaft of his penis bobbed lightly as he edged closer. She admired the dark, glistening head and, leaning forward, flicked her tongue experimentally over it. He jerked reflexively.

She smiled. "Mmm, you taste delicious."

Sliding her hands up the back of his hard thighs, she cupped his buttocks, and then slid one hand between his legs to gently caress his balls. She liked that they weren't overly huge, but hung nicely beneath his straining cock.

Angel groaned, and when Sedona glanced up, his handsome face was taut with desire. She closed her fingers around the base of his penis and admired how the thick veins bulged in response. Slowly, she slid her hand upward, even as she bent her head and swirled her tongue over the head.

He arched his back, made a low, growling noise deep in his throat, and buried his hands in her hair. He didn't force her head down as she'd thought he would. He merely used his fingers to caress her scalp and the sensitive skin behind her ears. That, and the sensation of him in her mouth, was incredible. She urged him closer, stroking the underside of his shaft with her tongue and using her lips to create friction.

As her fingers caressed him, she wrapped one hand firmly around the base of his penis and used every instinct she had to love him with her mouth. When he drew close to the edge, she'd pull away and give him time to cool down, softly licking his shaft and then blowing gently on his damp skin. Then she'd take him into her mouth again and use her lips and tongue to torture him, teasing the sensitive area just beneath the head, and easing her fist slowly along his length as she did so.

She knew he was close to losing control when he made a low, harsh noise in his throat and stiffened. Before she could protest, he dragged himself from her.

"I need to—I can't—Christ, *mina*," he half groaned, and collapsed onto the pillows beside her, sucking air into his lungs. "I don't want this to end so soon."

Raising himself on one elbow over her, he grabbed a

condom from where he'd left it on the bedside table and expertly covered himself. When he leaned down and kissed her, she wrapped her arms and legs around him so that he pressed against her sex.

It was a kiss that made no concessions. It was fiercely possessive and primal, and Sedona welcomed it, touching her tongue to his and arching against him. She wanted him so badly. She hadn't thought that pleasuring him with her mouth would be a total turn-on for her, as well.

With one surge, he penetrated her fully, burying himself in her. Sedona cried out and grasped his lean buttocks. He pulled his mouth from hers and swirled his tongue along the edge of her ear, causing shivers to chase along her spine.

With each bone-melting thrust of his hips, he murmured husky words into her ear in Spanish. Sedona didn't have to understand them to know they were words of endearment and encouragement.

She met his thrusts with an increasing urgency of her own, reveling in the smooth skin beneath her fingertips, loving the harshness of his breath against her throat. And when he gave a ragged shout of release and stiffened inside her, it was enough to push her over the edge, as well. She keened with pleasure and shuddered with each delicious spasm that rippled through her.

Angel rested his head on her shoulder and she hugged him fiercely, keeping her legs pulled tight around his lean hips. He might be the embodiment of every fantasy she'd ever had, but this was so much more. The reality of being with Angel exceeded all her dreams.

Not only was he heart-stoppingly handsome, but he had the ability to make her laugh. With him she felt sexy and cherished and protected.

A flutter of fear constricted her chest. She couldn't let

herself be this happy. Couldn't delude herself that this could last. This wasn't reality, it was just a brief interlude. In real life, guys like Angel Torres did *not* fall for women like her. This was just some bizarre twist of fate, where she was in the right place at the right time.

In fact, nothing had ever felt so right in her life. Angel's heart still beat heavily against her own, and his breath stirred the hair at her temple. She knew she couldn't keep him. Guys like Angel needed to be free, to spread their wings and fly. Eventually, she'd have to let him go. But for right now, he was completely hers.

She never wanted this moment to end. Her chest felt as if it was expanding. She was going to burst with the emotion that flooded her. Despite her relative lack of experience with the opposite sex, she recognized all the warning signs.

She was falling in love with Angel Torres.

IT WAS ALMOST midnight. Sedona leaned back against Angel's chest and let him squeeze the warm water from the washcloth over her breasts, making rivulets in the sudsy, fragrant froth that covered her and exposing the skin beneath.

"Mmm," she sighed, and stroked his thigh with her hand, captivated by the way the black hair flattened against his bronzed skin and then swirled upward again with the lapping of the water. "I can't recall the last time I took a bath. To think I once considered them a waste of time."

Angel laughed softly against her ear. "That's because baths are definitely meant to be shared."

Sedona looked down at their legs, where Angel's lay along the outside of her thighs.

"Hmm," she said. "Maybe in a bigger tub. This one is little short."

"That all depends on what it is you want to do." His hand

swept upward to cup her breasts and toy with the nipples until they stood rosy and stiff beneath his ministrations. Sedona gasped. His fingers were lean and brown against the pale creaminess of her breasts. The sight was erotic, causing a now-familiar tingling to begin between her legs.

When he rolled her nipples between his fingers, she felt his own response in the rise of flesh that pressed against her backside. Her breathing quickened when he ran one hand down over her belly and pressed it between her thighs to stroke her slick flesh.

"Ohmigod," she panted as she pushed against his hand, "what are you doing to me?"

He chuckled. "What does it look like?"

Sedona moaned. "You're turning me into a sex-crazed lunatic." She shivered when he caught her earlobe in his teeth and tugged gently.

"You say that like it's a bad thing," he murmured.

But Sedona wasn't prepared when he stood up, lifting her with him and sloshing water over the edge of the tub.

"What—"

"I want you again," he said roughly, "but this tub is definitely too short for that."

He stood her on the bath mat, and pulled a towel from the rack. Sedona's knees felt weak when she saw how ready for her he was. The man had no right to be so incredibly gorgeous. She had absolutely no willpower when it came to Angel Torres.

But when he turned to face her, she could only admire the sleekness of his skin and all the hard, muscled contours of his body. For the moment, anyway, he was all hers.

He lay the towel across the tank on the back of the toilet, and a second one over the closed seat. Then he tore open a condom that he'd put on the counter earlier and sheathed himself. Sedona smiled uncertainly.

"What are you doing?"

"Come here."

He drew her forward until she stood facing the toilet. She was helpless to prevent a giggle from escaping. "Sorry, but I'm still not getting it."

"Oh, you will, *mina*," Angel said. He stood close behind her until his erection pressed against the cleft of her buttocks. Keeping one hand on her abdomen, he used his other to bend her forward. "Look in the mirror."

Sedona looked sideways at the mirror that covered the wall over the sink. She gasped at the erotic sight they made. With her hands braced on the tank, her breasts hung down in clear view, and the curve of her bottom glistened wetly from the bathwater.

Angel stood behind her, his penis dark against the pale skin of her butt, his hands grasping her hips. She felt herself grow hot and wet at the sight. Slowly, watching their image in the mirror, Angel stroked a hand over one buttock, all the way down to the back of her knee, even as he cupped and kneaded one breast with his free hand.

Sedona's breathing quickened. Instinctively, she shifted to accommodate him. Angel smiled then, a sexy smile of male appreciation, and slid the head of his penis along her cleft. Sedona pushed back against him, feeling herself swell with desire. She was helpless to look away, even when Angel stroked her with one hand, and gently inserted a finger into her wet center.

"Oh, oh!" Sedona clenched her muscles around his hand, and cried out in protest when he withdrew. But her breath caught when he went down on one knee behind her.

"Bend over a little more, *mina*. That's it."

Sedona braced her elbows on the soft terry cloth and arched her back. She nearly swooned when Angel gently parted her folds with his fingers. But she couldn't prevent her cry of pleasure when his hot, talented tongue swept over her, swirling over her clitoris. The sight was the most incredibly erotic thing Sedona had ever seen. He continued to lick her, and then inserted his finger once more.

Her climax caught her by surprise, and she cried out, convulsing around his finger as her body was rocked by one of the most intense orgasms she had ever experienced. But even as she collapsed weakly forward with her head on her arms, Angel stood up.

"I want you to come again," he said, his voice rough with need.

Bending her forward over his arm, he drew her back to him. Sedona's eyes glazed over when she watched him enter her, one excruciatingly delicious inch at a time. He stretched her, filled her, rubbed against her already sensitized flesh until she was helpless to prevent the small, mewling sounds of need that came from her throat.

Angel threw his head back as he thrust into her, and Sedona thought she'd never seen anything quite as masculine or beautiful as the sight of this man, loving her so fiercely. As if on cue, Angel opened his eyes and captured her gaze.

"Watch me, *mina,*" he growled softly. "See what you do to me." His eyes were dark and hot. "I'm going to come, *mina,* can you feel me?"

His words were like a catalyst, and amazingly enough she *could* feel him. He seemed to swell within her, to grow thicker and longer. Her flesh gripped him, stroked him, until she was about to explode. She knew he was on the verge, too.

"Oh, please," she gasped, thrusting back against him, "please, don't stop."

As their eyes locked in the mirror, Sedona could have watched herself as she experienced her third shattering orgasm of the night, but she watched Angel instead. Watched him as he watched her climax again, and the expression on his face was one of pure, unadulterated male satisfaction.

Then, Angel bent forward and pressed a tender kiss between her shoulder blades, before withdrawing. He helped her straighten, and wrapped his arms around her, gazing at her in the mirror.

"You are the most amazing woman I've ever known," he said, his breathing was still ragged.

Sedona's heart rate pounded unevenly. "Oh, yeah?" she said with a smile. "You should see what I can do with a bidet."

Angel laughed, the sound sliding over her senses like warm honey. "Here," he murmured. "You're cold. Let's dry you off and get you into something warm."

He reached up and took another towel from the rack. Her sketchbook came down with it, landing with a thunk on the bathroom floor.

Faceup.

Open.

An image of Angel in all his nude, muscular glory stared up at them. The ensuing silence was almost deafening, and for a moment the world itself seemed to stop.

It wasn't until Angel bent to retrieve the book that Sedona was galvanized into action.

"Oh. Wow." She swiftly scooped it, snapped it closed and hugged it defensively against her chest. She laughed self-consciously. "I wonder how that got in here."

She couldn't meet Angel's eyes as he pulled another towel down and tied it around his hips. Maybe he hadn't gotten a good look at it. Maybe he hadn't recognized the drawing as himself.

"Sedona." His voice was quiet. Was that resignation she heard?

She smiled brightly and ignored him as she turned toward the door. "I'll just go put this away somewhere. Housekeeping must have gotten it mixed up with the towels, but geez, all that humidity will ruin the pages."

"Sedona, I already saw the book."

Her heart almost stopped. Heedless of her own nudity, she clutched the sketchbook and turned to face him. "You did?"

His smile was tender, his eyes warm and filled with emotion. "I came in earlier, looking for you. You'd left the book on your bed, and I—" He shrugged. "I looked at it."

"Oh." Sedona took the towel he held out to her, wishing the bathroom floor would suddenly open up and swallow her. Heat flooded her face. She swallowed. "How embarrassing."

"Actually," he said, moving closer and taking the sketchbook from her nerveless fingers, "I find it incredibly flattering." He let the book fall open in his hands, this time to the picture of himself standing in the entrance to the hangar. "These are really good, you know that? I mean, really good. There are military artists who sell their work for thousands and in my opinion, their work isn't nearly as good as yours."

Sedona felt her face get even redder. "They're just okay," she demurred. "I do my best work when I have a photo to work with, like those artists you see at the shopping malls." She shrugged. "But the only photo I have of you…"

"Is the group photo from the USS *Abraham Lincoln*," he finished. "I know. I saw that, too. The photo isn't great. Your drawings are."

She knew he was just trying to make her feel better. She was going to have to explain just why she had a sketchbook filled with pictures of him.

"Angel, I know how this looks, but…" She shrugged and pulled the sketchbook out of his hands and clutched it to her.

"Well, c'mon, let's admit it. You're pretty hot. Who wouldn't want to capture you on paper? I never tried to hide that I find you attractive." She raised her eyes to his. "In fact, I've pretty much been attracted to you since the first time I saw you down on the flight line. I won't pretend I wasn't."

Angel stepped close enough that she could smell the fragrance of his skin, still warm and slightly damp from their recent bath. He smiled almost ruefully and reached out to tuck a strand of wet hair behind her ear. "I don't want you to pretend you weren't. To be honest, I discovered something about myself tonight." He gave a self-deprecating laugh. "When I saw you with Larson…well, let's just say I didn't like it. And it made me realize I really want to make a go of this."

Sedona felt her heart stutter. "What do you mean?"

He caught her gently by the elbows and drew her forward until the sketchbook was wedged between their bodies. "I don't know, exactly… I just know I hated seeing you with somebody else, and I don't want this to end when we get back to the East Coast."

"Angel… I don't know what to say."

Except maybe, *hallelujah!* Sedona was stunned. She still had a hard time believing this incredible guy found her interesting and sexy enough to spend a night with. And now he wanted to try to make a relationship out of what essentially began as a one-night stand.

"Don't say anything," he murmured, sliding a hand under her damp hair to cup the nape of her neck and tilt her face up. "Just think about it, okay? Now kiss me."

And Sedona did.

14

"Angel, you don't have to do this."

"C'mon, it'll be fun."

Sedona stood at the foot of the bed and stared at Angel, stretched out on the sheet with his arms bent behind his head, wearing nothing but a towel draped over his hips.

"You don't have to do a beefcake pose. I can take a picture of you fully clothed and…" She blushed. "The rest I can do from memory. I only need a picture of your face."

Angel grinned. "If you're going to be drawing pictures of me without my shirt on, I'd just as soon you get it right."

"Oh!" Sedona gave an astonished laugh. "Are you saying I didn't do you justice?"

"I'm just saying I want to make sure you have all my…parts where they're supposed to be." A dimple teased the corner of his mouth.

"I refuse to take pictures of your *parts*," she said indignantly, but couldn't keep from smiling back at him.

"Take the damn picture, *mina*."

"Okaay." Quickly, before she could change her mind, she held up her small digital camera and centered him in the tiny display screen. "Mmm, that's good. Smile." The camera flashed, and Sedona peered at the display to see the results. "Actually, that's *really* good."

She sat down on the edge of the mattress and held the

camera so Angel could view the picture she'd taken. She was unprepared when he pulled her down beside him and wrested the camera from her fingers.

"Smile," he said cheerfully, and holding the camera at arm's length, took a picture of the two of them, sprawled laughing against the pillows.

"Angel," she protested, making a grab for the camera, "delete that picture right now. I'm not decent!"

"You're fine," he assured her, holding the camera out of reach.

"I'm wearing my *underwear.*"

"I've seen bathing suits that reveal more than your bra and panties." He grinned and sat up, pulling her with him. "C'mon, get dressed. I already told you, we have a big day ahead of us."

She watched as he disappeared through the connecting doors to get dressed before she collapsed back onto the mattress, unable to keep the silly grin off her face. He'd stayed the entire night in her room, his long limbs wrapped around her as they'd slept. And the way he'd woken her up… Her smile turned dreamy.

Angel had seen her sketchbook, and he hadn't run screaming for the hills. He'd actually encouraged her. Even let her take his picture so she could capture his likeness more accurately in her drawings. She knew it wasn't done out of vanity, but in an effort to please her. Had he guessed that she was falling for him?

He'd said he wanted to make a go of their relationship, but did he really mean it? It was one thing to profess your feelings during the intimate aftermath of lovemaking, but how would he feel once they returned to the East Coast and the first blush of romance had worn off? Sedona didn't need to guess; he'd pretend to still be interested, and maybe he actually would be. But eventually, he'd see how impossible any relationship between them was.

"Hey, c'mon, you're not even dressed yet."

Startled, Sedona looked up to see Angel leaning against the door frame between their rooms. He'd pulled on a pair of faded blue jeans and a black T-shirt that emphasized his dark good looks. His hands were shoved casually into his front pockets. He hadn't shaved and the dark blur of stubble on his jaw lent him a slightly piratical look.

She shivered.

"Sorry," she said, pushing herself upright. "I'll hurry."

"Okay, I'll pull the car around and meet you out front."

After he left, she rummaged through her dresser, undecided on what to wear. It was Sunday, and the inspection teams were working rotating shifts. Neither Angel nor Sedona had to report for work that day. Angel had said he had a surprise in store for her, and now she tried to guess what it might be.

She grabbed a pair of jeans and a scoop-necked gold T-shirt with a slender ribbon of satin piping at the neck. Casual, but still nice. Not overdressed. She almost gathered her hair back into a clip, but then let it fall loosely around her shoulders. Angel had said he liked it that way.

Satisfied, she took the elevator down to the lobby and stepped outside. Angel stood by the rental car, and his dark eyes gleamed with approval when she came around to the passenger side.

"You look great," he murmured into her ear as he opened her door for her. "Really."

"Thanks." She felt ridiculously pleased by the compliment. "So," she ventured, when they pulled on to the main road, "where're we going?"

He just smiled at her. "You'll see."

Sedona frowned when he drove onto the base, and turned in her seat to stare at him as they made their way down the now-familiar roads that led to the flight line.

"Oh! You tricked me. Unfair!"

"What?" Angel laughed as he looked over at her.

"Here I thought we were going to spend the day doing fun things, and all you want to do is work." She cast him a dark look. "Unless you're planning on doing wicked things to me in the backseat of one of those Coyotes, you can turn around right now."

"Actually, *mina*," he said as he parked the car next to one of the Coyote hangars, "I was planning to put you in the backseat of one of those Coyotes and take you for a ride."

Sedona stared at him, stunned. *"What?"*

Angel grinned. "You heard me. We're going for a ride."

"But how?" Sedona shook her head, bemused. "I mean, what are you talking about? You can't be serious."

Angel turned in his seat to face her, one arm draped over the steering wheel. "Oh, I'm completely serious." He shrugged. "I know it's something you've wanted to do, so I've been planning this for a few days."

He'd been planning…

To her utter horror, Sedona felt her eyes fill with tears and she blinked furiously, unwilling to let Angel see how much his unexpected gesture meant to her.

"Hey, what's wrong? You did say you've always wanted to ride in a Coyote, right?"

His voice was warm and concerned and Sedona knew if she saw the tenderness in his eyes, she'd lose it completely. She waved him away and turned to look out the window, swiping at her cheeks and laughing self-consciously.

On the opposite side of the flight line, a dozen Coyotes gleamed softly in the morning sun. To her eyes, they were incredibly beautiful, representing all the strength and courage of the U.S. Navy. Like the man sitting next to her. Until this past week, being close to either had only been a dream.

She swallowed hard and turned to give him a wobbly smile. "Yes, I did. It's just—it's just that I can't believe you remembered, and then actually went ahead and planned this."

Angel grinned, clearly relieved. "Hey, it's the least I can do. Besides, it wasn't all that difficult to arrange."

He pushed his door open and climbed out as Sedona stared at him. *The least he could do?* O-kay. Nothing like taking the fun out of it; he made fulfilling one of her dreams sound as mundane as giving her a lift to work.

She pushed down her disappointment in his reaction and tried instead to focus on what he had planned. She was going to take a ride in a Coyote! The prospect terrified her as much as it thrilled her.

He grabbed his flight bag out of the trunk. "You haven't eaten anything this morning, have you?"

"Well, when you told me not to eat breakfast, I thought it was because we were going out to eat. If I'd known…"

"What did you eat?"

She grimaced. "A banana. Was that bad?"

Angel laughed. "Actually, if you had to eat something, that was probably the best choice."

Sedona walked beside him as they made their way to the Coyote hangar. "Why is that? Because of the potassium? Does it help with altitude sickness or something?"

"Nope. It's just that bananas taste pretty much the same coming up as they do going down."

"Oh!" Sedona stared at him, horrified.

"Relax," he said, putting an arm around her shoulders and giving her a brief, hard hug. "I'll go easy on you. Besides, you may not even need the air-sickness bags."

"I think I want to change my mind," she moaned.

"Too late," Angel said cheerfully. "We've already scheduled your preflight brief."

He opened the side door to the hangar and sure enough, there was a Coyote flight crew waiting inside for them. She had to sign some release forms, and then the crew went to work ensuring she had at least a basic understanding of what would happen once she sat down in the rear seat of the Coyote.

One of the grounded jets became a perfunctory classroom as the crew chief escorted her up the ladder and helped settle her into the seat directly behind the pilot.

Sergeant Dwight Nelson was a master mechanic, on loan from the Marine Corps flight program to assist with the investigation. He didn't talk; he barked. His voice was loud and gruff, and combined with his shaved head and Marine Corps tattoos, it made him the epitome of a Hollywood drill sergeant.

"This is a small camera mounted on the back of Diablo's seat." Sergeant Nelson sat perched on the edge of the cockpit with his feet resting on the wing as he prepared her for the flight. He indicated a tiny lens affixed directly in front of her face. "It will record the entire flight and capture every scream, squeal, hurl and blackout you experience, so remember to smile every so often."

Sedona gave him a withering look. "I will not *squeal,* and I certainly will not hurl."

Nelson laughed. "Yeah, right. I've seen marines completely incapacitated by the g-forces this baby pulls. It's no big deal."

Sedona glanced down to where Angel stood at the foot of the ladder, arms crossed as he watched them. He shrugged and grinned at her expression of horror.

"Okay," Nelson continued, "this is your seat belt and it straps you in like this." He deftly pulled several straps across her chest and another one up between her thighs until they buckled near her midriff. "You're sitting on top of live explosives, so whatever you do, *do not* touch this handle, here, unless you want a bonus ride." He pointed to a bright-yellow-and-black-striped handle next to her seat.

Sedona looked quizzically at the lever. "A bonus ride?"

"Yep. That's the free ride you'll get should Diablo decide you need to leave the aircraft during the flight. A free ride aboard your own rocket-propelled ejection seat. Pulling up on this handle will eject you from the aircraft with enough force to compress your spine and cause you to black out." He grinned into her shocked eyes. "I'm sure you won't need to use it."

Sedona made a mental note not to touch the yellow handle under any circumstances. Under Nelson's tutelage, she learned about the physical effects the flight would have on her body, and how to counter the g-forces so she wouldn't pass out. She practiced drawing deep breaths and squeezing her leg muscles to keep her circulation flowing during intense maneuvers.

"You want to tighten those muscles," Nelson explained, "to keep the blood from rushing out of your head to pool in your legs. It's the number-one cause of blackouts."

"Wonderful."

It was several hours later when Angel helped her climb out of the seat and down the ladder.

"Here's a flight suit for you," he smiled, handing her a dark-green jumpsuit and a pair of flight boots. "We took the liberty of assigning you a call sign."

Sedona's eyes widened, and she held the suit up by the shoulders to admire the name tag they'd affixed to the front.

Sedona "Flygirl" Stewart. Oddly, she felt her chest constrict. Angel had given her a call sign.

"It's perfect," she murmured. And it was. "Do I get to keep the suit after the flight?"

"Well," Angel drawled, "we don't have too many calls for suits in a size small with extra room in the rear and chest."

"Oh!" She smacked him playfully on the arm, then grinned. "I'll just go change."

It wasn't until they were on the flight line and standing next to the actual Coyote that would rocket them into the skies, that Sedona felt the first real frisson of fear finger its way along her spine. The Coyote engines were already whining with life, and the flight crew was prepping the aircraft. Standing below the jet, looking up at the blue sky and white clouds reflected on the glass surface of the canopy, she wondered if she really had the nerve to do this.

"C'mon, darling, we have a schedule to keep."

Sergeant Nelson indicated the ladder, and with a sense of foreboding, Sedona climbed up. With Nelson's assistance, she sat down in the snug seat and let him buckle her in. He fitted a helmet onto her head and fastened it beneath her chin, and then rechecked all the safety straps one last time. He was like a mother making sure her child was safely buckled into a car seat. His ministrations made her feel both small and cherished, and she gave him a grateful smile.

As he turned to climb down the ladder, she grasped his arm. "Can you…can you tell me who the plane captain is for this jet?" she asked, hoping her voice didn't betray her fear.

"I did the final inspections myself," Nelson assured her. "Diablo took this jet for a test flight yesterday and it's in perfect condition. You're in good hands."

As long as it wasn't Airman Laudano, she was satisfied. After what Lieutenant Palmer had told her about him, she didn't trust the guy, plain and simple. There was no way she'd voluntarily go up in a jet under his watch. "Right." She gave Nelson a grateful smile. "Well then, I guess that's it."

"Have a good flight, ma'am," he said, and gave her a brief salute before disappearing over the side of the Coyote.

Angel came swiftly up the ladder and before he climbed into the cockpit, he stood looking down at her. "Are you okay?"

He was silhouetted against the backdrop of brilliant blue sky, all wide shoulders and chest. Sedona gave him what she hoped was a confident smile. "Of course. After all, I'm flying with a Top Gun, right?"

"Okay, then." His coffee-dark eyes swept over her, and he smiled, his dimples denting his cheeks. "You look good in there."

Sedona rolled her eyes. "Yeah, right. If my butt was two centimeters wider, I wouldn't be able to fit into this seat."

Angel laughed, a low, rich sound that slid along her senses like melted chocolate. "The seats are supposed to be snug, *nina*. That way, you don't slide around. Nelson showed you where the air-sickness bags are located, right?"

Grimacing, Sedona nodded. "Yes. Please don't do anything that will make me have to use one."

"I'll try. Here's what will happen. We're going up with two other jets. Splatt will be piloting one, and my buddy, Tuna, will be in the other one. We'll begin by doing some basic maneuvers, and then we'll segue into a mock dogfight." He tapped the side of her helmet. "You'll be able to hear me through your headset. Listen for my instructions, and remember to breathe. You'll be fine."

She drew in a deep breath and smiled. "Okay, then. Let's do this."

Angel grinned and gave her a thumbs-up, before shoving

his own helmet down over his head and climbing nimbly
into the cockpit. There were several more minutes of tense
anticipation for Sedona as he meticulously checked and rechecked his controls, and then she heard his voice in her ear,
the sound so close he might as well have been curled up
around her.

"Okay, Flygirl, here we go. The canopy is coming down.
We'll accelerate to 350 knots, and then go into a vertical
14,000-foot-per-minute climb, and level out at 12,000 feet."

Sedona watched as the glass canopy slowly lowered, near
enough to her head that for a brief instant she was certain it
was going to hit her. She expelled the breath she'd been
holding, and tried to control the nervousness that caused her
heartbeat to pulse hotly in her ears. The canopy closed with
a whoosh and a click. Then it was just her and Angel
cocooned together in the cockpit of the Coyote.

Glancing out through the glass, she watched as two of the
maintenance crew pulled the blocks from beneath the wheels.
The jet throbbed once as Angel kicked the engines into gear
and they roared into life. Then they were slowly moving
forward, taxiing onto the runway as a crew member guided
them.

"And here we go." Angel's voice was calm, assured.

They began to accelerate down the flight line until the surrounding countryside was nothing more than a blur, and then
bam! They weren't just airborne, they were rocketing straight
up into the stratosphere.

Whatever Sedona had expected, it wasn't to be pinned against
her seat back by the sheer force of their upward momentum.
She'd been to Walt Disney World once, had experienced the g
forces of the Mission to Mars ride, but nothing could have
prepared her for the sense of helplessness she now felt.

Her heart was slamming in her rib cage and her entire

world was reduced to the tiny bubble she sat in, her gaze locked with desperation onto the back of Angel's seat and the small bit of his helmet that she could see.

"Okay, now we're leveling out. Give you a chance to enjoy the scenery. How're you doing back there?"

"Good," she squeaked.

And they *had* leveled out. Sedona could actually lift her head enough to peer through the glass at the earth below. It was the loveliest thing she'd ever seen—sweeping carpets of brown, beige and occasional green, and at the very edge of the horizon, shimmering under the sun, she could actually see the ocean. She was just beginning to relax a tiny bit, when another Coyote drew alongside them.

"Are they supposed to be that close?" she squealed, her voice sounding frightened, even to her own ears.

"That's Splatt," Angel responded, sounding relaxed and unconcerned. "If you look out the left side of the canopy, you'll see Tuna."

Sedona looked, and sure enough, there was another Coyote on their left flank. As she stared, the pilot gave them a thumbs-up and she could have sworn he grinned.

"Okay, here we go," Angel said. "We'll accelerate into a vertical climb, invert into a 360-degree roll, and then drop out through the bottom. Ready?"

Sedona closed her eyes for a brief second. Damn, the maneuver sounded deadly. "Okay." Her voice was breathless.

"Take a deep breath, squeeze your legs, and…here we go."

Sedona knew a moment of sheer terror as she was pressed back into her seat, and then her head seemed to lift free from her body. Her eyes rolled back in their sockets and blackness fluttered at the edge of her vision.

When she opened her eyes again, the Coyote had leveled out.

"Are you back with me?"

Angel's voice was calm and steady.

"Did I leave?" A vague feeling of nausea settled in the pit of her stomach.

"You blacked out, but just for a moment. It happens, nothing to worry about." Angel's warm assurance filled her ears.

"Oh, God, I'm going to be sick." She grabbed the air-sickness bag and to her shame, discovered bananas really *did* taste the same coming back up. She clutched the bag in her hands and tried to concentrate on drawing in deep, cleansing breaths.

"Okay, now?"

She could hear the concern in Angel's voice, and the last thing she wanted was to distract him. She needed him to be one hundred percent focused on his flying.

"Yes," she assured him, trying to sound normal. "I'm good."

"Okay, great," Angel replied, "because now comes the challenging part of the ride. We'll do a mock dogfight with Splatt. First we'll be the chase plane, and then we'll switch and be the ones chased. Ready?"

Sedona closed her eyes and concentrated on her breathing, and tried not to think about the fact she was shooting through the sky like a bullet, completely at the mercy of Angel's piloting skills.

"Three, two, one…fight's on."

The next forty minutes were the most horrific of Sedona's life. At times, they were upside down and Sedona completely lost sight of the horizon. Twice, she experienced tunnel vision, and nausea threatened once more.

Angel pressed the Coyote through a series of maneuvers that made her briefly consider pulling the ejection handle—anything to get her out of this torture chamber and back onto the ground. She gritted her teeth and endured the seemingly endless flight as best she could, but just one thought kept pounding through her head: she was an idiot. A complete and utter idiot.

While she'd truly wanted to ride in a Coyote, the reality was she couldn't handle it. She'd been fooling herself to think she could. The Coyote was sleek and beautiful and powerful, and completely out of her league.

Just like the man who piloted it.

"Okay, Flygirl." His deep, warm voice penetrated her thoughts. "We'll head back home now. A hard brake to slow us down and put us into landing pattern, and then we'll be on the ground."

Sedona fought to maintain consciousness as the braking maneuver exerted yet more g-forces on her already exhausted body. She hardly felt the wheels touch the ground, and closed her eyes with a grateful sigh. Finally, they drew to a stop and a half dozen or more of the maintenance crew immediately converged upon the jet. The canopy opened over her head, and Crew Chief Nelson's smiling face appeared over the edge of the cockpit.

"Welcome back, ma'am." He grinned down at her. "Have a good flight?"

Casting him a baleful look, Sedona reached up with trembling fingers and fumbled with the fastening of her helmet. Nelson brushed her hands aside and with deft movements, removed the helmet and released the safety harness.

"Easy," he said as she pushed herself to a standing position.

Sedona swayed. Her legs wobbled and her head floated about two feet above her shoulders. She flung out an arm to support herself, and the crew chief gripped her firmly by one arm and helped her out of the cockpit and down the ladder.

"Easy does it." He looked sharply at her. "You okay? Maybe you want to go sit down somewhere." Without waiting for a response, he turned to a nearby crew member. "Heil-muller!" he barked. "Accompany Ms. Stewart to the ladies' room, please."

Suppressing a groan, Sedona looked up to see the perky maintenance officer standing to one side as she prepared to help shut down the Coyote.

"Not feeling well?" Heilmuller asked sweetly, her eyes dancing with devilry. "Well, it just goes to show, you really do need the right stuff in order to sit in one of these babies." She extended an arm to Sedona. "I'll walk with you to the hangar. There's a couch in the bathroom where you can lie down for a few minutes and get your land legs back under you."

"No, thanks." Sedona ignored her arm. "I'll be fine, I just need a minute." No way was she going to toss her cookies in front of the sweetly smug petty officer.

"Okay," Heilmuller said, stepping back. "Have it your way."

She turned away, but not before Sedona saw the specula-tive gleam in her blue eyes. She was only vaguely aware of Angel pulling himself out of the jet and speaking briefly with the crew members. She didn't wait for him, but instead forced herself to walk toward the hangar. Her legs felt like Jell-O, and she was just barely keeping her stomach in check when Angel fell into step beside her.

Sedona cast him one sideways glance. He had his helmet tucked beneath his arm, and his face bore an expression of both satisfaction and pride. Sunlight glinted off his black hair, and she could see her reflection in the mirrored lenses of his aviator sunglasses. His flight suit, with its bulky survival vest, made him seem even bigger, if possible. He looked incredibly handsome. He could have been on the cover of *Life* magazine as the epitome of the all-American hero.

Swallowing hard, she ducked her head and continued walking.

"Hey, hold up a minute." He caught her by the arm and drew her to a halt on the tarmac. "You okay?"

Sedona tipped her head back to look at him. "Yes, thanks. It—it was a great ride. Thrilling. Really." She laughed weakly and held up the air-sickness bag. "I even have a souvenir."

She would have pulled away from him, but he refused to let her go. He yanked his sunglasses off, his dark eyes reflecting both concern and bemusement. "Listen, getting sick isn't uncommon. It's nothing to be ashamed of. Are you sure you're okay?"

"I just—I'm not feeling well."

"That's normal, *mina*. Your body isn't accustomed to the stresses of a flight like that. But you did great."

"Yeah. Sure."

Angel blew out his breath in exasperation. "What the hell is it, Sedona? Were you expecting something less intense? Was it too much for you?" He spread his free hand in a gesture of apology. "I'm sorry. Maybe I got a little carried away. It's just that you seemed to be doing so well back there. I didn't realize you weren't enjoying yourself."

Sedona felt a tightness in her throat and chest. She had to say it and be quick, before she started to cry. "That's just it, don't you see?"

"See what?" He was clearly puzzled.

Sedona spread her arms. "I'm completely out of my element here. I thought I really wanted to go up in that Coyote, and I appreciate you making it happen for me, I really do. But the truth is, I hated it. It *was* too intense. It was more than I could handle."

"Okay," he said, and he smiled at her, a smile that was tender. "So it was a little more extreme than you were prepared for. It's no big deal. It typically takes months of training to be able to do what you just did." He tipped his head down so that he was at eye level with her. "You. Did. Great."

Sedona made a sound of frustration and pulled her arm free. She began walking toward the hangar again, with Angel striding alongside. "I can't do this, Angel."

"What can't you do?"

"Any of it. All of it. Us. *You.*"

"Now hold on just a damn minute." This time there was no escaping his grip as he caught her by the wrist and spun her around. "How is this about us? I thought we were talking about the Coyote ride."

Sedona stared at him, feeling a familiar burning sensation behind her eyes. "We were. But don't you see? Being up there just made me realize what it is you do for a living. Guys like you—you're not normal." She gestured jerkily toward the jet, where Petty Officer Heilmuller's derriere was displayed to full advantage as she leaned deeply into the cockpit of the Coyote to secure the ejection seats. "You're better suited to somebody like *her.*"

"*What?*" His voice was incredulous and there was no more tenderness in his expression, only bewilderment and the beginning of what might have been anger.

"Don't you understand?" Sedona searched his eyes. "I can't be with a guy who takes the kind of risks you take on a daily basis, Angel. That little jaunt through the clouds scared the hell out of me. Maybe right now you're just doing test flights, but at some point you're going to be recalled to combat duty, and I don't know if I can handle that. Just the thought of you doing that…with the enemy firing at you…"

Sedona turned away abruptly and swiped at her eyes.

When Angel finally spoke, his voice was hard and rough, and his accent more pronounced. "So what are you saying, *mina?* We're through?"

She shrugged, not looking at him. "I think it's for the best, don't you? I think we both knew this was going to happen eventually. I mean, how long do you think you'd be happy with someone like me?" She laughed humorlessly, recalling Mike Sullivan's mocking words when she'd first discovered the existence of the Membership. "After all, my idea of excitement is finding a mint on my hotel pillow."

"Sedona." He placed his helmet on the ground beside them and moved forward to grip both her shoulders in his hands, turning her to face him and searching her eyes with an intensity that left her breathless. "Christ. I don't know what's gotten into you, but if you think you can't make me happy, you're *wrong*. You do make me happy."

"Angel—"

"I'll admit," he rushed on, "when I first saw you in the workout room, my intentions were, well, less than honorable. I figured we could have a good time together while we were here, and then go our separate ways after the inspections were done." His hands tightened on her shoulders. "I swore I wouldn't commit myself to a woman while I was still on active duty. But you know what? I *like* being with you." He chuckled ruefully. "Okay, I *love* being with you. I can't wait until the day's over so I can be with you again. Doesn't that mean anything?"

Sedona's gaze slid from his face and fastened on the zipper of his flight suit. She couldn't meet his eyes, not when his expression was so earnest. "It's just lust, Angel. That and convenience. I mean, look at you. You could have any woman you want. You're only with me right now because I came on to you pretty strong." She wet her lips nervously. "I didn't give you much choice in the matter."

"Oh, come on, Sedona." His voice was full of contempt. "Is that really what you believe? That this—this *thing* we have is nothing more than lust?"

She forced herself to meet his eyes without flinching. "Yes. Because one day you're going to look at me and wonder what the hell it was you ever saw in me. This isn't real, Angel. It's like—like a fairy tale or something. It's better to just end it now, while we're still feeling good about each other."

Angel let his hands drop to his sides and took a step back from her, looking at her as if he had no idea who she was.

"You're wrong," he finally told her. "I think you're an amazing woman. You're beautiful and brilliant, and I think we're good together." He rubbed a hand over his head. "Hell, we're *great* together, and what's more, you know we are."

Sedona shook her head. "It would never work, and you know it. You're like that jet you fly—more than most people can handle and best appreciated from a distance." She shrugged helplessly. "I realize…you and the Coyote are a package deal. It's the price of admission, but you know what? I can't afford it."

She turned away, wanting only to escape before she said or did something really stupid. Like throw herself at him and tell him she was completely, foolishly, head over heels in love with him. He tried to forestall her with a hand on her arm, but she pulled away, refusing to look at him, and continued to walk toward the hangar.

"You know what the problem is, Sedona?" he snarled softly. "You're a coward. You're afraid to take risks, afraid to reach out and grab your dreams with both hands and make them come true. Like that sketchbook of yours, you hide them away and hope nobody finds out about them."

Sedona's step faltered and she stopped for just a moment, but she didn't turn around. Her heart was thudding hot and loud in her ears, but not enough to drown out the painful truth of his words. After a second, she started walking again, determined this time not to stop. Not to listen.

"But you know what, *mina?*" His voice was low and bitter. "Those drawings of me won't keep you warm at night. Go ahead and carry them around with you, but they're not me. They're nothing but a flat caricature of the real thing. Kinda like you."

She made it maybe another dozen steps before she stopped and turned around. Angel was striding away from her, back toward the Coyote and the maintenance crew, and the other two pilots who had landed behind them. His steps were hard and the set of his broad shoulders was rigid with anger.

For an instant, she almost called his name. She wanted to run after him and tell him…what? That she'd just made a huge mistake, and of course she was the right woman for him? A frown hitched between her brows and she chewed her lower lip. Better to let him go now than to see him grow bored and turn away from her later. And he would. Eventually, he'd need more excitement than she'd be able to provide. Guys like Angel Torres didn't live happily ever after with plain-Jane engineers like herself.

She turned away, his words repeating themselves in her head. You're a coward…a flat caricature of the real thing… afraid to take risks.

She was going to be sick.

She ran the last few yards to the hangar and barely made it to the ladies' room before she began retching. But there was nothing left in her stomach and after a few minutes she collapsed, weak and gasping, onto the sofa in the small, adjoining room. She swiped at the tears that blurred her vision, and sniffed loudly, staring up at the ceiling.

Her entire body ached. She felt nauseous and dizzy. Her head hurt. But even those physical discomforts didn't match the gnawing ache that had settled in the center of her chest. With a small moan of distress, she curled onto her side.

You're a coward.

The words mocked her, taunted her. Made her want to shrivel up and die of shame.

Angel was right. She *was* a coward, and in more ways than he knew. If she was honest with herself—and the cowardly part of her didn't want to be honest—she'd been a complete wimp for most of her life.

All her life, really. For as far back as she could remember, she'd done things to make others happy. Never once had she stood up and done something to please herself. As a teenager, she'd been too afraid of defying her father to pursue a career in the arts. She'd been too afraid of his censure to purchase those fabulously feminine outfits with the short skirts and matching pumps. And she'd been too afraid of failure to try to make a go of a relationship with Angel.

She'd been too afraid for too long.

For a brief instant, she saw her entire life stretched out before her, filled with all the wrong choices she would make because of her own cowardice. Oh, she'd do okay. She'd have a good career and a nice place to live. But she'd be miserable and unfulfilled. Empty.

Like she felt right now.

With a groan of self-disgust, she swung her legs off the sofa and sat up, scrubbing her hands over her face. Even her decision to leave the agency was based on her own cowardice, because she didn't have the guts to do what was required to expose the Membership.

Well, no more. God, she'd been such a moron.

She might not have the courage to make her relationship with Angel work, but that didn't mean she had to be a coward in every other aspect of her life. It was time she took control, and she knew just where to start.

15

"HEY, STEWART, you have a call on line three."

Sedona turned away from the glass window that separated the calibration room from the test cell, where she'd been watching two of the maintenance crew prepare an engine for testing.

"Okay, thanks." She acknowledged the engineering technician with a brief smile and picked up the receiver.

"Miss Stewart?" It was a deep, male voice and for just an instant, her heart leaped, until she realized that, of course, it wasn't Angel. She hadn't seen or heard from him since their ugly confrontation four days earlier.

Her entire body ached with longing for him.

"Yes, this is Stewart."

"Ma'am, this is Senior Chief Hamlin over in Hangar 74. We're conducting an engine teardown, and you asked me to contact you if I found anything...interesting."

Sedona's breath caught. "Yes? What did you find?"

There was a brief pause. "Maybe you'd better come over and check it out for yourself."

"I'm on my way. Who else have you contacted?"

"Captain Dawson came over with a couple of his guys and took a look. He's gone now, but he was pretty pissed. He's called for a full investigation and is sending over a security unit. My guess is they'll cordon off this hangar once they see what I've found. I'd hurry if I were you."

"I'll be right there."

She replaced the receiver and turned to the engineering technician. "I have to go over to Hangar 74. Give Ken Larson a call and ask him to come up and oversee this test." She gave him an apologetic smile. "I'd do it myself, but I'm in a hurry."

He shrugged. "No problem, ma'am. I'll call him right now."

Sedona hurried from the test cell, wincing as she stepped outside into a blinding rainstorm. The sullen clouds, clustered on the horizon all morning, had finally moved directly overhead, drenching the air base with sheeting rain. The dismal weather completely matched her mood.

She hadn't seen Angel during the three days since their confrontation on the flight line. He'd even packed his gear and moved out of his hotel room and into the Bachelor Office Quarters on base. Not that she blamed him. She'd been a complete bitch, taking all her fear and insecurities out on him.

She didn't know how long she would have been able to resist him had he remained in the room next to hers. She'd picked up her cell phone more than a dozen times, intending to apologize and beg his forgiveness—anything to have him back in her life. But each time, she remembered his expression of contempt as he accused her of being a coward. He was right. She'd put the phone away without hitting the Send button.

She bent her head, bracing herself against the soaking onslaught of rain. Wind howled across the open space, and through the downpour, Sedona could see the Coyotes sitting on the flight line, their profiles blurred by the spray of water.

Was Angel flying in this weather? She told herself it didn't matter; he'd fly well above the cloud bank and would hardly be affected by the storm.

Shielding her eyes against the stinging rain, she skirted the far side of the building where Ken Larson was overseeing the removal of a Coyote engine. The last thing she wanted was to run into him. He'd demand to know where she was going, and there was no way she wanted him tagging along.

She entered Hangar 74 and paused for a moment to swipe at the rain that still dripped from her hair and down her face. As she did so, the sound of low, angry voices drifted toward her from the other side of a large compressor.

Cautiously, she peered around the edge of the machine. Airman Laudano, his face drawn in harsh lines, had Airman Wheeler shoved up against the wall of the hangar as he spoke in hushed, fierce tones to the other man.

"You say my sister means everything to you. Well, now's the time to prove it. You screw this up and you'll never see her again." He gave Wheeler a brief, hard shake. "You have my promise on that."

He let go of the other man, taking a moment to smooth the fabric of Wheeler's flight suit where he'd had it bunched in his hand. Then he turned and walked away.

As if sensing her scrutiny, Wheeler turned his head and his eyes locked with Sedona's. They stared at each other for a long moment. He was pale except for two patches of color that rode high on his cheekbones. For a moment, Sedona thought he would speak, would say something to explain the bizarre interaction she'd just witnessed. His mouth opened, then closed, and before she could say anything, he turned and followed Laudano toward the rear of the hangar.

She watched him go. Was Wheeler dating Laudano's sister? What had Laudano meant by Wheeler not screwing this up? Had he been referring to Wheeler's relationship with the sister, or something more sinister?

Thoughtful, Sedona turned and made her way to where several maintenance-crew members gathered around a Coyote. One of the engines hung suspended from a lift several feet away. Senior Chief Hamlin bent over the remaining engine, still installed in the jet, while the other technicians strained to peer over his shoulder.

"Hey," she said as she approached the group. She tucked several loose strands of wet hair behind her ears. "I came as fast as I could. What do you have?"

The senior chief backed carefully out of the engine compartment, carrying a small mirror in one hand. "Well, this particular jet was out on the flight line this morning, and was mistakenly put into the queue for flight testing."

"Did one of our pilots take it up?" She glanced out the enormous doors of the hangar to where the jets were parked. Where was Angel right now?

"No, ma'am," Hamlin replied. "We caught the problem in time, but if someone *had* taken this jet up, it could have resulted in a catastrophic engine failure."

Sedona's breath caught. "Why?"

He held out his hand. Lying in his palm were three small, metal balls. "I found these inside the fan module."

Sedona frowned. "You found three ball bearings just rolling around? Wasn't that the cause of damage to the fan blades on the last engine we looked at?"

"Yes, ma'am." Hamlin's voice was grim. "But these weren't just rolling around." He drew her aside and lowered his voice. "These were actually fastened to the back side of the fan blades with adhesive."

Sedona stared at him, bewildered. *"What?"*

"I've seen this before. It's usually done to cause engine damage before the jet leaves the ground. However, in this case the adhesive is of such high quality, I believe the ball bearings would remain in place until the jet was airborne. Eventually, the sheer force of the fan suction would cause the adhesive to fatigue. When that happens, the ball bearings would get sucked through the fan modules and the afterburner, trashing the engine on their way out."

"Enough to cause an in-flight failure," Sedona said softly, her eyes wide.

"Exactly."

Sedona met the senior chief's grim expression. "Sabotage?"

"No question."

"Whoever did this believed this particular jet was going to be flight-tested today."

He nodded. "It would seem so. If we hadn't pulled it from the lineup, the jet would have gone up."

Angel. "Oh my God," she breathed. "How many jets are in the air right now?"

"We've implemented a no-fly procedure until the remaining jets can be cleared, and the commander is sending a unit out to secure the entire area, but we have four pilots conducting test flights right now."

"And they are…?"

Hamlin shook his head. "I don't have that information." Something on the flight line caught his attention. "There's Captain Dawson now, with Lieutenant Palmer. You might ask them. Looks like they're heading up to the control tower."

Sedona followed his gaze and saw Captain Dawson and Lieutenant Palmer surrounded by several other naval officers, heads bent and black umbrellas tipped against the driving rain as they strode across the tarmac toward the building that housed the control tower for the naval base.

"Do they know?"

"Oh, yeah."

"Okay, thanks." She began to turn away, when a thought struck her. "Senior Chief, do you happen to know what the relationship is between Airman Laudano and Airman Wheeler?"

"Excuse me?" His expression was bewildered.

"Is Airman Wheeler dating Laudano's sister?"

"Oh, yeah." The senior chief gave a brief grin. "Actually, I think Wheeler is engaged to Laudano's sister. Met her when Laudano brought him home for Thanksgiving one year."

"Thanks. I was just curious."

Her mind spun as she turned away, alarm bells jangling in her head. It had certainly sounded like Laudano was blackmailing Wheeler, and she didn't have to guess why. As a plane captain, Laudano had access to the Coyote engines. He could easily have planted those ball bearings.

Maybe Airman Wheeler had discovered what his future brother-in-law was up to, and had threatened to expose him. But even if Wheeler lacked the courage to do the right thing, she didn't. She would go directly to the military police and tell them what she suspected. But first, she had to make sure Angel wasn't up there, flying a jet that Laudano had inspected.

By the time she reached the control tower, she was drenched through to the skin and Captain Dawson and his entourage had already vanished inside. She pressed the buzzer next to the secure entrance, gasping for breath from her dash across the base.

"Yes?"

Sedona blinked up at the security camera mounted above the door and spoke into the small speaker beneath the buzzer. "Um, this is Sedona Stewart. I'm part of the Coyote inspection team, and I need to speak with Captain Dawson or Lieutenant Palmer. Right away."

There was a momentary silence.

"Come on up, Miss Stewart." The door buzzed.

She pushed it open and took the stairs two at a time as they wound upward, until her thighs cramped in protest and she thought her lungs would burst. By the time she reached the top of the stairs, she'd climbed eight flights. She paused in front of another door of dark, smoked glass. She pressed the buzzer and this time the door opened immediately.

The control room was cool and dark, dimly lit by neon-blue halogen lights. Sedona struggled to check her ragged breathing as she climbed the last flight of steps. Through the observation windows, the air traffic controllers had unobstructed views of the flight line and the surrounding countryside, only slightly obscured by the sheeting rain that drummed against the glass.

The entire perimeter of the small room was occupied by a vast array of computer displays and digital readouts. Three men, each of them wearing a headset, rolled their chairs between the various monitors, watching the blips on the screens and dictating coordinates and flight instructions into their mouthpieces.

Leaning over them, crowding the small space, were Captain Dawson, Lieutenant Palmer and two other naval officers. They all turned to look at her as she rounded the last step and entered the room.

"Captain Dawson." She paused to catch her breath. "Thank you for seeing me."

"Miss Stewart." His voice betrayed his astonishment as he took in her disheveled appearance. "Is there something I can help you with?"

"Actually, yes." She glanced out the window toward the distant Coyote hangar, where she could still see the senior chief standing next to the sabotaged engine. "I, uh, just came from the Coyote hangar, where I saw evidence of sabotage. I need to know if you have any Coyotes in the air right now."

Captain Dawson considered her for a moment, and Sedona thought he was actually going to tell her what she needed to know. But then his lips compressed in what might have been sympathy, before turning back to the controls. "Thank you for your concern, Miss Stewart, but we have everything in hand."

It was a dismissal. Sedona glanced at Lieutenant Palmer, but he stared resolutely through the windows and refused to meet her eyes.

"I understand, sir," she forced herself to say, "but I have reason to believe the Coyotes scheduled for today's test flights may also be compromised." She stopped just short of demanding to know if Angel was up in one of those jets.

"We've already contacted the authorities, Miss Stewart," Captain Dawson replied. "We have the situation contained."

It seemed she wasn't going to get any information from him, and she rubbed her hand across the back of her neck in an effort to dispel some of her tension. "Okay." She sighed. "Can you at least tell me if Lieutenant Torres is up there? We're…friends. I'm concerned for his safety."

One of the men swiveled in his chair to face her, pulling one side of his headset away from his ear. "Hello, ma'am," he said, extending a hand toward her. "I'm Tim Colletti, the flight commander. In answer to your question, yes, Diablo is up there, but I assure you, there's nothing to worry about. I served with him aboard the *Lincoln,* and he was the best damn stick in the squadron."

"Did somebody go over his jet before it went up? Who was the last person to check it, to touch it before it went up?"

Lieutenant Palmer finally turned to face her. "It wasn't Airman Laudano, if that's what you're thinking. He hasn't been on duty since yesterday, and he didn't oversee any of the jets that went up today." His voice held a note of defiance and more than a little smugness, but Sedona hardly noticed for the relief that flooded her. That Laudano apparently had not been on duty that morning, and hadn't been near Angel's jet, allowed her to breathe easier, if only a little.

"So, who was the plane captain for Lieutenant Torres's jet?" she persisted.

Lieutenant Palmer leaned back in his chair and crossed his arms over his chest, looking at Captain Dawson for approval, before turning his attention back to Sedona.

"It was Airman Wheeler," he finally said. "He performed the final inspections. We already spoke with him. Everything seemed in order."

Sedona nodded. "Okay, then." Thank God.

They were each looking expectantly at her, and she shoved her hands into her pockets and took two steps backward toward the stairs. "I just, you know, wanted to make sure he was okay up there, but it seems like you have everything under control, so I'll just be going."

She felt like an idiot, and knew both Captain Dawson and Lieutenant Palmer would have been in complete agreement with that sentiment, but she no longer cared. Angel was safe and that was all that mattered.

She had just turned away when the sound of Angel's voice on the control-tower radio caused her to stop in her tracks.

"Roadrunner, this is Diablo. I have a problem."

Sedona stood, riveted, as every man in the room converged on the instrument panels.

"This is Roadrunner," replied the flight boss. "Go ahead, Diablo."

"I've lost my left engine. It's blown to hell. I have FOD tearing through the fuselage. I have one good engine, but I'm losing altitude."

"Roger that, Diablo. Start ejection sequence."

Even as Commander Colletti began speaking, Sedona heard Captain Dawson swear softly beneath his breath. He turned to Lieutenant Palmer. "Get those other aircraft back on the ground. *Now.*"

"Yessir." Lieutenant Palmer snatched up a spare headset and began contacting the other pilots, commanding them to return to base.

"Negative on ejection." Angel's voice was eerily calm. "I have civilian population below…attempting to reach open water."

"Jesus," breathed Lieutenant Palmer, looking up at Captain Dawson. "If he's already breaking up, he'll never make it."

Together they watched the tiny green blip on the radar screen that was Angel's jet. Without realizing she did so, Sedona moved closer to stare with horrified fascination at the small dot as it blinked across the monitor. She knew the jet was traveling at hundreds of miles per hour, but it appeared to travel at a snail's pace across the screen.

Sedona felt light-headed. This couldn't be happening. The very scenario she had dreaded was unfolding before her eyes. She saw the perimeter of the land mass faintly outlined on the radar screen, and though Angel was closing the distance to the water, she also saw he was rapidly losing altitude.

"Roadrunner, this is Splatt. I have Diablo covered at five o'clock and it doesn't look good. He's spewing body parts and fuel."

Sedona gasped. *Body parts?*

Commander Colletti yanked his mouthpiece away and met her horrified gaze. "Pieces of the aircraft are breaking away," he explained grimly. He shoved the mouthpiece back into place. "Eject, Diablo. Repeat, eject."

"Negative, sir. I can still make open water."

"Diablo, this is a direct order. *Eject.*"

"Roadrunner, this is Splatt. Diablo still in control of aircraft and accelerating toward open water." An instant later, "Belay that message, Roadrunner. He's losing control of the jet. Hard yaw to the left…now back to the right. He's overcompensated. Aircraft in a flat spin. Looks like an out-of-control Frisbee. He's shooting flames and throwing debris. The aircraft is over open water."

"Dammit, Diablo, *eject!*"

There was a momentary silence. Every person in the control tower leaned forward. Sedona passed a hand over her eyes, feeling ill. Even if Angel did eject, could he do it in time to avoid serious injury? She'd read numerous accident reports during her years with Aerospace International and she knew how dangerous ejection could be to the pilot. With the aircraft in a spin, Angel could inadvertently eject directly into the water and be killed instantly. Even if he ejected correctly, he could be rendered unconscious and drown before they could rescue him.

"Roadrunner, this is Splatt. Aircraft down over open water. Pilot ejected. Repeat, pilot ejected and in the water."

Sedona didn't wait to hear more. With a muttered curse, she turned on her heel toward the stairs.

"Miss Stewart!" Captain Dawson's voice stopped her in her tracks. "Where are you going?"

She looked up, directly into the captain's eyes, and didn't try to hide the tears of fury that blurred her vision. "I'm going to find the son of a bitch who sabotaged that aircraft."

THE CENTRIFUGAL FORCE was enough to pin Angel to the instrument panel as the aircraft yawed in a corkscrew motion. Full thrust on his one good engine swung the tail around and the aircraft veered in the other direction. The sound of screaming engine and twisting metal filled the cockpit, and the acrid stench of burning jet fuel filled his nostrils.

He slammed the stick left to compensate, but it wasn't enough. The vortex of the falling jet caused his one good engine to flame out, and then he dropped below the canopy of clouds and into the thick soup of the coastal storm.

Through a break in the clouds below him, Angel glimpsed the churning waters of the Pacific as the earth rose to meet him. Using every bit of strength he had to push against the g-forces that held him immobile, he reached back and wrapped his hand around the ejection handle and began the ejection sequence.

Almost immediately, the Coyote's canopy blasted away, sucked upward into the turbulent skies. Angel yanked the handle. He slammed back into his seat as the ejection-seat straps responded. One. Two. The rockets beneath the seat blasted him out of the jet. The stunning impact jarred his teeth and caused his head to snap back. Then he was tumbling, free-falling through the stormy skies.

Instinctively, he reached up and groped for the straps that held him pinned to the seat. He pulled on them sharply, then the seat tumbled away and his chute streamed out. He glanced upward, saw it balloon open and gritted his teeth against the violent snap that stopped his fall and jerked him upward until he was floating, suspended in his harness beneath the open chute. He drifted for scant seconds as rain sluiced over his helmet and into his face, before he plunged into the sea.

Something in his ankle snapped, but before he could think about it, his heavy gear sucked him down and the dark waters of the Pacific closed over his head. Almost immediately, the life preserver that was built into his survival vest inflated around his neck, pressing against his jaw. Using his arms and legs, he fought to propel himself upward. Before he could reach the surface, he was yanked hard to one side as the wind caught his chute, dragging him through the churning waters and twisting him in the straps. He was turning over and over as he struggled desperately to release himself from the tangled line.

He burst through to the surface and sucked in huge gulps of air, heedless of the rain that lashed his face. Reaching up, he fumbled with the release snaps, and fell back into the water as the parachute finally broke free and whipped across the waves like a giant kite.

The sea was rough, with eight-foot chops. Gusts of wind blew blinding spray into his face. At one point, when a large wave buoyed him up, he thought he glimpsed debris from his jet floating a short distance away. His heavy gear threatened to drag him beneath the surface once again. His own harsh breathing filled his ears. His body felt battered, almost too weak to continue treading water, and he became aware of the throbbing pain in his left ankle.

Summoning up his last bit of strength, he twisted and fumbled with fingers that were cold and numb, until he located the inflatable raft attached to his harness. He pulled the cord and the orange raft burst open with a hiss until it bounced beside him on the surface.

Angel hooked an arm over the side, pulled himself into the small opening, ignoring the screaming protest of his injured leg, and collapsed onto his back, exhausted. He flung an arm over his eyes and breathed heavily, letting the undulating waves soothe his body.

He was alive.

Pushing to a sitting position, he braced himself against the side of the raft and bent over to examine his injured leg. Gritting his teeth against the shooting pain, he unlaced his boot and peeled the wet fabric of his flight suit back far enough to assess the damage. It looked to be a compound fracture of his ankle. The skin around the protruding bone was ragged and inflamed, but there was little blood and, if he didn't move too much, the pain was bearable. The bone must have snapped on impact with the water, though he barely recalled feeling it at the time. He eased the fabric back into place and sank back against the edge of the raft.

He was alive.

Despite the loss of the Coyote, and the pain in his ankle, he smiled. He'd managed to push the aircraft, even with the damage she'd sustained, to the safety of the open ocean. When he'd first heard the terrifying *boom* of the engine, seen the warning lights begin to flash, and then felt the aircraft shudder and falter as the foreign object tore through the engine compartment and shredded the turbofans, he'd known he wasn't going to be landing. He just wanted to ensure the inevitable crash didn't take innocent lives. But damn, he regretted the loss of the Coyote.

Where was Sedona right now? Had she heard about the crash? God, he hoped not. It would only confirm her belief that his job was too dangerous.

An image of her floated behind his closed eyes—Sedona smiling, laughing, doing things that completely blew his mind and made him ache to take her. Her words echoed in his head. *"Guys like you—you're not normal...I can't be with a guy who takes the kind of risks you take on a daily basis."*

He lifted his arm from his face and stared into the pewter clouds overhead, letting the rain wash against his skin.

He was alive.

Despite the pain in his leg, and despite the fact he was floating somewhere out in the middle of the goddamn ocean with a monsoon pouring down on him, he felt great. Maybe he'd gambled with his life today, but it had shown him how precious that life was. And way too short to go it alone.

For an instant, when he'd been unsure if the Coyote was going to stay airborne long enough to push her out over the water, when he didn't know if he'd be able to eject safely, one thought had consumed him: if he didn't survive, Sedona would never know he loved her.

He'd already known he was falling for her, and fast.

Despite his resolve not to become seriously involved, he hadn't counted on his heart having other plans. He'd told Sedona he wanted a relationship with her, but maybe if he'd told her he loved her she wouldn't have walked away.

He needed to talk to her, convince her to give them a chance. As soon as he got back to Lemoore, he'd tell her how he felt about her. He'd even give up combat flying. Maybe he could get an assignment as a flight instructor, either at Lemoore or Oceana. As an instructor, he could experience the thrill of combat flight every day.

The thought of being grounded long enough to actually establish roots brought him a profound sense of well-being. He and Sedona belonged together, and it was way past time he told her so.

16

SEDONA MADE IT all the way back to the Coyote hangar before Lieutenant Palmer caught up with her. He grabbed her by the arm and dragged her to a stop just outside the hangar.

"Just what the hell do you think you're doing, Ms. Stewart?"

Sedona turned to face him, squinting through the rain that lashed her face and whipped hair into her eyes. "I'm going to find Airman Laudano," she said, wreathing her words with a patently false smile, "and then I'm going to wring the little bastard's neck until he confesses."

"I already told you," Lieutenant Palmer said between gritted teeth, "Laudano didn't inspect those jets."

"I know. You already said Airman Wheeler did. But I can't believe he sabotaged those jets. My money's still on Laudano." She bit the words out and wrenched her arm free of his grasp at the same time.

Casting a baleful glance up at the sky, Lieutenant Palmer grimaced and shoved her ahead of him into the shelter of the hangar. "Let's get the hell out of this rain, then we'll talk."

Inside the hangar, Sedona shook the water from her arms and hands, and used her fingers to wipe the moisture from her face. She turned to look at Lieutenant Palmer, who was squeezing the water out of his hat.

"Okay," she said, impatience edging her voice. "I'm listening."

The lieutenant glanced around as if someone might overhear them. "I didn't want to say anything until I was sure, but…" His voice dropped and he cast an uneasy glance over his shoulder. "I have reason to believe Wheeler *is* the one sabotaging the jets."

Sedona's eyebrows flew up. "*Wheeler?* But—"

"*Shh!*" Lieutenant Palmer gestured furiously for her to keep her voice down. "It's only a suspicion I have."

A frown hitched between Sedona's brows. "Well, have you talked to the investigators about your suspicions? I mean, Christ, Angel's jet is down!"

A tightening in her throat, accompanied by a sudden burning sensation at the back of her eyes, forced her to look away. She had to get a grip on herself or she was going to lose it. She blinked rapidly. The man she loved was somewhere in the waters of the Pacific, and she didn't even know if he was alive. Swallowing hard, she composed her features and turned back to Palmer. "Just when were you planning on sharing this bit of information?"

Palmer shifted uncomfortably, and his eyes slid away from hers. "Soon. Right away. I just wanted to be sure. And I am." He nodded his head, as if to convince himself. "Yeah, I'm pretty sure it's Wheeler."

Sedona recalled the plane captain's wholesome good looks and shy nature. There was no way she could envision him doing anything as treacherous as sabotaging the Coyotes. During the exchange she'd witnessed earlier, it had sure looked like Laudano was threatening Wheeler. Had those threats been related to the Coyotes?

She narrowed her eyes at the lieutenant. "What about Laudano? If he's already on restriction because of some offense, wouldn't it make sense to look at him first? Maybe this is some twisted attempt at revenge. Besides, I heard him threatening Wheeler. Maybe it was to keep him quiet."

"I already told you, he wasn't the last one to inspect the jets. Wheeler was."

Sedona turned away and pinched the bridge of her nose. It made no sense. What possible reason could Wheeler have for wanting to jeopardize the lives of the Coyote pilots? She'd been so certain that if anyone was responsible for sabotaging those jets, it was Laudano.

"I just don't get it," she muttered. "Why would Wheeler do such a thing?" She turned back to Palmer, who watched her closely. "Where is Laudano now?"

"You can't talk to him. He's on restriction and I'm sure the investigation team is prohibiting contact with any of the plane captains until they've had the chance to question them."

Loud voices drifted to Sedona from across the hangar, momentarily distracting her. A team of military police strode through the hangar, barking directions to seal off the Coyotes and quarantine the area.

"Well, it's about time," she said darkly. "I'll just bet those MPs will be interested in hearing your theories about Wheeler." Without waiting for a reply, she moved toward them with long, determined strides.

"No, wait!" Lieutenant Palmer took two swift steps after her and grabbed her upper arm, spinning her around.

"What—?" Sedona tried to wrench free.

"Just *wait,* dammit!" Palmer's eyes looked wild and unfocused. He tightened his grip on her arm. "I have to tell you—"

"Let me go," Sedona said, her voice low and tight. *"Now."* She stared at Palmer, and even with the military police just steps away, a frisson of fear feathered its way up her spine as she watched his eyes. He didn't release her; instead, he began to haul her toward him and Sedona had a vision of him dragging her out of the hangar before she had a chance to speak to the police.

"Hey!" She resisted, twisting her arm in his grasp and straining to pull away from him. "I said let me go!"

"No, wait. Please!"

At the same instant she managed to jerk her arm free, she stepped back, directly onto a patch of oil-slickened floor. Her foot flew out from beneath her and she teetered precariously. With a sharp cry, she grabbed at Lieutenant Palmer's shirtfront. Unbalanced, he cartwheeled his arms and in the next instant they both toppled to the floor. Sedona landed heavily on her backside with the lieutenant on top of her. She shoved at Palmer's shoulders. He groaned and rolled to his back beside her.

"Ma'am?"

Looking up, she saw a burly MP bending over them. He extended a hand and hauled her to her feet.

"Oh, man," she said ruefully, "that hurt."

She rubbed her posterior and looked down at Palmer as he sat up. His shirt was partially pulled out of his waistband and several buttons had popped free where she had grabbed him. He leaned forward and pushed himself to his feet. As he did so, a handful of small metal balls fell out of his breast pocket and skittered madly across the concrete floor, like beads from a broken necklace.

Stopping one with her foot, Sedona bent down and picked it up. "What is this, Lieutenant Palmer? A ball bearing?"

Palmer stared at the small sphere that rested in her palm, before his glance shot to the military police with something like panic. "I—I know what you're thinking, but this isn't what it looks like."

Sedona stared at him in dawning horror. "Did *you* do it? Did you put those ball bearings on the back of the fans?"

His eyes shifted to the military-police officer who stood beside her, and his hand pressed furtively against the pocket of his trousers.

"What do you have in your pocket, Lieutenant?" she asked. "Anything you'd care to show us? Maybe some more ball bearings? Is that what you were doing when I saw you on the flight line that night?"

"I—I don't know what you're talking about," he stammered. His gaze flicked between her and the MPs who now ringed them.

Sedona held out her hand. "Then you won't mind showing us what's in your pocket."

When it seemed he might actually refuse, one of the military police took a step forward. "Sir, please empty your pockets."

Palmer looked desperately around, as if seeking some escape. Seeing none, his shoulders sagged. He reached into his pocket and withdrew what looked like a trial-size tube of toothpaste.

"I never meant to hurt anyone," he muttered.

The MP took the tube and turned it over in his hands. "Industrial-strength adhesive," he murmured, reading the words on the outside of the tube. He looked back at Palmer, his eyes hard. "I'm sorry, sir, but you'll need to come with us and answer a few questions."

"Wait a minute," Sedona interrupted. "I just want to know one thing, Lieutenant Palmer." She stared at him, as if by searching his eyes she might glean some understanding of what would prompt him to commit such a crime. "Why?"

"I think I can answer that for you."

Sedona whirled around. Standing several feet away was Airman Wheeler. His face was grim.

"Please tell me you're not involved in this," Sedona breathed.

He flushed. "No, ma'am, except as a potential scapegoat." He gave Palmer one brief glance, filled with both sympathy and disgust. "I found out Laudano's been buying drugs for this guy." He grimaced. "I even agreed to keep quiet about it since we're almost family, but Laudano got caught bringing some of that crap back onto the base. He refused to implicate the good lieutenant here, but it looks like neither one of them trusted me to keep my mouth shut."

Sedona knew her own mouth was open, but she couldn't help it. "That's what all this is about?" She turned to face Palmer. "Because you have a drug problem, you'd be willing to sabotage the Coyotes and set Wheeler up to take the blame?"

The military police moved to either side of Palmer. He offered no resistance when they drew his arms behind his back and secured them.

"You think it was just about the drugs, Stewart?" His voice was filled with contempt. "Those sons of bitches at Top Gun owe me. They *owe* me! Do you know how many years I spent trying to make the cut? And those bastards kept denying me. Do you know what that does to your psyche? To your self-esteem? To be looked down on by guys like Diablo and Tuna?"

Crew members began to drift over from their workstations to witness the unfolding drama as the police led him away. He twisted to look at her over his shoulder. "I'm a good pilot!" he cried. "I could have been up there with the best if they'd only given me a chance! But they wouldn't, and for that they had to pay! *Someone* had to pay!"

"It's not just about being good enough," Sedona replied. "It's about having the right character." She stood and stared after him, but it wasn't until he had disappeared from sight that she realized she was shaking.

"Ma'am?"

She turned to see Airman Wheeler looking at her with concern. She passed a hand over her eyes. "I'm sorry. I—I have to get out of here. I need to find out about Diablo."

"Yes, ma'am. Is there anything I can do?"

"Yes." She gave him a trembling smile. "Next time, have enough guts to do the right thing."

He looked shamefaced. "Yes, ma'am. I only kept quiet because I didn't want to get Laudano in any more trouble. I'm going to marry his sister, and if she thought—"

"If she loves you, she'll understand. She'll stand by you, no matter what."

"Is that what you'd do? Stand beside your man, no matter what?"

Sedona gave a shaky laugh, feeling tears spring to her eyes. "Yes. If he'll have me. If he's still—"

For the first time, a ghost of a smile touched Wheeler's mouth. "Ma'am, the reason I came here was to tell you they just recovered Diablo. He's on his way to the hospital right now."

SEDONA STOOD beside the hospital bed and watched Angel as he slept. The room was dark except for one dim light over the adjoining-bathroom door, but despite the dimness, she thought she could see faint shadows beneath his closed eyes.

A rescue helicopter had plucked him from the churning sea and transported him back to Lemoore Naval Air Station, where he'd undergone surgery to repair the damage to his shattered ankle. Encased in a cast, his lower leg rested in a padded sling suspended over his bed. They'd had to use screws and pins to hold the fractured bones together, but she'd been assured he would make a full recovery.

It was the middle of the night, but Sedona hadn't been able to leave the hospital. The thought of going back to her empty hotel room was completely depressing. She also had an irrational fear that if she didn't stand watch by his bedside, death might still find a way to take him from her. She wanted to be with Angel—*needed* to be with Angel—and when the nurses on duty had seen her determination, they'd reluctantly allowed her to stay on the condition that she did not wake him.

She dragged a chair close to the bed and she sank onto it. Even now, she could scarcely believe he'd survived.

Reaching out, she took his hand in hers and gently stroked the back of it, admiring the long fingers. She loved his hands, loved how strong and capable they were. Loved how gentle they could be.

She started when his fingers closed around her own and squeezed gently. Jerking her gaze upward, she saw his eyes were open. He watched her with a quiet intensity, as if he half expected her to bolt. But there was no way she was leaving.

"Hey," she said softly, and leaned closer, cupping his hand between hers. "How're you feeling?"

"What are you doing here?" His voice was raspy and low, and the sound of it caressed her like a warm flame. "What time is it?"

"It's just after midnight. Everyone else went home. Splatt and Tuna, Captain Dawson…just about everyone from the Coyote flight line was here earlier. Even Petty Officer Heilmuller." She rolled her eyes and smiled. "She was actually here the longest." Sedona didn't tell Angel the other woman had left less than an hour earlier. She'd seemed determined to be at Angel's side when he regained consciousness, insisting he'd want to see a friendly face. Sedona was certain her own less-than-friendly demeanor had finally driven her away. "I—I couldn't leave." Sedona swallowed and dropped her gaze. "I wanted to be with you."

His fingers squeezed hers, and when she looked up, his eyes were warm. "I'm glad you're here. We need to talk."

Sedona shook her head and laid two fingers across his lips.

"No, it's okay. You don't need to say anything. You were right about everything. I'm a complete coward. About us, about my life…about everything." To her horror, tears stung her eyes and blurred her vision. "You're a phenomenal pilot, Angel. Nobody could have done what you did up there today." She swallowed hard. "The Navy needs guys like you."

"And what about you, *mina?* Do you need a guy like me?"

"Angel…don't." Her voice broke.

"Come here."

She didn't protest when he pulled her hard across his chest and enclosed her in the warmth of his arms. Her face lay buried against his neck and she breathed in his scent and savored the feel of him against her.

"I love you, Sedona Stewart," he murmured, and she felt him press a lingering kiss against her hair. "I know you're scared by what I do for a living, so I made some decisions."

Sedona felt as if her heart had stopped beating. She lifted her head to gaze down at him, searching his dark eyes. He loved her? He'd made some decisions? She held her breath.

"I'm requesting a transfer to the Top Gun school as an instructor." He smiled at her. "Any combat flight I do will be strictly educational."

"Oh my God…" His features blurred as the tears that had threatened finally spilled over. She swiped at them with one hand. "Angel, you don't have to do this…"

"Shh. Don't you get it? I *want* to." He ran a hand over her hair. "I'm crazy about you. I want you in my life and besides, it's way past time I settled down." He used his thumbs to wipe the tears from her cheeks, and then cradled her face in his hands, searching her eyes. "That is, if you'll have me, *mina*."

Sedona gave a choked sob. "*Have you?* Are you kidding? I love you so much, Angel Torres." Her voice was husky with emotion. "I think I have since I first saw you. And when I knew you were up there, in that jet… I've never been so afraid in my entire life. I just—I just—"

He frowned. "What?"

She laughed self-consciously. "I just can't believe you really love me. I can't get used to hearing you say it…"

Angel laughed and drew her down. "I love you," he growled, nuzzling her neck. "I love you."

And then his lips slanted across hers, claiming her with a fierceness that told her how much he wanted her. He buried his hands in her hair as he deepened the kiss, sweeping his tongue against hers and drawing a soft moan from her. She had one palm pressed against his chest and could feel the heavy beat of his heart. Her own quickened in response.

After several long moments, she pushed away. She was breathless and slightly dizzy from the intensity of his kiss. She braced herself over him and gazed down into his eyes. They smoldered with heat, and something else. Something that caused her heart to trip unsteadily and then swell within her chest.

She cupped his jaw, shadowed with stubble, and stroked her hand tenderly along his cheek. He smiled, turned his face into her hand and pressed a fervent kiss against her palm.

"Stay with me tonight," he whispered. He shifted his weight to one side of the narrow hospital bed. "Here, there's more than enough room. I know you don't want to go back to the hotel, and I don't want you to, either."

"Angel…" She hesitated. "Of course I want to, but what if I bump your leg? Hurt you? Besides, I'm sure there's some kind of hospital rule against overnight guests."

Angel chuckled and drew her down until she was curled against his side with her head resting on his shoulder. "It's the middle of the night and there are only two nurses on duty. Nobody is going to come in tonight," he murmured against her temple, "and even if they did, I think it's safe to say they wouldn't bother us."

Using her feet, Sedona shucked her shoes and stretched out on the narrow mattress next to Angel, careful not to disturb his injured leg. She could hear the strong, reassuring thump of his heart, feel the hard warmth of his body next to her own, and in that moment was so profoundly grateful for both, she wanted to weep.

"I was in the control tower when your distress call came in," she said quietly, tracing a pattern on his chest with her finger.

"Ah, *mina*…I'm sorry."

"I was so frightened. I was so sure you'd be killed, and I'd never get the chance to tell you how much I love you, or that I didn't mean those awful things I said to you the other day after you took me up in the Coyote." She shivered and burrowed closer. "But as scary as it all was, it wasn't nearly as frightening as the thought of going through the rest of my life without you."

His arm tightened around her. "Don't think about it anymore. It's over and we're both here. Together. That's the important thing."

"They've arrested Lieutenant Palmer in connection with the sabotage. There will be an inquest."

"I know. I spoke briefly with Captain Dawson before they brought me into surgery. After he chewed my ass for not ejecting sooner, that is." He gave a snort of disbelief. "I'd have never guessed Palmer carried so much resentment and anger."

Sedona lifted her head to look at Angel, and used her fingers to smooth the frown between his brows. "I guess you never really know what goes on inside another person's head. Or their heart."

Angel brushed a tendril of hair back from her face. "I guess not. I'll try and make sure you're never in any doubt about what's in my heart." He pressed another kiss against her forehead. "The good news is that it's over. Once all the jets are checked over and cleared, the Navy can get them back in the air where they belong. It's over, *mina.*"

"Thank God for that," Sedona breathed fervently. "Your last test flight was too close a call for me." She yawned, suddenly overcome by fatigue.

"Let's get some sleep," Angel said, and tipped her face up for a brief, hard kiss.

"Mmm," she sighed, smiling at him. "I *am* tired, but it's probably nothing compared to how you must feel. You've had quite a day."

Angel shook his head. "As bad as it was, it could have been a lot worse. You won't hear any complaints from me."

"I should probably leave." She burrowed deeper into his warmth. "You need your rest, and I can't help feeling I shouldn't be here."

Angel put a finger under her chin and tipped her face up to look into her eyes. "You're here with me, *mina,* which is exactly where you should be."

As Sedona searched his eyes and saw the tenderness reflected there, she knew he was right. She relaxed against him. He was safe, and they were together. Beyond that, nothing else seemed important. Her arm tightened briefly around him as she let sleep slowly overtake her. She'd made a mistake by shutting him out of her life once; she wouldn't do it again.

17

SEDONA SAT at her desk and fingered the photos in her hands. There was the photo of Angel in her bed, lounging back against the pillows with nothing more than a towel wrapped around his lean hips. He had one arm bent behind his head as he grinned into the camera. She traced a fingertip over the photo. From his bulging biceps to his taut, washboard stomach, he looked altogether delicious.

The second picture was of the two of them, faces close together as he snapped the picture from arm's length. Her face was flushed and laughing. She looked like a woman in love.

Turning the photos facedown on the desk, she pressed her hands against her eyes. She couldn't do it. There was no way she could use the intimate photos of Angel to expose the Membership and their disgusting practices.

"Hey, you okay?"

Sedona pulled her hands away from her face and looked up. She'd arrived back at her office two days earlier and had contacted Agent Denton at the Defense Criminal Investigative Service. She told him she'd had a change of heart regarding the Membership, and together they'd worked out a plan to fully expose the club and end their sordid promotion tactics. All she had to do now was confront the members. Sedona was done hiding; this would be the first courageous step she took toward her new life.

She was scared to death.

She looked up at Agent Denton. "I really hope I'm doing the right thing."

Denton was old enough to be her father, but there was nothing remotely fatherly about him. He looked tough and uncompromising, and she wondered just what experiences he'd been through to carve such deep lines into his face.

"No waffling allowed, Miss Stewart. Either you're committed to this, or you're not. You've already turned in your resignation. What do you have to lose?"

Nothing, except my self-respect. She just hoped Angel never discovered how she'd used the photos they'd taken. He hated deception. He'd be furious if he knew. Not that there was any chance of that. He wasn't due back from Lemoore for another three days, and he wouldn't be returning to the flight line at Aerospace International until after his ankle had fully mended. By then, this would be nothing more than a distant memory.

"You're right," she acknowledged, looking at Agent Denton. "I have nothing to lose. So…let's do this thing."

"Agent Bates checked your wire?"

"Yes. She said it's good to go." Sedona touched a hand to her midsection where Agent Bates had used first-aid tape to fasten a hidden recording device against her skin. "Hopefully she's a little smarter than I am, and won't forget to turn the thing on."

A spark of amusement lit Agent Denton's hard eyes. "It's already recording." He checked his watch. "We have five minutes. Ready to go?"

Sedona drew in a deep breath in an effort to calm her nerves. "Yes, ready."

"Okay, now stop second-guessing yourself. You'll be fine. Sullivan expects you to be triumphant, even a little aggressive, so don't be afraid to work it. Throw those photos in his face and demand the promotion they promised you. Right?"

She wiped her damp palms on her skirt. "Right."

"You told Mike Sullivan to get the members together in the F/A-44 conference room?"

Sedona scooped the photos up from the desk. "Yes. It's sort of out of the way, and offers more privacy than the other conference rooms. I—I refused to meet them in the men's bathroom."

Agent Denton checked his watch once more. "You should be on your way. I'll be listening right here, and Agent Bates should already be in position across the hall from the conference room." He compressed his lips in what Sedona guessed was his form of an encouraging smile. "You can do this."

Leaving her office, Sedona walked briskly past Linda, who practically leaped from her chair upon seeing her. "Oh, Sedona, I have a message for you."

Sedona held up her hand to stop the other woman. "Sorry, Linda. I'm late for a meeting. I'll catch you on my way back."

Yeah, right. The only thing she was going to catch was a train home. Ignoring Linda's look of dismay, she continued through the hallways, skirting the manufacturing bays until she reached the conference room where the Membership had agreed to meet.

Sedona paused outside the door to collect herself. She glanced quickly over her shoulder at the door across the hall, but it remained firmly closed. The corridor behind her was empty. Before she could change her mind, she pushed open the conference-room door and stepped inside.

ANGEL TRIED to curb his impatience. "Did you give her my message?"

It was clear the plump administrative assistant was completely flustered by his presence, but he didn't care. He was anxious to see Sedona, and missing her by mere minutes hadn't improved his disposition.

"I tried to give her your message, sir, but she was in such a hurry."

"Okay." He rubbed a hand over his face. He'd pushed himself hard over the past week, both physically and mentally, to get released from the hospital and complete his statements to the investigators. He'd been overjoyed when the lead investigator finally seemed satisfied with his report and said he was free to go home. He'd managed to catch an early flight out of Lemoore that morning. From Logan Airport, he'd caught a taxi directly to Aerospace International. "Can you tell me where the meeting is? I really need to see her."

The woman looked slightly dazed as she stared up at him. "I'm not sure…sir. There was no meeting scheduled on the calendar. It looked like she was headed to the manufacturing bay."

Angel gave her a quick smile and swung away on his crutches. "Thanks, I know where she's going."

The F/A-44 conference room, located on the far side of the manufacturing bay. Whatever meeting she was attending, he'd just slip into the back of the room and wait for her to finish. It had been three days since he'd seen her and he was going crazy.

Bracing himself on his crutches, he swung silently through the corridors. Since he was officially off duty, and out of consideration for the bulky cast on his foot, he wore a pair of loose cargo pants and a T-shirt. He was grateful he didn't run into anyone he knew.

As he neared the conference room, voices drifted toward him through the partially open door. He was just debating poking his head in to see if Sedona was there, when the sound of his name being spoken froze him where he stood.

"So you're telling me you were getting it on with Lieutenant Commander Torres the entire time we were out at

Lemoore? Well, hell, Stewart, that's all you needed to tell me. Why make me feel like it was a personal rejection?"

What in hell? That was Larson's voice.

"Because if Lieutenant Torres even suspected my true reasons for being with him, it would have been all over. But he didn't suspect a thing, and I have the proof."

Angel recoiled.

"Okay, let's see this 'proof.'"

Angel thought he recognized this new voice. It sounded like Mike "Hound Dog" Sullivan, one of the lead engineers for the Coyote program. Angel didn't know the man well, but he was familiar with Sullivan's reputation.

"Oh," Sedona crooned, "you'll get your proof." Her voice hardened. "Just as soon as I get my guarantee that the next promotion is mine. I mean, that was the deal, right? I screw some guy's brains out while I'm on business travel, bring back proof of the deed, and you guys make sure I get promoted. So I ask again—where's my guarantee?"

Angel heard several male voices as they talked in raised, excited tones. He stood immobile, stunned. He felt like someone had just kicked him in the gut. Hard.

"Okay, Stewart," Sullivan drawled. "Show us the proof, and if it's like you say it is, then sure…the next promotion is yours."

"Well, then, here you go, boys."

There was the sound of paper being slapped down on the surface of the table, and then several long, low whistles.

"I'm impressed, Stewart," Larson said. "You really *were* banging Torres. These photos are…inspiring."

"Yes, I think so, too. Now, about that promotion…"

Angel turned away, sickened. Part of him wanted to shove his way into that conference room and confront Sedona. He wanted to throw the deceitful little witch over his shoulder and carry her to some private place where he could wring the truth out of her lying lips; she belonged to him.

Another part of him wanted to go in there and smash a fist into Larson's face. Anything to wipe off the smug expression he knew he'd find there.

Instead, he turned away. He didn't know if he had the stomach to face Sedona, not when he'd been so certain what they'd shared had been special…magical.

She'd told him about the Membership, but she'd left out the fact that she was campaigning for her own position within the club. To find out she'd used him to satisfy some twisted, sexual prerequisite to advance her career was mind-boggling. He felt defiled.

Without waiting to hear more, he retraced his steps as swiftly as his crutches would allow. He was an idiot, a total idiot to have been so completely duped by her. To think, he'd fallen hook, line and sinker for her sweet, sultry come-ons. He didn't know if he'd ever manage to accept that she'd seduced him in order to get ahead.

He thumped his way along the corridor, remembering how she'd protested his taking the pictures. He'd played right into her hands, thinking he was helping her with her artwork. At the time, he'd have done anything she wanted, given her anything. Christ, he'd practically begged her to take the photos.

He snorted derisively. After he'd taken her up in the Coyote, she'd told him what they had together was nothing more than lust, but he'd refused to believe it. He'd been so convinced their relationship was the real thing, but in reality, it had been nothing but a cheap knockoff. She'd fooled him once. It wouldn't happen again.

18

"WELL, I GUESS that does it." Sedona closed the top of the cardboard box that held the last of her personal items, and ran a strip of packing tape along the seam, pressing it into place with her fingers. She looked up at Agent Denton. "Would you mind walking out to the parking lot with me? Since The Incident, I'm pretty much persona non grata around here."

Agent Denton scooped up the larger of the two boxes. "It couldn't have gone any better," he commented. "We got everything on tape, and Mike Sullivan gave us the names of the members on the Promotion Selection Board. I think it's fair to say none of them will ever get another job with the Department of Defense."

It had been three days since Sedona had confronted the members. Immediately following their "meeting," federal agents had converged on the conference room and arrested each of the men on illegal labor practices and sexual-harassment charges.

Sedona was just glad it was finally over. She didn't even regret leaving the agency. She hefted the remaining box into her arms and followed Agent Denton out of the office.

Nope, not a single regret.

She'd been given a second chance and she wasn't about to screw it up. This time, she'd find a job doing what she loved. She'd already e-mailed samples of her drawings to a magazine that specialized in military art. The executive editor had expressed interest in her drawings of the Coyote jets, and had indicated they were in the market for a senior illustrator.

Beyond that, the only thing she wanted was to be with the man she loved. She'd spent the past five years committed to her career, but now she'd been given a second chance and there was no way she was going to blow it.

Angel was due to fly in from Lemoore that evening. It felt like forever since she'd seen him. She'd tried calling him numerous times, but hadn't been able to get through. She told herself it was the time difference. That, and he was still providing information to the Coyote investigation team.

But there was a part of her that was hurt that he hadn't returned any of her calls, or bothered to let her know exactly when his flight was due in. With his broken ankle, he'd need somebody to pick him up at the airport and drive him home.

If not her, then who?

As she followed Agent Denton out of the office, she became aware of those who came to stand in the doorways of their offices and cubicles to watch her leave. She hadn't made any true friends during her five years with the agency, and now couldn't bring herself to look at her former coworkers. As she passed Linda, however, she thought she heard the other woman whisper, "Good job."

In the parking lot, she opened her trunk and waited while Agent Denton deposited his box inside, before sliding her own in beside it. She slammed the trunk closed, and turned to face him, shoving her hands into her pockets.

"Well, I guess I'll be seeing you around," she said, squinting at him in the bright sunlight.

"You did the right thing, Sedona."

She scuffed the ground with her toe and then shrugged. "I know. I mean, what they were doing was wrong. Still…"

"What?"

"Once the press gets wind of what happened, their careers will be over. They'll never get another job, either in government or private industry. Not to mention what it will do to their marriages."

Agent Denton didn't smile. "They brought it on themselves." He glanced at his watch. "I have to get going. One of our people will be in touch with you. Maybe I'll see you in court, okay?"

"Okay." She took his proffered hand. "Thank you for everything, Agent Denton."

"Good luck, Sedona."

She watched as he climbed into his car and drove away before glancing at her watch. It was only midmorning. Had Angel already left for the airport, or was he still at the Lemoore hotel? She pulled her cell phone out and punched in his number, frustrated when there was no answer.

She stood, undecided for a moment, unable to deny the growing sense that she was being ignored.

Or dumped.

But why? When she had left Angel at the hospital, he'd been so determined to get released, to wrap up the loose ends of the investigation and get on the next flight east to be with her. He'd kissed her thoroughly, had told her he loved her. Not once, but several times. And when she'd finally had to leave, she could tell he didn't want her to go.

She tapped her keys against the palm of her hand. If Angel wasn't going to let her know what was going on, she would have to find out on her own. She stared across the parking lot to the building where the navy test pilots maintained their own offices. She debated with herself for maybe a second before she set off in the direction of the building.

She found two of the pilots in the office, preparing their

flight plans for the afternoon. One of them looked up, surprised, when she entered.

"Miss Stewart." He rose to his feet. "Can I help you?"

"Yes—" she glanced at his name badge "—Lieutenant Brodie. I'm here about Lieutenant Torres."

She paused, and he looked at her expectantly. "What about him?"

"Well, it's just that he's due to fly into Logan this afternoon, and I was supposed to meet his flight, only I lost his flight number and I can't seem to reach him. I was wondering if perhaps he contacted either you or one of the other guys with his travel plans. I'd hate to miss his flight and have him waiting at the airport for me."

The pilot looked dismayed. "Miss Stewart, I thought you knew…I mean…"

"What? Thought I knew what?"

The man made a helpless gesture. "Diablo is gone."

"What?" Fear gripped her, making her knees go weak. "What do you mean, *gone?*" She refused to believe it. Aside from his injured ankle, Angel had been fine the last time she'd seen him. The doctors had assured her he would make a full recovery.

The lieutenant glanced around desperately, clearly wishing he was anywhere else. "I mean he's been reassigned. He came back two days ago, but didn't stay. He just packed up his gear and said he was going back to the West Coast."

Sedona stared at the man, unable to believe what he was saying. "No, you must be mistaken, Angel wasn't even due to come back until today."

Lieutenant Brodie looked down at the paperwork on his desk and shuffled it, avoiding her eyes. "He came back two days ago. I thought you knew…he said he was going over to your office. He wasn't gone long, and he came back pretty pissed off." He shrugged and looked chagrined. "I figured you two had words."

"Words?" Sedona stared, bemused. "I never even *saw* him, are you sure it was two days ago? I mean, what time was it? How could I have missed him? Why didn't he wait, or try to find me?"

"I don't know, except he was pretty psyched to be back early. I think he wanted to surprise you."

And then it hit her.

If he had come back two days ago, the only possible reason he could have for leaving without contacting her and for refusing to either accept or return any of her calls, was that he'd somehow discovered her confrontation with the Membership, or how she'd used the photos of him to entrap them.

"Oh, God," she breathed. "I need to find him. Did he leave a forwarding address? Anything?"

The pilot shrugged. "Maybe, but not with me. You might want to check with his XO."

"Okay. Where do I find the XO?"

"He's located down in Newport. We only ever see him when it's time for our evaluations, or when we're due to transfer to a new assignment." The lieutenant opened a desk drawer and took out a small planner. He flipped it open and scribbled a number on a sheet of paper, tearing it off and handing it to her. "Here's his phone number. If anyone knows where Diablo is, it's him."

Sedona took the paper, feeling dazed. She walked to the parking lot, then sat in her car and stared blindly at the phone number, unable to accept that he'd come and gone without even giving her the opportunity to explain what had happened. He'd said he loved her, but apparently not enough to trust her.

Before she could chicken out and change her mind, she

pulled her cell phone from her bag and punched in the XO's number.

"Commander Schiffer." The voice was deep and slightly distracted, as if the commander had other, more important things to do.

"Sir, I was told you could tell me how to reach Lieutenant Commander Angel Torres."

There was a brief silence. "I'm sorry…who is this?"

"My name is Sedona Stewart. I worked on the recent Coyote investigation with Lieutenant Commander Torres." She swallowed against the small white lie she was about to utter. "He…still owes me several flight-test reports, but I can't seem to reach him. I understand he's been reassigned to Lemoore Naval Air Station."

"Yes, actually, he has. Sedona Stewart, you said?" There was a brief pause, as if he was looking through some paperwork. "Ah, yes. I see you were the lead engineer for the engine-calibration tests during the investigation. You say he owes you several reports? I was told he had completed his reports."

"These are just some small, er, calculations that we somehow overlooked during our initial inspections."

"I understand." There was doubt in the commander's voice. "Lieutenant Torres requested reassignment to Lemoore, and considering he is currently unable to perform his duties as a flight-test pilot, the Navy has agreed to assign him as an instructor at the Top Gun school."

"Oh." Sedona couldn't keep the shock out of her voice. "The decision was…very sudden, wasn't it?"

"Yes, it was. But it made sense to send Lieutenant Torres where he could do the most good. I don't yet have a duty number for him, but I do have his cell phone, which I can give you."

Damn. She didn't need his cell phone number; she already

had that. She also knew he wouldn't answer if he thought it was her calling.

"Actually, Commander Schiffer, I'm going back out to Lemoore to, uh, meet with the investigation team one last time. I could always meet Lieutenant Torres there and pick up the reports I need. That is, if I knew where at Lemoore he was located."

There was a brief silence. "To the best of my knowledge, Miss Stewart, he's residing at the Bachelor Officers' Quarters until he can locate appropriate housing. He'll be working out of the Top Gun training facilities at Lemoore. I'm sorry, but that's the best I can tell you."

"Of course. Thank you very much, Commander."

"Would you like me to contact Lieutenant Torres and let him know you're coming?"

"Oh. No, thank you. I'm not exactly sure when I'll be leaving, so I'll just contact him when I get there. Thank you again for your help."

She closed her cell phone, tilted her head back against the seat and blew out her breath in frustration. It seemed there was no other option; she would be on the next available flight to Lemoore.

SEDONA STOOD before the closed door of the small apartment where Angel was staying. It was part of a complex of apartments built to quarter unmarried or unaccompanied naval officers.

She had arrived in California just hours earlier and had driven straight to Lemoore. All she'd brought with her was a change of clothes, stuffed into an oversize shoulder bag.

Was he home? What would she do if he wasn't? And what would his reaction be if he found her waiting on his doorstep like some forlorn kitten? She drew in a fortifying breath. If he didn't answer the door, she would simply go and check into a nearby hotel and return when he was home. But there was no way she was leaving without confronting him. He owed her the courtesy of telling her to her face that he was no longer interested.

Before she could change her mind, she raised her fist and knocked on the door. For one long, agonizing minute she thought he might not be in, and then the door swung open and he was standing there.

He looked disheveled and tired, with dark stubble on his jaw and lines of fatigue etched around his eyes and mouth. He wore a T-shirt and a pair of shorts, and except for the white cast on his foot, his hard-muscled, bronzed legs were bare.

In the brief instant before his expression changed, Sedona swore she saw pleasure in his dark eyes, and it gave her hope. Then his expression changed and his brows drew together. He raked her with one brief, contemptuous look before he swung away and turned back into the apartment, leaving the door open.

She followed him in.

"What are you doing here?" he growled, using one crutch to shove a duffel bag out of the way.

"I—I came because I had to," she said, glancing around the tiny room. It was bare of anything warm or personal, containing only military-issue furniture and a small television that sat on the counter separating the living area from the tiny galley kitchen. "I think you may have gotten the wrong impression about what happened in that conference room the other day." She paused, but he refused to turn and look at her. "Angel, why didn't you tell me you were coming in early? And, for God's sake, why did you leave without letting me explain?"

He swung to face her then and Sedona recoiled at the raw

fury she saw on his face. "Explain what, Sedona? How you manipulated me? How you—what were the words you used—spent the entire time screwing some guy's brains out?" His hands fisted on the crutches. "If all you wanted was some stud to help you get your promotion, why'd you have to pick me? We were on a naval base, sweetheart, with squadrons of horny guys, I'm sure any one of them would have loved to play the porn star for you. In fact, Larson seemed like a prime candidate."

Sedona gasped. "Is that what you think?"

"What else am I supposed to think?" He took a step toward her, his expression harsh. "From the first night at Lemoore, you made it perfectly clear you wanted to have sex with me. I actually thought—Christ!" He scrubbed a hand over his face and turned away again. "Just get the hell out of here. I'm not interested in any more of your lies. Go on." He turned his face partially toward her, and his voice was little more than a snarl. "Get out."

Sedona flung her arms out. "So that's it? You tell me to just get out, and I do it, and that's the end?"

"What did you expect?"

"Well, jeez, I don't know." Her voice was rising and she knew she sounded more than a little hysterical, but she couldn't seem to help herself. "I expected a little more than a 'don't let the door hit you on the ass on your way out,' though. I guess I came all the way out here expecting you'd at least let me explain. Let me tell you that what you *think* you heard in that conference room wasn't real."

"It sounded pretty goddamn real to me."

"It wasn't! I swear to you, Angel, it wasn't real. When I told you about the Membership and how they were illegally promoting people—men—based on their sexual exploits, I'd already decided I wanted nothing to do with them. It wasn't until—" To her horror, her voice broke. "It wasn't until you called me a coward that I decided I needed to do something about it. I already had the photos we'd taken that morning…" Her voice trailed off, grew small. "I—I was part of a sting operation to expose them. That's all."

"And you just thought you could use compromising pictures of me to really stick it to them, is that it?"

Sedona stared at him, and the full awareness of his disappointment hit her. She could see it in his eyes, in the weary sag of his shoulders as he faced her.

"Angel, listen to me." She reached a hand toward him, but when he flinched, she jerked it back. "Okay. You're right, I did want to sleep with you, but it had nothing to do with the Membership or proving anything to those men."

A muscle in his jaw worked convulsively, but he didn't say anything, just continued to watch her. The fact that he didn't physically throw her out gave her courage.

"I wasn't lying when I told you I had a—a thing for you from the first time I saw you," she hurried on. "But my being with you had nothing to do with the Membership and their disgusting promotion requirements." She paused and looked away, unable to meet his eyes. "You see, I'd fantasized about being with you, but…" She allowed her gaze to drift back to his.

Angel's attention was riveted on her, but his voice was cool. "I'm listening."

Sedona drew in a deep breath. "But I never thought it would ever amount to anything more than that—a fantasy. The reality of being with you was like a dream come true. I was glad to finally tell you about the Membership and why Larson kept harassing me. It was a relief for you to know the truth."

Angel snorted. "You just conveniently left out the part where you planned to use our relationship to nail them, huh?"

"*No!* Of course not." Sedona laid a hand on his arm, and this time he didn't pull away. "I never wanted to hurt you, but the photos were the only way I could get the Membership to believe I wanted to be part of their club. I should have told you what I intended to do. I wish to God I had." She gave a small laugh. "Regardless of the Membership, I would have given my right arm to be with you, even though I knew it couldn't last."

Angel frowned. "Why couldn't it last?"

"Well, look at you. You're every woman's fantasy, while I'm—well, look at me." She smiled ruefully.

Angel took a step toward her. "I'm looking, *mina.*"

Sedona's breath caught at the expression in his eyes, but she determinedly forged ahead. "The entire time we were together, I knew the day would come when you'd fly off to bluer skies. I just wanted as much of you as I could get in the short time we had. I was glad we took those pictures. I was so sure that eventually, they'd be all I had of you."

"Sedona—"

"No, please. Let me finish." She stared up at him, letting her love for him show in her eyes. "When you were up in that jet, and I thought I might lose you forever, I realized how much I loved you. I still do. So if you want to end what we have together, let it be because you don't have feelings for me, but not because you think I used you."

To her utter amazement, Angel leaned his weight on his crutches and reached out to cup her face in his hands. "You think I don't have feelings for you, *mina?*" There was no laughter in his eyes. "When I heard you in that conference room, reducing our relationship to the equivalent of a quick screw in a dark alley, I couldn't believe I'd misread you so completely. I freaked."

Sedona covered his hands with her own, pressing her

cheek against his palm. "I wish you had let me explain. You see, I was wearing a wire. There was a federal agent hiding in the room right across the hall, and three more waiting for those men to incriminate themselves before they could move in and arrest them."

Angel stroked a thumb over her cheek, and there was both regret and relief in his eyes. "I'm sorry, *mina*. I didn't want to hear that what we'd had was nothing but sex. You see…I fell in love with you, and I didn't think I'd have the strength or courage to see you, knowing you didn't feel the same way."

"So you left."

"Yes."

"But now you know…"

"I know I can't keep flying solo, *mina*. I need a copilot, a navigator. But, more than that, I need someone to keep me grounded."

Tears blurred Sedona's vision as she hugged him fiercely. "I love you so much, Angel. And I'm so sorry I didn't tell you about my plan to expose the Membership."

"Shh. It's okay. I should have trusted you. I shouldn't have left without at least talking with you first."

Looking up at him, she ran a hand across his stubbled cheek. "You look like hell."

Angel laughed, and this time there was real humor in his eyes. "I haven't eaten or slept since I first got on that plane to Boston. First because I couldn't wait to see you again, and then because…because I thought I'd lost you." His hands where they cupped her face tightened, and he ran a thumb over her lips.

"You haven't lost me." She searched his eyes, letting him see the truth. "In fact, I'm sort of between jobs right now, so if you know of a place where I could hang out for a while…?"

"What happened to your job?"

Sedona smiled into his eyes. "I handed in my resignation before we left for Lemoore. I knew I couldn't continue to work for the agency, but agreed to complete the inspection of the jets before I left."

"So there was never going to be any promotion for you, whether you brought back photos, or not."

"No," she agreed.

"Then, yes, I can think of a place for you to stay." He tossed away one crutch and used his free arm to pull her in close. "Right here with me. I love you, Sedona Stewart. I also know that the senior brass here at Lemoore were pretty impressed with the work you did while you were here. I'd be willing to bet they might have a job for you, if you're interested."

"Actually," she confessed shyly, "I applied for a position as senior illustrator for a military magazine."

Angel pulled back just a little and looked at her with admiration. "I'm impressed."

Sedona smiled. "I'm just taking the advice someone once gave me, and grabbing my dreams with both hands. All of my dreams." She reached up to run her fingers over his firm jaw. "I've got you now, flyboy, and I'm not about to let you go."

Angel smiled at her, a seductive slanting of his lips that caused a slow, melting warmth to spread along her veins. "You don't have to, *mina*. This flyboy has fallen, and hard."

He buried his hands in the mass of her hair and tipped her face up, and Sedona's lashes drifted closed as his lips claimed hers in a kiss that was both intensely sweet and searingly hot.

He pulled away and gazed down at her, and Sedona saw the love reflected there.

"So," she said huskily, running a hand over his hard chest. "Are you going to give me a tour of your new place, or what?"

He smiled into her eyes, his eyes full of promise. "Well,

this arrangement is only until I can find a permanent place to live. A place to settle down and raise a family. The only room here you haven't seen is the bedroom. Of course, I can show that to you, if you insist."

"Oh," Sedona murmured against his lips, "I insist. I really, really insist you show me."

And he did just that.

* * * * *

Melita had been expecting a chaste quick kiss of the generic variety. But this kiss with Sully was the kind that sparked a dying flame to life. The kind of kiss you can't plan for. The kind of kiss memories are built on.

The memory of her murdered lover, Nemo, came to her then and she made a starved little noise in the back of her throat. She raised her arms and threaded her fingers through Sully's hair, pulled him closer. Felt his body settle, then melt into her.

In that instant her hunger for him grew, and his for her. She pressed herself to him with more urgency, and he responded in kind.

Melita came out of her kiss-induced memory of Nemo with a start. "Wait a minute." She pushed Sully away from her. "You bastard!"

She spit two nasty words at him in Greek, then wiped his kiss from her lips.

"I thought you deserved some solid proof that I'm still in one piece." He started for the door. "The clock's ticking, honey. Come on, let's get out of here."

"That's it? You sucker me into kissing you, and that's all you have to say?"

"I'm sorry. How's that?"

He didn't sound sorry in the least. "You're—"

"Getting out of this godforsaken prison cell. Stop whining and let's go."

"Not if I was being shot at sunrise. Go. You deserve whatever you get if you walk out that door."

He turned back. "Freedom is what I'm going to get."

"A second of freedom before the guards in the hall shoot you." She jammed her hands on her hips. "And to think I was worried about you."

"If you're staying behind, it's no skin off my ass."

"Wait! What about our deal?"

"You just said you're not coming. Make up your mind."

"Have you forgotten we need a boat?"

"How could I? You keep harping on it."

"I'm not going without a boat. And those guards out there aren't going to just let you walk out of here. You need me and we need a plan."

"I already have a plan. I'm getting out of here. That's the plan."

"I should have realized that you never intended to take me with you from the very beginning. You're a liar and a coward."

Of everything she had read, there was nothing in Sully Paxton's file that hinted he was a coward, but it was the one word that seemed to register in that one-track mind of his. The look he nailed her with a second later was pure venom.

He came at her so quickly she didn't have time to get out of his way. "You know I'm not a coward."

"Prove it. Give me until dawn. I need one more night to put everything in place before we leave the island."

"You're asking me to stay in this cell one more night...and trust you?"

"Yes."

He snorted. "Yesterday you knew they were planning to harm me, but instead of doing something about it you went to bed and never gave me a second thought. Suppose tonight you do the same. By tomorrow I might damn well be in my grave."

"Okay, I screwed up. I won't do it again." Melita sucked in a ragged breath. "I can't leave this minute. Dawn, Sully. Wait until dawn." When he looked as if he was about to say no, she pleaded, "Please wait for me."

"You're asking a lot. The door's open now. I would be a fool to hang around here and trust that you'll be back."

"What you can trust is that I want off this island as badly as you do, and you're my only hope."

"I must be crazy."

"Is that a yes?"

"Dammit!" He turned his back on her. Swore twice more.

"You won't be sorry."

He turned around. "I already am. How about we seal this new deal?"

He was staring at her lips. Suddenly Melita knew what he expected. "We already sealed it."

"One more. You enjoyed it. Admit it."

"I enjoyed it because I was kissing someone else."

He laughed. "That's a good one."

"It's true. It might have been your lips, but it wasn't you I was kissing."

"If that's your excuse for wanting to kiss me, then—"

"I was kissing Nemo."

"What's a nemo?"

Melita gave Sully a look that clearly told him that he was trespassing on sacred ground. She was about to enforce it with a warning when a voice in the hall jerked them both to attention.

She bolted away from the wall. "Get back in bed. Hurry. I'll be here before dawn."

She didn't reach the door before he snagged her arm, pulled her up against him and planted a kiss on her lips that took her completely by surprise.

When he released her, he said, "If you're confused about who just kissed you, the name's Sully. I'll be here waiting at dawn. Don't be late."

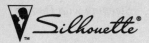

Romantic
SUSPENSE

**Sparked by Danger,
Fueled by Passion.**

Onyxx agent Sully Paxton's only chance of
survival lies in the hands of his enemy's daughter
Melita Krizova. He doesn't know he's a pawn in the
beautiful island girl's own plan for escape. Can
they survive their ruses and their fiery attraction?

**Look for the next installment in the
Spy Games miniseries,**

Sleeping with Danger

by Wendy Rosnau

Available November 2007 wherever you buy books.

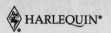

REQUEST YOUR FREE BOOKS!

2 FREE NOVELS PLUS 2 FREE GIFTS!

HARLEQUIN®

Blaze®

Red-hot reads!

YES! Please send me 2 FREE Harlequin® Blaze® novels and my 2 FREE gifts. After receiving them, if I don't wish to receive any more books, I can return the shipping statement marked "cancel." If I don't cancel, I will receive 6 brand-new novels every month and be billed just $3.99 per book in the U.S., or $4.47 per book in Canada, plus 25¢ shipping and handling per book and applicable taxes, if any*. That's a savings of at least 15% off the cover price! I understand that accepting the 2 free books and gifts places me under no obligation to buy anything. I can always return a shipment and cancel at any time. Even if I never buy another book from Harlequin, the two free books and gifts are mine to keep forever.

151 HDN EF3W 351 HDN EF3X

Name	(PLEASE PRINT)	
Address		Apt.
City	State/Prov.	Zip/Postal Code

Signature (if under 18, a parent or guardian must sign)

Mail to the **Harlequin Reader Service®:**

IN U.S.A.: P.O. Box 1867, Buffalo, NY 14240-1867
IN CANADA: P.O. Box 609, Fort Erie, Ontario L2A 5X3

Not valid to current Harlequin Blaze subscribers.

Want to try two free books from another line?
Call 1-800-873-8635 or visit www.morefreebooks.com.

* Terms and prices subject to change without notice. NY residents add applicable sales tax. Canadian residents will be charged applicable provincial taxes and GST. This offer is limited to one order per household. All orders subject to approval. Credit or debit balances in a customer's account(s) may be offset by any other outstanding balance owed by or to the customer. Please allow 4 to 6 weeks for delivery.

Your Privacy: Harlequin is committed to protecting your privacy. Our Privacy Policy is available online at www.eHarlequin.com or upon request from the Reader Service. From time to time we make our lists of customers available to reputable firms who may have a product or service of interest to you. If you would prefer we not share your name and address, please check here. ☐

HB07

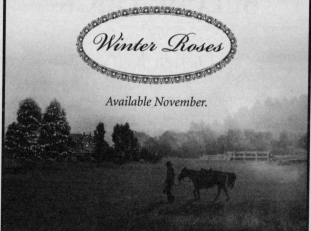

HARLEQUIN®

Mediterranean
NIGHTS™

Not everything is above board
on Alexandra's Dream!

Enjoy plenty of secrets, drama and sensuality
in the latest from Mediterranean Nights.

Coming in November 2007...

BELOW DECK

by

Dorien Kelly

Determined to protect her young son,
widow Mei Lin Wang keeps him hidden
aboard *Alexandra's Dream* under cover of
her job. But life gets extremely complicated
when the ship's security officer, Gideon Dayan,
is piqued by the mystery surrounding this
beautiful, haunted woman....

HM38965

Silhouette

SPECIAL EDITION™

**brings you a heartwarming
new McKettrick's story from**

NEW YORK TIMES **BESTSELLING AUTHOR**

LINDA LAEL MILLER

THE MᶜKETTRICK
Way

Meg McKettrick is surprised to be reunited
with her high school flame, Brad O'Ballivan,
who has returned home to his family's
neighboring ranch. After seeing Meg again,
Brad realizes he still loves her. But the pride
of both manage to interfere with love...until
an unexpected matchmaker gets involved.

—— **McKettrick Women** ——

Available December wherever you buy books.

Visit Silhouette Books at www.eHarlequin.com SSEIBC24867

HARLEQUIN®

Blaze™

COMING NEXT MONTH

#357 SEX BOMB Jamie Sobrato
Elle Jameson can wield a .38 as fiercely as a makeup brush. But there's not a big demand for her eclectic skill set. Then Christian Navarro appears to recruit her to a secret spy agency. A chance to use her talents *and* a superhot guy to train her? She is so there!

#358 DEAD SEXY Kimberly Raye
Love at First Bite, Bk. 1
Hairdresser Nikki Braxton has had it with dating losers. So when she falls desperately in lust with sexy cowboy Jake McMann, she's thrilled. Jake is the real deal, a man's man. Too bad he's also a vampire....

#359 DANGEROUS... Tori Carrington
Extreme
When undercover agent Lucas Paretti agreed to infiltrate the mafia, he never dreamed he'd have another chance with his first love, Gia Trainello. Or that his still unbelievably sexy Gia would be the new Lady Boss of the family he's vowed to bring down...

#360 WILD CHILD Cindi Myers
Sex on the Beach, Bk. 3
Sara Montgomery needs this vacation in the biggest way. But getting unplugged from the cell phone and laptop is proving tricky. Luckily for her, hottie surfer guy Drew Jamison arrives as the perfect distraction. Who can think about work with this kind of temptation?

#361 FEELING THE HEAT Rhonda Nelson
Big, Bad Bounty Hunters, Bk. 1
Bounty hunter Linc Stone always gets his man. But when irresistibly sexy Georgia Hart joins him, insisting on helping him track down her louse of an ex-boyfriend, Linc can't help thinking he'd like to get his woman—*this* woman—too. Into bed, that is...

#362 TALL, DARK AND FILTHY RICH Jill Monroe
Million Dollar Secrets, Bk. 5
"There's always dirt." That's female P.I. Jessie Huell's mantra. But when she uncovers a serious scandal involving Cole Crawford—her long-term crush—will she be so quick to reveal it? Especially when it might ruin her shot at finally bedding the gorgeous TV producer?

www.eHarlequin.com

HBCNM1007